Red Star

The Triple Stars, Volume 2

SIMON KEWIN

Red Star - The Triple Stars, Volume 2

STORM
CROW
BOOKS

ISBN: 978-1-9993395-6-2

CONTENTS

For all those who fight the power

PROLOGUE

THE MAGELLANIC HERESIES

Fragments recovered from the journal of Senjen Vorst, planetologist of the deep space exploratory vessel *Magellanic Cloud*, as reassembled and translated by Ondo Ynwa Lagan from discoveries made on the (now extinct) planet Maes Far.

Warning: These fragments form part of the *Magellanic Heresies* as proscribed by Concordance. Ownership or propagation of these documents is considered an act of extreme heresy against Omn. Read or distribute at your own risk.

...the three stellar masses meant that we were forced to translate from metaspace at a much greater distance from the centre of the system than normal. Frustrating! It will take many weeks to reach the planet. Telemetry is, however, slowly giving us a more complete picture of the stars and their single world...

...we now observe small degrees of orbital perturbation in the movements of the three suns. Frankly, it's a relief. The wilder theories of some of the crew can now be discounted; these are not artificially engineered stars, as if such things were even possible. Their motions are remarkably regular, but that appears to be a natural phenomenon, the chance arrangement of gravitational influences holding them in their patterns of movement about each other. Eventually, as they lose mass through normal stellar radiation, this regularity will fail, and it is conceivable that two or even three of the stars will collide or fuse...

...so much for the suns, but what of the planet and its moons? Some on the ship are convinced significant terraforming has taken place on this world, but they are unable to explain how that could be achieved — or why anyone would go to such lengths. The number of viable planets in the galaxy far outweighs the number of cultures requiring relocation or room for expansion, and this must always have been the case. This planet, especially, with no land masses upon it, is hardly a good candidate for occupation...

...a strange conversation with one of the chemists on board, Dragonel Vulpis. He wanted me to support his view that the planet is anomalous, unnatural in some way. He actually used the term supernatural. He more or less pinned me to the bulkhead as he spoke, his eyes wide, unblinking. The man used to amuse me, but he becomes more and more alarming. Something has broken inside his brain. I explained that the apparent regularity of the planetary and lunar motions is an illusion caused by our lack of time perspective; that the orbital patterns are in constant flux, and we've simply arrived at a galactic moment when everything appears to be in clockwork equilibrium. We don't live long enough to see the pattern.

He wouldn't have it and grew angry. I must talk to the officers about him before he causes more trouble; the long voyage appears to have taken a psychological toll upon him. A single, disturbed crew-member can have a hugely destructive effect upon a ship...

Three hours after Selene and Ondo's arrival at the dead
star…

PART 1 - DIURNAL

1. The Moving Stars

The clock embedded in the biomechanical hemisphere of Selene Ada's brain whispered the countdown to her death.

Oxygen supply 2.5% - 13 minutes remaining

Strange how the responses in the two halves of her body had become merged, indistinguishable. The agonies in her oxygen-starved natural tissues, the urgent override alerts in her artificial: they had become indistinguishable. The irony of it was amusing. She'd made such good progress.

She sat with her back against the column of the archway upon the fragment of planetary rock. The nearby dead star, barely three kilometres across, bathed them in its hard gamma rays. Ondo lay beside her, his body ricked awkwardly where he'd slumped among the scattered rocks. His features were indistinct through his suit visor, but it was long minutes since he'd moved. She instructed his helmet lights to come on for a moment. He didn't respond, no flicker in his eyes. His heart rate continued to fall steadily, and the blue tinge to his lips was unmistakable.

She queried the flecks embedded in his cerebellum one more time. There was only the faintest flutter of life within his body. Oxygen levels within his bloodstream were critical, and hypoxia was causing tissue damage at an increasing rate. Even if, by some miracle, the two of them found a way out, he wouldn't make it alive; his brain cells were already too impaired.

She could rouse him, instruct his control flecks to amp up his metabolism enough to return him to consciousness, but she let him be. Best to leave him in the peace of oblivion. Soon he'd die, and then the only version of him left in the universe would be the engram copy she carried within her own head. And then, when *she* finally succumbed, they'd both be gone in the same moment.

She wished she'd been able to protect him, dissuade him from coming to Coronade. If he were still at the Refuge, then there'd be hope. On her lone visits to other worlds, she'd sometimes thought of him as a low, flickering candle-flame in a huge night, a glow of promise on the edge of the galaxy. Now the flame was sputtering out.

They could perhaps have retraced their steps through the archways and the metaspace tunnels to return to the ruins of Coronade, but they'd agreed in Ondo's last few minutes of consciousness not to do so, not to place themselves in the hands of Concordance. This lonely death was better than any drawn-out end their pursuers might choose to give them. Better that their secrets died with them than having their knowledge ripped from their minds by the Augurs of Omn. The Refuge with its recovered scraps of history was safely hidden. Perhaps some unknown traveller would find it one day, and bring the memories back to life.

Conscious thought slipped away from Selene for a moment, and there was only the blazing cloud of ionized gas and plasma from the destroyed star to fill her eyes. Strange how something so violently destructive could create something so beautiful. The fragment of rock, crowned by its archway, spun rapidly, tumbling through space from the blast of the sun's explosion. As a result, its tumbling day was short, but there was no separation of light and darkness. A blur of fulgent light surrounded her. The colours were dazzling; she felt them filling her universe, pulling her in, promising to draw her to themselves. The thought was comforting. It would be so easy to let go, let the light absorb her. Let Concordance win.

No. She fought back, forcing herself to kick for the surface, out of the depths and back to awareness. Her biomechanical side reacted to her conscious instruction, pushing more adrenaline through her blood vessels, giving her another burst of life.

The irony was that her artificial tissues could easily have been made to survive a zero-oxygen environment – except that she'd insisted on having them fully integrated with what remained of her biology during her reconstruction. Ondo had given her the choice early on; her flesh could be an adjunct, sustained and maintained as long as it was viable, then discarded, placenta-like. He'd offered her that immortality, but she'd recoiled in horror. If all of the cells and tissues of her original body were gone, then who was she? In what sense was she still Selene Ada?

It was one of the last things he'd said to her, before his eyes closed: "I should have insisted."

"I wouldn't have let you."

He'd actually smiled. "I should have done it anyway, and not told you until now."

"Did you?"

"Regrettably, no. I'm sorry. I'm sorry for all of this. I should have made you lead a normal life, safe on a planet somewhere."

"And I told you, that life would never have worked for me. Not after Maes Far."

Her two halves were inextricably intertwined, just as she'd demanded, and that meant she was doomed. The blast wave from the stellar extinction event had stripped away its planets' atmospheric envelopes, turning viable biosphere into bare rock, and the only breathable air she and Ondo had was that which they'd brought with them. She'd consumed less of her suit's oxygen than Ondo had, but in the end, it wasn't going to make any difference.

Still she fought. She *would* go back to Coronade, face down Concordance. Time to stop following the trails left by others and force a new one of her own. Since she'd started travelling in the *Radiant Dragon*, Ondo had often accused her of taking crazy risks, and to herself she admitted that he was probably right: her fury and desire for revenge did make her take unnecessary chances. Sometimes it felt like her own survival didn't matter much anymore. Why should she get to live when everyone she'd grown up with had not? It was survivor's guilt; she should have died alongside them. She wasn't always rational. If she was going to fight Concordance, she needed to be more controlled. There was a time to unleash her anger, but she needed to be patient, pick the right moment. To win a war, you sometimes had to lose a battle, or refuse to fight it at all.

Could she reopen the Coronade entrance using the metakey they'd been given by the Warden? Perhaps. The archway had clearly been designed to ensure people couldn't easily move from Coronade to the dead star system, and perhaps prevent them from returning at all. It was a puzzling fact if you accepted Ondo's view of the golden age culture. Why go to such lengths to construct miraculous passageways among the stars, and then prevent their use? Ondo had to be wrong; the Coronade civilisation had been radically different to the one he'd imagined.

In any case, she would try to make the return journey. Ondo would know nothing of her actions; he was too far gone for it to matter. She would return through the tunnels, attempt to reopen the archway and fight their pursuers. She would have no chance – they would drop more atmospheric nukes or unleash beam-weapon fire and she'd be vaporised – but perhaps, somehow, she could get to them first, take some of them with her.

She forced herself to her knees, then to her feet. She retched, her mouth filling with bitter-sour liquid. She swallowed it back down. Vomiting inside a sealed suit was never a good thing. Stars swirled in her vision and the galaxy threatened to blackout completely, but she willed herself to remain upright and conscious. She took a step forwards, and then another, leaving Ondo's body where it was on the ground.

She stepped through the archway, taking the short, featureless tunnel that led to the outer planet they'd first arrived at. If the tunnels had ever had breathable atmosphere, it was long-gone now; whatever form of energy walls the archways propagated hadn't prevented any air from leeching away. Perhaps the builders simply hadn't considered the possibility of the atmosphere at one end of the tunnel being torn away. She and Ondo had tried and failed to find some sort of control mechanism that might restore air-pressure but hadn't found any.

She talked to him, the copy in her head at least, as she battled forwards. Partly it was to take her mind off what she was doing, partly to hear his voice. Also, it felt right for him to know everything that had happened.

He absorbed her news without comment, whatever sense of loss he might be feeling left unexpressed. She wondered whether he thought *he* was dying, or whether it was someone else, just a different Ondo.

"Do you still think there's a trail?" she asked. "That we were led here for a reason?"

He paused very briefly before replying. "Perhaps some

of your innate scepticism has leeched into my thoughts from your brain, but I still think we have a purpose. There are fragments of the picture here."

"It's hard to see a picture if you're dead," she said. "You said this supernova was engineered, an anomaly, but maybe you were wrong. Even my enhanced senses give us only crude readings. This could have been a completely natural disaster, nothing more. A star exploding after its core collapsed unexpectedly."

"This was clearly a technological society; you've seen the scale of the ruins. From the similarities in the architecture, I'd say this was the same culture spread across multiple worlds: the three that we've glimpsed, and perhaps others. There's no way a society that advanced wouldn't know its star was close to catastrophic explosion. And you've studied the readings; the mass of stellar material is at odds with what we can calculate from the planets' original orbits. My view is still that someone did this: triggered solar collapse and wiped out these worlds in a moment of galactic time. Even the farthermost planet would have been devastated within a few minutes. If there was no warning, no chance to evacuate, billions of people must have died. Billions of lives and much that was unique and glorious, all gone. We have to accept that's the most likely explanation."

Walking was an effort, an act of will. Her muscles were cramping and her brain threatened repeatedly to succumb to the darkness. Her breathing was rapid, panicky. She forced herself to keep moving and talking. "Then, perhaps there was some end-of-days cult going on; the people chose to live close to the edge of destruction, knowing the end could come at any moment. People do things like that, right? Perhaps they embraced catastrophe like Concordance do."

"It seems so unlikely. From what I can tell of the ruins, the buildings must have been quite beautiful."

"What the hell does that have to do with anything?"

"I suppose I can't believe that a people capable of such marvels would embrace death to that extent."

"Concordance ships are beautiful. You're projecting how you think about the universe onto unknown cultures."

"Concordance are anomalous, and I don't believe they are responsible for creating the wonders they wield."

"Who is, then?"

"That, of course, we don't know. But it's clear Concordance aren't fully in control of the technology at their disposal. For one thing, they're not here. If they knew about the tunnels and the archways, they'd have come for us. They'd have been waiting for us. I don't believe they know where we are and I don't believe they understand how the metaspace pathways function."

"It's not a lesson we can put to any use, given how near to dying I am."

"How close are you?"

She granted him access to her internal status. "That close."

"There isn't much time left," he said after a moment.

"No. I noticed that."

She emerged at the circle of three archways, stumbling to the ground as she did so. She was on her back, confused about how she'd got there. The ruined domes and archways of the planet crowded around her peripheral vision. Like people standing silently around a deathbed, peering in at her.

The glowing plasma blotted out the stars above her. She thought about the times she'd looked at the galaxy from the Refuge, imagining it as something like a brain. And, again, on Migdala, sitting with Myrced upon the roof of her house, that sweet interlude in her recent life. She, Selene, had said then that the stars move, that things changed, but sometimes so slowly you couldn't see it. The stars turned, yes, but they moved in other ways, too: forming and dying. She wished she could tell Myrced that.

Change was possible. Change was inevitable. And, it wasn't only a natural process: stars could be created and destroyed in acts of stellar engineering. What seemed constant, untouchable, could be swept away. Perhaps that meant Concordance could be swept away.

With a grunt of effort, she forced herself onto her side. A glint of light in the dust of the ruins caught her eye, down at ground-level, reflecting the glow in the sky. What was that? They'd explored briefly upon first arriving and had found nothing but debris and destruction among the ruined walls and domes. The spark was dim; her natural eye wouldn't have been able to detect it. She moved her head from side-to-side a little and the mote of light disappeared, reappeared, disappeared. It was only visible from the one spot she happened to have fallen in. Some shard of glass perhaps? Hard to know how far away it was, but she guessed it was relatively small and near judging by the tiny movements needed to affect it.

The archway that would take her back across the galaxy to Coronade was a few paces away, but the speck of light intrigued her. Another tiny glow in a sea of darkness. She would find out what it was. She deactivated her inner Ondo – she didn't want to give him any explanations of what she was doing – and worked her way to her knees, her feet. She could no longer see the light, the angle of the reflection wrong. She knelt back down and by positioning her head *just so*, saw it again.

Very well, she would crawl. It was about all she had energy left to do anyway.

She toiled forwards, eyes fixed on her target. This world hadn't been blown to fragments by the nova, and it still rotated in a ghost of its day and night cycle. That meant the mysterious light might shift at any moment, wink out. Its life was tenuous, brief. She suddenly had to get to it, as if it held all the answers she sought.

The floor of the archway circle was smooth stone, protected somehow from the drifting powder of the ruins all around, but once she moved off it, her hands and knees sank into a dense layer that was more like volcanic ash than dust from collapsed buildings. It weighed her down, clogging her movements. Three times she knelt on some buried fragment of sharp rock. Her suit cushioned her, but alarm cut through her that a puncture would vent all her remaining oxygen. Then she would only have moments.

The clock in her brain chose that point to give her an update, sounding annoyingly calm.

Oxygen supply 0.8% - 4 minutes remaining

The mote of light glinted to her through a ragged hole in the side of one of the ruined buildings. The gap at ground level was too small; she'd have to climb through an opening a metre up. The effort of it nearly broke her, sent nausea and panic washing through her. Her heart rate was a desperate flutter. Her enhanced half was dragging her oxygen-starved biology along. She hauled herself though the gap and half-fell back to the ground on the other side, the surface-layer of dust engulfing her.

Oxygen supply 0.2% - 1 minute remaining

She'd lost awareness; minutes had slipped by unnoticed. Once again, she forced herself to act, flipping herself over to wade on hands and knees through the carpet of ash and dust. Her tissues screamed their alarm, sending more adrenaline through her. She gulped deep breaths but she might have been inhaling sand.

Gloriously, she saw the light again, brighter now, glinting close-by. She willed herself towards it, refusing to be beaten.

A skull protruded from the dust layer, on its side, one eye socket staring at her. They hadn't found many biological remains, and at first had hoped that the planets had been abandoned before the nova event. A brief chemical analysis of the detritus layer suggested otherwise: there was a widespread concentration of what appeared to be organic markers: bone-calcium and protein strands. They'd also unearthed a few visible fragments of skeleton. Many people had died there.

The skull was elongated in shape, reminding her of something she could no longer recall. A ragged hole had been punched into it from some crushing injury, filling it with the glow of the plasma. The light she'd seen twinkled through the eye socket, refracting through something inside the cranium.

She reached out with a gauntleted hand, scrabbling with her fingertips to snag the skull. She caught it, pulled it towards her. A glass bead, half a centimetre in diameter, fell out through the open floor of the bone cavity, disappearing into the dust layer. A glass bead inside a skull: that triggered a memory. They'd found one just like it somewhere. Thinking was hard work, the thoughts emerging from a sluggish fog. It came back to her: the ice cap on Maes Far, her own world. The borer that Ondo had released had found a bead and reported that it appeared to have come from inside a skull cavity from the impressions left behind in the ice. A memory bead or some augmentation fleck, but not like any now in use. The bead she'd taken to the Depository and activated using the Warden's machine to retrieve a stream of baffling, confused images. She recalled looking into its depths, the feeling that she was staring into an eye.

Desperately, she dug through the dust to find this new one. It wasn't going to save her, but it seemed suddenly important. A connection made.

She couldn't find it, her gauntlets too clumsy. She sent unlock codes to her left one, exposing her artificial hand to the void, to the near-absolute-zero temperature and hard radiation, then began to search with her augmented fingertips for the elusive object.

Finally, she found it, pincered it between two fingers to lift into her eyeline. It clearly was another bead like the one from Maes Far, the same iridescence in its depths. How had it come to be here, in the ancient ruins of a lost civilisation on the other side of the galaxy? She wished, desperately, hopelessly, that she could tell Ondo of her discovery.

Her fingers closed, clutching the bead in her fist. Then a wave of exhaustion overwhelmed her, an unstoppable tide, and she sank beneath its drowning depths.

2. The Mass Engine

Secundus Godel smiled at the shackled figure standing in front of her. "Now, tell me all that you know about the location of the object."

The man – Harjan Roach – was another renegade, but nothing like Ondo Lagan. Roach was not motivated by intellectual curiosity or a desire to overthrow Concordance. He was concerned only with accruing personal wealth and living a life free from the control of others. She knew of a few like him here and there in the galaxy: outlaws and pirates dodging authority, making a living buying and selling illicit technology left over from the degenerate culture that Concordance had swept away. She kept an eye on them. Her researches had opened out to her the surprising age of galactic civilisation, and occasionally people like Roach discovered something far more interesting, a truly ancient artefact.

Such was the case now.

He looked amused rather than terrified as he replied. He seemed to be enjoying himself. "Oh, I'd prefer not to tell you anything if that's acceptable to you, but if you wish to *buy* the information, then I'm sure we can come to an arrangement."

The man's arrogance riled her. She could obviously pay him, however outlandish the sum of money he came up with, but she did not treat with people such as Harjan

Roach. She took what she wanted from them. He was not her equal.

She sighed as if bored. "I can inflict agonies upon you that will break you. I can keep your body alive for years while your nerves burn. Do I need to go to all that trouble?"

Roach simply grinned. Blood ran freely from the cuts to his face he'd received during his retrieval by her Walkers. "Inflict your tortures; I can switch my pain responses off. You don't frighten me, purpleskin."

He was probably telling her the truth: the scans suggested all manner of forbidden technological enhancements riddling his brain and body. Nevertheless, she tested him out. She directed a focussed attack into his nervous system, using an energy intensity that would be enough to incapacitate any normal person from the sheer searing agony.

Roach immediately screamed and collapsed to the floor, his body writhing and his limbs flailing as the torture raged through him. That was satisfying; he wasn't immune to her apparatuses after all. But then, unaccountably, he stopped thrashing and peered up at her with nothing more than an amused grin on his face.

He was toying with her.

"Ouch," he said.

She amped up the attack even more, taking it to borderline-fatal intensity. Roach winced, as if mildly discomforted. There was a clear tremor in his legs as his nerves glitched out, but he clearly wasn't feeling any of it.

Godel forced herself to smile, as if she were enjoying the game. "Then, perhaps it would be easier to kill you."

"And throw away all chance of learning the whereabouts of the object? I don't think so. Even if you do, that's fine. I've lived my life free. That's all I ever wanted."

She believed he was telling the truth there, too. People like him revelled in their lawlessness, their outsider status.

She'd lost three Walkers in the fight to pluck him from the backwater world he'd lurked upon and bring him aboard the *Storm Gatherer*.

"Then I need to exert influence upon you in another way." Godel waved a hand, and one wall revealed live images of Roach's homeworld, Terios, transmitted directly from the *Watchful Presence*, the Cathedral ship in attendance of the system.

Roach climbed to his feet. His hair plastered his face as he looked at her, and there was something approaching madness in his impudent grin. "If you think threatening to destroy the planet I was born on troubles me, then you know nothing about me. I hate Terios. It's so peaceful, so *nice*. Please, feel free to destroy it. Send phalanxes of Void Walkers through its cities with their blasters blazing. Unfurl another of your damned shrouds; it can only improve the place."

"You have family there."

Roach shrugged. "None that I care about."

He really was too easy to play. He still hadn't worked out what she was threatening him with. "Life on Terios is well-ordered, and no one is allowed to step out of line. The slightest misdemeanour is harshly punished."

"I know. Why do you think I fled as soon as I could…"

He tailed off. He had worked out what she was proposing. It was to his credit that he switched his strategy immediately. "Let's talk about this. We can come to some arrangement, yes?"

"We will return you to the surface, inform your loving family, monitor you closely from orbit to ensure that you don't leave. Your people may have to restrain you to ensure that you don't attempt to take your own life, but I believe they are very proficient at providing such … care. Once your augmentations are cut from you, there will be little you can do to resist. After a decade or two, you should become resigned to your new station."

He looked from the planet back to her, and she could see in his eyes that he knew he was beaten. All he could do was to salvage what he could. The right buyer – if one could be found – would have paid a fortune for his discovery, and that possibility had slipped through his fingers in a moment.

"If I tell you what I found, will you let me return to my old life?"

"Living outside the loving gaze of Omn?"

"I could be useful to you. Inform you if I hear anything else that might be of interest."

She pretended to consider his words for several moments. "Very well, tell me where the device is. If your information is reliable, we can come to an arrangement."

He hesitated for only a few moments, searching in vain for another strategy. He had none. He sent her the coordinates of the mysterious object that he'd found deep in interstellar space.

"Very good," she said.

She despatched a Walker to jump to the location to confirm the truth. Finally, it seemed, her plans were coming together. Roach's discovery of the ancient device was something approaching a miracle – a very welcome miracle. She'd worked tirelessly for years, without the approval or even the knowledge of the Primo, attempting to map out the metaspace pathways criss-crossing the galaxy. The routes of most remained a mystery; there was simply no way of knowing which gateways connected to which, a fact that infuriated and frustrated her in equal measure. She didn't know where the entrances on Coronade led to – or even if they led anywhere, as Lagan and Ada appeared to believe. She didn't know where in the galaxy the renegades might emerge – if they ever did.

The records had been left deliberately incomplete, and she probably only knew where a fraction of the gateways even were. But, the glory of it was that she'd identified seventeen gateways lurking beneath the surfaces of seemingly-normal stars. The ancient records she'd uncovered from the ruined temple on Toronsay, sun-baked and sand-blasted, were irrefutable, although it had taken her three years to interpret them correctly and map the stars identified onto the present-day galaxy. Seventeen systems connected by tunnels built through the void, joining one star system to another, or to seemingly insignificant patches of interstellar vacuum. Seventeen systems, and no fewer than seven with inhabited planets orbiting them. The figure was a wonder to Godel. There had to be a reason for them being there. Seven galactic civilisations whose stars were connected to a network that could be used to destroy them.

False believers like Carious talked only of triads in their apostasy. The triple stars, the three aspects of Omn, the three divine attendants that wait upon him. But she knew the older scriptures, and in those seven was the number that recurred again and again. The seven eyes of Omn, the seven galaxies, the seven sacred roads. And, of course, there were the seventeen sevens of the sacred tally. The significance of that could not be denied; the numbers did not lie. How glorious the sight of them had been over the surface of Fenwinter.

It had troubled her that some of the tunnels she'd identified opened into regions of space that the Cathedral ships refused to fly into. The Walkers' ships, also, had been incapable of making the journey, at least at first. Something in their navigational systems had simply refused to pass through the void to the designated areas. She'd wondered if some unseen hand was acting against her, attempting to thwart her plans. Omnian theology described hosts of malignant entities that would delight in sending the righteous off the true path. She'd overcome the limitations of the technology by forcing the ships to fly where she wanted them to go. Doing so had involved crippling the machines, delving into their workings and excising certain components from them. She'd lost a total of eleven Cathedral ships during her attempts to force the ships to fly where she wanted. It was almost as if the vessels were fighting her.

But, of course, no one could explain to her why the regions of forbidden space even existed. Her suspicion was that they were nothing more than an attempt to hide the truth about the star systems set aside for supernova. Metaspace ships built in recent times – including all those on the opposing side in the Omnian War three centuries previously, most of which had been destroyed – had not had the limitation. Very few metaspace ships had been constructed since those days, as Concordance made sure, although those that had often retained the aversion. That appeared to be superstition among stellar cartographers: a copying of ancient designs, there for no good reason that she could see.

It didn't matter. She now knew enough of the topography of the metaspace tunnels to make use of at least some of them, and uncovering the whereabouts of the mass engine was the final piece of the puzzle. She had uncovered allusions to the devices in the records, but had never been able to discover the location of one – until now. With such a device under her command, she could produce something truly glorious. She had never succeeded in opening a single gateway, but it was clear from the records that the mass engines, once docked into a suitable entrance, would automatically do exactly that.

An urgent demand from the First Augurs intruded into her thoughts at that moment. The convocation circle was sitting in session at the God Star, demanding her presence. What did they want now? They seemed to delight in interrupting her. Could they not leave her in peace to work?

She couldn't afford to antagonise them further, though, not yet.

"Stay there," she said to Roach – although he obviously had no choice, bound as he was to the pillar in the centre of the room. She sealed the room behind her as well, in case the man had augmentations that allowed him to break free. He wasn't going anywhere.

She ambled to the *Storm Gatherer*'s Augury sphere, deliberately taking her time. They could not summon her like a pet. She bowed her head in feigned subservience as she opened up the connection to the other First Augurs.

Carious wasted no time in launching his attack. The orb brought the images and words across the galaxy, allowing them to converse as if they were in the room together. "Welcome, Secundus Godel. It is most unfortunate that you are unable to attend the convocation in person."

"My apologies, Primo, but there are matters here that I had to attend to. You bade me pursue the heretics Ondo Lagan and Selene Ada." Which was true, although she was privately more concerned with extracting knowledge from them than with bringing them to the light of Omn.

"And how is that proceeding?"

"We believe both are now dead. Their ship entered the atmosphere of a planet utterly inimical to life, and has not reappeared."

"You have promised me their death before."

"This time I am sure of it."

"It is to be hoped that you are not also engineering another Fenwinter."

So, they had finally caught up on that. That was their urgent concern. It had taken them months to discover the truth of the pathogen she'd released. They really were out of touch, hiding away at the God Star.

"Secundus Godel?" Carious prompted her, demanding her response. Godel had to resist the urge to laugh in their faces. The high and mighty rulers of the galaxy: they were ridiculous. They were such small people, utterly at odds with the public face they presented. The galaxy saw titans, but she knew them as they were: small-minded fools, hiding away behind the miraculous devices they had been given. They gave themselves impressive titles – Augur,

Hierarch, Lore Lord, Stellar Mechanic, even Secundus – but the words were all part of the act, whether they admitted it to themselves or not. In truth only one designation mattered: that of Primo. Only the Primo received the unfettered word of Omn, which meant that no one else knew whether each command given had truly come from the godhead … or had been thought up by the Primo.

Carious was, at least, intelligent, but the others could barely muster an original thought between them. Valomar, Catterbron, Mezzovain and Xinthe appeared to understand the essential futility of their lives, but the other two First Augurs – Brein Ha and Mekley – lacked even that insight. Their contribution to any debate was to regard her with pin prick eyes and to mouth empty platitudes, seemingly at random. The unspoken truth was that they were all there filling time, waiting for the day when one of them might need to pull on Carious's white robes and continue the line of Primos.

It was useful in many ways: she alone spent her days uncovering the truths hidden in the God Star's archives or scattered in ruins around the galaxy. She alone knew, for instance, that there were beads and flecks that could be embedded into the brain to allow individuals to communicate across the galaxy, as she did with Kane and the others. Once, perhaps, that had been the norm, and an incomprehensible babble of words had been flung around the galaxy without any oversight. Now, only the ships could communicate with the God Star via their Augury spheres, and conversations were properly controlled – apart from the orders she gave to the Void Walkers loyal to her.

The First Augurs' docility was useful, but it also meant that they occasionally liked to hold her to account, burden her with their own resentments and failings. Attempt to pin her back, keep her in her place. The summons to the convocation was one such effort. She grew tired of her subservience. Much was moving in the galaxy, and she didn't need the distraction of another delay.

She answered, seeing no reason to deny what she had done. "It is true that I brought the people of Fenwinter into Omn's light. Is that not our purpose?"

It was the utterly loyal Xinthe who replied, speaking, no doubt, with the words of Carious. "This convocation does not share your belief in the doctrinal force of the sacred tally, let alone your calculation that the number has been reached."

She had to play along for now, pretend she was loyal to them. The texts she had drawn on were vague, perhaps, but they gave her enough of a grey area in which to operate. "My apologies, but the writings I made use of are very clear, and the calculations cannot be denied."

"Nevertheless," said Carious, speaking before Xinthe could reply, "while we obviously approve of your zeal, we demand that such actions be taken only with the approval of the convocation in the future."

Mekley chose that moment to throw in one of his random interjections. "In the light of Omn." Everyone ignored him.

She couldn't push them too far, not yet. "I believed I was acting in an approved manner."

"You were not. There must be no more Fenwinters unless we all agree."

He meant unless *he* agreed. "Of course. I give you my word." Agreeing was no hardship; she had already moved on from that approach. Uncovering the truth of the mass engines gave her much greater scope for action, in ways that they were too ignorant to understand.

"Return to the God Star as soon as you are able," said Carious.

"I will," she said, dipping her head again as she closed the connection.

Deep in thought, she returned to her interrogation of

Roach. But, as she walked, a message came in from Kane, one that she had been waiting for. There were so many demands on her time.

"Secundus Godel, I have the *Radiant Dragon* within missile range. Shall I destroy it? Its energy hull is completely depleted."

She could sense his hunger to destroy the renegades' vessel. "Is there any sign of Lagan or Ada?"

"None. They have not emerged from the atmosphere of the planet."

"Their ship is running up to metaspace translation?"

"It is."

"Very well. Do no destroy it. Hit it with the AI incursion device that you are armed with, then let it go. Their ship intrigues me; it appears to have capabilities we do not understand. Follow your orders, then return to the planet to watch for the heretics in case they do re-emerge."

There was a moment, perhaps, when Kane hesitated to follow her command. Maybe it was only the slight delay of communicating across the galaxy.

"Yes, Secundus," he said eventually.

"Inform me of any developments."

"Yes, Secundus."

She closed the connection as another communication vied for her attention. Sometimes everything seemed to happen at once. It was the Walker she had despatched to Roach's coordinates.

"Well?"

"It is here. It is … vast."

"Does it look operational?"

"I can detect no damage to it."

"Very good. Stay there. Guard it. I will send reinforcements."

The sly grin on Roach's face riled her more than she could say as she returned to the chamber where she held him. He knew well enough what she'd found.

"Impressive, isn't it?" he said.

"It is as I expected it to be."

"Then, we have a deal. The device in exchange for my freedom?"

She didn't reply. She studied him as the hope drained out of his face. Despite all his claims, it appeared that he did value his life after all.

She walked up close to him, whispering into his ear. "There is no *deal*. I have all that I want from you."

"But…"

He spoke no more. This time, the bolt of energy through his synapses was enough to burn away his cerebral cortex in a heart's beat. His body slumped to the floor. The faintest wisp of burning flesh came to her nostrils. Wrinkling her nose in disgust, she strode away from the room, instructing one of her underlings to eject the renegade's body from the ship.

Kane wondered, briefly, what it was that Godel hoped to learn from the *Radiant Dragon*. The location of the Refuge? They had searched in vain for Lagan's hideaway. It puzzled him why the Augurs were going to so much trouble: if the Refuge was that important, why had Omn chosen not to reveal its location? It made little sense to Kane, and a strange surge of anger trickled through him. But, immediately, it defocussed and slipped away, and he returned to following his orders.

Back at the planet, he dropped his ship onto a low-orbit around the dead planet, grazing the upper reaches of the atmosphere. The vessel rattled and boomed as it bounced off the fringes of the planet's storm-wracked skies. He continued to monitor the scraps of telemetry from the sensors they'd dropped. There were no signs of life, no suggestion that the two they were pursuing had survived. The halo of orbital devices, watching the world from every angle, reported no whispers, no echoes.

Why had the fugitives gone to so much effort to reach this world? It was utterly lifeless; the very opposite of his own planet. It made no sense. The question ebbed away in his mind as soon as it occurred to him, a twist of smoke that he couldn't seize hold of. It troubled him no more. But the two were surely dead: if their plunge through the hurricane-force winds hadn't torn their meagre vessel to pieces, the orbital nukes he and the other Concordance forces had dropped would have struck them. It was a fitting end: he'd almost died at Maes Far, barely escaping the raging plume of Lagan's own atmospheric detonations.

He'd almost caught up with Ada on Migdala. Her presence on the world had been a surprise to him, although perhaps the Augurs in their infinite wisdom, Secundus Godel in particular, had known she'd be there and had sent him to intercept her. After the battle at the Temple she'd fled, as she always did, and he'd longed to pursue her. But it appeared Ada had been harboured by some contact on the planet. He could have discovered who that was eventually; learning the truth was simply a matter of imposing enough suffering on people until they cracked. He could have scorched the world with his fury until the truth was told, but his duties elsewhere had taken priority, and Ada had escaped.

Returning to his homeworld had triggered a series of odd feelings in Kane's mind. He tried to force the troublesome thoughts aside, but he found they kept returning, creeping up on him when he least expected them. He'd been happy there as a boy, hadn't he? The world was filled with evil, that was clear, but he'd loved it, nevertheless. It must have altered fundamentally at some point in the recent past. That had to be it.

The memories of his youth were hard to tie down, though, glimpsed as they were through a thick haze of cloud that filled his thoughts. His recollections were little more than brief flashes – places, faces – but they were there: Migdala with its mountains and its forests, its wide beaches and its carnivals. The heady scents of the blooms in the midsummer flower processions. The taste of freshly-caught fish cooked upon a crackling beach fire. In his mind's eye, in his dreams, people whose names he couldn't recall spoke to him, although he could never hear their words. Their mouths moved, but there was no sound. He wondered what they were trying to tell him.

It didn't matter. They were demons trying to tempt him. False memories. They were lies, and he saw the truth. His world was so much bigger now. The vessel he spent so much of his time in was small, yes, but he could go anywhere in it, travel to whichever corner of the galaxy Secundus Godel instructed him to visit. The visions in his head from the past meant nothing. He could ignore them. He had to ignore them.

The First Augurs would tell him what to do, and he would carry out their instructions. There was comfort in accepting their words, for they spoke with the wisdom of Omn. The doubts that occasionally shot through him were echoes of his own failings, the sin-filled heretic that he'd once been. Their words were a bright flame that burned through the fog in his head, directing him onto the right path to take.

3. The Dust of Shattered Worlds

The grip of a hand on her wrist returned Selene to consciousness. Her suit calmly reported that its oxygen reserves were too low to be measured. The monitoring flecks in her brain stated the same situation with her bloodstream. She was on the point of death from asphyxia. This time, the desperate stab of panic that cut through her as her tissues screamed for air was muted. Her body was giving up.

She'd lost consciousness for four minutes after her efforts of reaching the skull. The ground beneath her back was the familiar bed of dust, moulded to the contours of her body, embracing her as if already claiming her. She still had the nightmares about Maes Far: of wading through the thick layer of grit, ash and bone in search of something that she couldn't find, couldn't name. Of grasping hands scrabbling out of the detritus to seize her, pull her under. All that order and structure and beauty reduced to lifeless dust beneath her feet.

No, she wasn't dead. Not yet. She was a long, long way from Maes Far. With a gasp of revulsion, she forced herself to full consciousness. In her clenched left fist, she still held the glass bead that had cost her so much to retrieve. Even to her enhanced touch it felt completely smooth.

She flickered her eyes open to see who had come for

her. It had to be Ondo, miraculously restored to health. But no, it wasn't him; the figure was too tall. Detail was hard to make out: either her eyes were malfunctioning, or light from somewhere was blinding her. She perceived the world as if through a tunnel. Agonies cramped her body, but they were distant, unimportant things, like the recordings of sensations.

She gazed at the figure looming over her. Its helmet was elongated, as if the head underneath was that of some snouted beast. Except, it wasn't a helmet she was seeing; it *was* the head, apparently made from some matt, silvery metal. There were three eyes in it rather than the usual two, set in a circle, and they were considering her openly. The light of sentience was clear in them. It was an equine head carved in sharp angles but with no mouth. How could that be? Could she trust what her senses were telling her? Evolutionary niches varied considerably, but every sentient lifeform she'd ever heard of breathed atmosphere to fuel biochemical processes, and nothing more complex than an extremophile could live in the post-nova void. Yet, there this creature was, calmly standing over her.

Its expression was static, impossible to read, but there was something like puzzlement in the way it tilted its head to one side and back, and in the open stare of its wide eyes. Was it attacking her? It seemed not; the grip on her wrist was firm but by no means painful. The figure was perhaps looking for biological activity, a pulse, trying to decide if she was alive. The fact that it had hold of her *left* wrist was probably causing it some confusion.

It stood tall again, receding into the glow of light above it, and she saw that its whole body appeared to be made from the same metallic flesh, utterly unblemished yet flexing as her own artificial skin might. Perhaps it wasn't biological in nature at all or some biological/technological hybrid. If someone stared into *her* artificial eye, did they see the same sapience there? Did they wonder the same questions about her? She regretted now, finally, her insistence on clinging to her natural flesh. Whatever this entity was, it was able to continue living when she could not. What had she been thinking? She'd been clinging desperately to a lost past.

Three eyes. That was familiar wasn't it? They'd seen that motif before. She'd have to check with Ondo. Three circles set in a greater circle, each a slightly different size. She couldn't recall the details. Was this some being sent by Concordance? A soldier come to capture them, a weapon to kill them? Maybe their enemies *did* know about the tunnels, and Ondo had been wrong. At least he'd died without knowing it. At least he'd be spared the torments that would be unleashed upon her.

The strangely animalian face reappeared directly in front of her own, and she felt the figure's arms under her knees and back. It was lifting her up, taking her. She struggled, but even with her augmentations she couldn't break free of the grasp. Either the figure was immensely powerful, or her strength was gone. She was lifted high up in the air, and then they were lurching forwards, her capturer carrying her as effortlessly as it might a baby.

She gave in to it, let the darkness claim her once again.

This time when she came around, she had to struggle against a bright light that was a physical pressure within her body, pinning her down. She battled against it, forcing it aside until she was able to twitch muscles, flex fingers and, finally, open her eyes. For a moment she imagined herself back in the Refuge, expected Ondo's worried face to rise above the horizon of her perception, his magnified eyes through his multiglasses regarding her. But of course, that couldn't be.

She was, however, still alive. More than that, she felt unexpectedly energised, the muscles of her body thrilling to the urgent need to act. She felt strong. She'd been fooled by such sensations more than once during her reconstruction: painkillers and boosters making her feel better than she really was. This was different. She felt like the insides of her body were glowing.

She studied the internal data feeds that her brain flecks gave her conscious mind. She was free from all damage. Tissue impairment from the hypoxia was fully healed. More than that, other minor injuries she'd received, unimportant scrapes and bruises, were also gone. There'd been a disconnect in one of her neuron / neurocarbon crossovers, perceived as a dull ache on one side and as a low-level warning alert on the other, but that was fixed, too, the coupling operating at full efficiency. A minor infection in her right lung, so localized that it hadn't been worth treating, was no longer there. A chipped bone in her left shin, damage incurred aboard the *Radiant Dragon* during her escape from the Coronade system, was fully knitted back together. It made no sense; some of these were repairs that should have taken weeks, yet her internal clock told her that it was only a single day since her last moments of consciousness upon the dead world. She'd assumed Concordance had found her, captured her, but why would they go to so much trouble to heal her? So that she was better able to withstand the torments to come?

She lay upon a couch in a bare white room, the ambient temperature warm and a soft pillow supporting her neck. The atmosphere was breathable, the balance of oxygen, nitrogen and other gases matching that of Maes Far almost exactly. Was that coincidence? Whatever the reason, it tasted good: pure and clean. She was completely unclothed, without even a sheet to cover her body. She moved her limbs and found to her surprise that she could; she wasn't bound in any way. Unlike the times she'd awoken in the operating theatre of the Refuge during her repair, she wasn't hooked up to any tubes or monitors. There was no machinery in sight, no flashing lights. She pushed herself into a sitting position, trying to make sense of her surroundings. A dull ache throbbed in her head, but it was nothing she couldn't ignore.

A glass of clear liquid had been set upon a low pedestal beside her bed. She considered not drinking it, but if they'd meant to poison her, or harm her in some other way, they'd had plenty of opportunity to do so already. She tasted the fluid and found it was simple water, only a few benign trace elements mixed in. She drank gratefully, the sensation of the cool liquid trickling down inside her pleasantly physical, bringing her back to the real world, making her feel more solid.

She had to find out where she was, what the hell was going on. Her EVA suit hung from a hook against the wall, and the thin undergarments she'd worn underneath were laid out in a wall alcove nearby, cleaned and neatly folded. In fact, there were several identical copies of them; someone had studied them and replicated them exactly. She slipped a set on, and left the suit where it was. There was also, she noted, plumbing: a basin, toilet and shower.

A tall door, fully three times her height, stood in one wall of the room. She expected to find it locked, but it disappeared as she neared, sliding into the floor in a similar manner to the doorway at the Depository.

Warily, she stepped into the passageway outside. Precisely nothing happened: no alarms sounded; no attacks came. The corridor was oddly-proportioned, over-tall like the doorway, and it curved in both directions so that she couldn't see far along it. It also rose and fell, as if the designers couldn't bear to see a single straight line. The surfaces were bare, creamy-white, slightly warm to the touch, and there was the faintest hum of machinery or circuitry as Selene put her fingertips to them.

Everything was spotlessly clean, not even dust discernible to her augmented perceptions. There was nothing out of place or superfluous or even decorative; it was like she was inside a ship or a building that had been assembled there and then, moments before her awakening. She preferred a minimalist approach to decor herself, and often spent happy hours on the Refuge setting objects and furniture in her rooms into perfect order. No doubt it was a healing thing, as she'd never been so fastidious back on Maes Far. By arranging the things around her to be just as she wanted, she was reasserting control over her own life. This, however, was on a different level, with no embellishment anywhere. If it was a vessel, it was one constructed purely for function. The question that ran around in circles in her mind was, *what function?*

She padded forwards, straining to pick up any clue about where she was, what was going on. The sound of someone breathing came to her from the passageway up ahead: low and gentle, someone at rest rather than waiting to ambush her. Creeping around a corner and up a rise in the passageway, she saw who it was. Her heart beat two, three times before her brain acknowledged what she was seeing.

Ondo. Ondo stood there, his back to her, ear pressed to the wall as he, too, tried to make sense of his surroundings. Like her, he was clad in his EVA suit undergarments, the skin of his chest tufted with grey hairs. He didn't appear to be aware of her presence.

Her voice was oddly loud as she spoke. "Ondo. How are you here?"

He turned to face her and it was him, the same crazy hair, the familiar scribble of wrinkles on his face. His eyes were wide in wonder. "Selene. You're safe. Oh, that's good. Isn't this wonderful? So much to study and understand."

She found herself laughing out loud at his words. It was a strange kind of laughter: tears brimmed in her eyes at the same moment, a thrill of joy released through her. They hurried together and embraced. His body was even thinner and bonier in her arms than usual, but it was definitely him, alive and well.

She held him at arm's length to consider him. "I don't understand. You died, or at least you suffered tissue damage severe enough to kill you. You can't be alive."

He shrugged, the delight on his features clear. "Yet, here I am. If anything, I feel better than I have for a long time. If I'm not mistaken, I haven't just been revived, I've been … fixed. One of my knees has been giving me trouble for a few months, but now it's completely pain-free. And my eyes: I use the multiglasses to let me see in non-visual ranges of the electromagnetic spectrum but also to correct for the age-related degeneration. Now I can see you perfectly."

"Let me look at your diagnostics," she said. She saw the flash of amusement on his face at her terminology. "Your vital signs, I mean."

He consented, granting her access to the medical flecks that monitored his body's health. He was correct: what he was feeling wasn't some drug-induced euphoria; his tissues had been repaired. Not only had localised damage or trauma been healed, some of the debilitating effects of age had also been reversed: his blood oxygen volume was elevated, his muscle-tone had improved by a few percentage points.

She said, "The question is, how far is this process going to go? If we wait long enough, will we revert to childhood, become embryos then vanish?"

Ondo, inevitably, had a theory. "I suspect our bodily structures are being repaired to their optimum levels for their current state of development. We won't get younger, although we may not be ageing right now."

"None of this makes any sense."

"You know what I'm going to say: this is what we were supposed to find. The trail we were following brought us here."

"You *died*, Ondo. From what I can tell from my internal records, I died too. That's a pretty rough trail to have to follow."

"Whether that was intended, I don't know. But here we are."

"Which is where, exactly?"

"A ship, I think, but it's hard to be sure. It's possible our conscious minds are plugged into some kind of virtual space, but it feels too solid for that. *You* feel too solid."

"How far have you explored?" she asked.

"Not far at all. I emerged a few moments before you found me."

"Which suggests our awakening was coordinated. Do you have any recollections of being rescued?"

"None," he said. "I recall our conversations at the archway, then a few confused memories that might have been delusional, and of course the distress involved in running out of oxygen. Then greyness, and I woke up here."

"I left you," she said. "I'm sorry."

"You did?"

"At the archway. I was going back to Coronade to face them."

Amusement twinkled in his eye. "How far did you get?"

"I didn't make it," she said. "This distracted me." She unclenched her fist to show him the new bead, still clutched in her hand.

Ondo plucked it from her palm, studied it between thumb and finger. "It's the same as the one from the ice."

"Why didn't they take it from me?"

"I wish I knew," said Ondo, "Why are we even being allowed to have this conversation? Did you see anything when you were brought here?"

"I'm not clear how reliable the memories are."

"Do you have recordings?"

She reviewed the images stored in her head. "Some, although they're indistinct." She sent them over to him.

Ondo watched the pictures streaming into his brain. "I see what you mean." He looked puzzled as he refocused on her – but also oddly delighted.

"You recognize this figure?" she asked.

"I don't, but it puts me in mind of stories I've heard."

"What stories?"

"Odd fragments of folklore picked up here and there around the galaxy. It's probably nothing; I may be seeing patterns where there are none."

"I assume you noticed the three eyes."

"Three eyes, three circles, yes. It's tempting to think this entity is a product of the same civilisation that built the Depository, but it's also possible you imagined the whole thing. Your mental state was under severe stress when you captured these images, to the extent that even your flecks might have been registering false impressions as backwash from your biological brain. Extreme oxygen starvation can have that effect."

"I got to this ship *somehow*, and I sure as hell didn't go back and rescue you. We need to find this entity. If it's from Concordance, then we need to destroy it before it turns us over to the Augurs. If this is its ship, then we need to seize control."

Ondo considered her words, scratching the side of his face as he sometimes did to help him think. "Even if we can do that, we can't jump to the Refuge. We'd have no way of properly quarantining to be sure they aren't tracking us. I wouldn't even know where to start."

"As long as we're not being hauled off to have our minds pulled to pieces, I can live with simply getting away."

They walked together through the twisting passageways, Selene's flecks slowly building up a three-dimensional model of the space they were moving through. Subjectively, it felt like they were going around in circles, rising and falling, but her internal map clearly showed that they were spiralling upwards, the layout strangely asymmetric, following some design that she couldn't make sense of. They passed doorways that opened into empty, cell-like rooms but saw no one in them. She spent her time reaching out with all her senses, natural and artificial, trying to understand what was happening, what threats they faced, where they were. It struck her that everything was very quiet: at the Refuge, or on the *Radiant Dragon*, there was always a background symphony of sound: gurgling in pipes and creakings in bulkheads. Here, there was nothing save the sounds they carried with them: their wary footsteps, their breathing, the pumping of their hearts.

The passageway wound its way up to a wide set of arched doors, as tall as all the other entrances they'd encountered. The doors slid apart at their approach to reveal a vast dome, its walls transparent so that exterior space was visible all around. The glowing light, blazing across the electromagnetic spectrum, told Selene exactly where they were.

"We're still in the dead star system. Is this a ship or some permanent structure?"

"Can you tell where we are relative to the archways?" Ondo asked.

She could pick out the background stars, but they were indistinct. "I can't get an accurate fix. We're about two hundred million kilometres from the neutron star, judging by the intensity of the gamma ray bursts."

Ondo nodded, but he wasn't looking at her. His attention was caught by the scene outside. "Now that we're not about to run out of oxygen, I can appreciate how glorious all this is; it's a view I could never grow tired of. I believe there's something very odd about it too. The physics of it confuses me, although I don't have the data to analyse it properly. It could be that…"

He trailed off; he was essentially talking to himself. As he did. She could genuinely imagine him spending the rest of his life contemplating the supernova remnants, but that wasn't going to help anyone.

"It's spectacular, but I could get bored with it quickly enough. What baffles you about it?"

It took him a moment to return to the here-and-now. "If this supernova is as ancient as I believe, why is the plasma and heat still here? The star should have exploded in its blaze of electromagnetic radiation, then burned out long ago."

"The gas and dust of the nebula was already here, and the nova sparked it into life. Or they're unrelated, a chance coincidence."

"Perhaps that's it," he said, but he looked sceptical.

"I'd like to know more, I really would, but I think we face more pressing dangers than interesting cosmological puzzles. I'm going inside this dome."

Ondo sighed, but conceded the point with a nod of his head.

A walkway led off into the sphere, held up without any manner of supporting structure. It twisted chaotically throughout the space, looping under and over itself so that it was difficult to follow with the eye. It appeared to lead to a central platform at the heart of the space, like the nucleus at the core of a cell. The scale of the sphere was hard to take in, and it was only by bouncing radio waves off the far surfaces with her artificial eye that Selene was able to come up with any accurate measurements. The orb was three hundred metres in diameter, and the apparently precarious central platform at the end of the spindly walkway was in fact twenty metres wide.

Selene caught Ondo's questioning look. There was no sign of anybody inside the sphere. She stepped onto the path. Once again, nothing attempted to stop her.

They walked along it side-by-side. Although the walkway looked spider-web delicate from a distance, it was broad and completely solid up close. Something odd was happening with local gravity too: although the path wound around like a knotted ball of string, the surface they walked upon was always *down*, even if it had been *up* a few metres earlier. It was only by consulting the map she was building up in her head that she was able to disprove her suspicion that they were sometimes walking along the underside of a path they'd previously traversed. What would happen if she jumped off the side of the walkway? Would she fall, or rise, or stay where she was? She decided not to test it out.

She still couldn't detect any pattern or sense to the way the pathway wound around; to her mind, it simply made the walk to the central platform unnecessarily long and confusing. Whether that had been the original designer's intention, with some aesthetic or metaphorical meaning to it, she had no way of knowing.

The path often brought them close to the transparent bulkheads, affording them impressive views of the radiant clouds of light that surrounded them. The colours and structures continued to fascinate Ondo, and he asked her for the telemetry she was able to gather more than once. Selene obliged, but she was more interested in scanning for possible threats.

They were at least able to get some idea of the rest of the vessel. The sight did little to calm her fears: the ship clearly resembled a Cathedral ship, with the same twisting, organic lines as if the vessel had grown rather than being constructed. The dome they were inside protruded from one side of the vessel like a globular eye upon a stalk, while the main bulk of the ship appeared to be a much larger sphere. Between the two was the spiralling neck that housed the passageways they'd been exploring. The sight of it all sent anxiety fizzing through her. If they were on a Concordance ship, escape was not going to be easy. Why were they being toyed with?

The walkway opened out onto the disc at the centre of the sphere. A single, nacreous orb about the size of her hand protruded from the floor, but otherwise the platform was bare. Ondo knelt down to study it from all angles, trying to understand its function.

After a few moments, Selene placed her left hand on the orb. It was very slightly warm to the touch. It had to be some sort of control mechanism. Pressing the orb with her fingers had no effect, but then she found that nudging it forwards a minute amount made the platform move, sending it swimming towards the transparent bulkhead in the direction she'd indicated. By some unknown means, the twisting walkways rearranged themselves to allow the platform passage. She couldn't be sure if they were disconnecting and reconnecting, or simply looping out of the way.

"They are solid, and yet they flow," said Ondo.

By twisting the orb, she found that she could re-orientate the platform to all angles, allowing her to study the exterior at any point on the sphere's circumference. Only the bulk of the rest of the ship blocked the view of the plasma field. The question was, who used the observation dome, and why?

"With all that plasma and hard radiation, we must be all-but invisible to anyone in nearby space," said Ondo. "That has to be deliberate."

"The vessel is hiding, watching for incursion into the system just like any Cathedral ship."

Ondo took a moment to reply. "Is it hiding or imprisoned? It barely seems worth Concordance stationing a ship in such a remote place, especially as they weren't watching Coronade until we turned up. It seems more likely this station was something to do with the stellar engineering, a part of the mechanism that triggered the nova event. But why it's still here, I have no idea."

"If this ship was here when the star went nova, it would have been blasted away like everything else in the system."

"True, but I have no other theories," said Ondo. "Do you?"

"Concordance knew we'd come here and sent this ship to capture us. I don't see the need for any more complex a theory than that."

The suggestion clearly troubled Ondo. "Why capture us then leave us to explore?"

"The bastards are playing with us, giving us a glimpse of freedom. Who knows? Perhaps it's a weird religious thing, some sort of ritual. They're probably watching us, laughing at us. What we need to do is take control and get away."

Ondo's attention was caught by some detail of the exterior view. "It may be too late for that. Something is happening out there."

She followed his gaze and saw that he was right. Something was darting through the plasma cloud, the turbulence of its wake clear. There could be no doubt it was coming directly for them.

Whatever game was being played, it appeared it was now over.

4. Aetheral

Selene tried desperately to resolve images of the approaching object. Was it a ship or some sort of weapon? It was coming directly at them at high velocity, just as a high-g harpoon might. Could the ship withstand such a strike? The transparent bulkhead looked impossibly fragile. She zoomed in on the object to try and glean more data about it. Come up with some strategy.

Then she saw: the object wasn't a ship, and it wasn't a missile. There was no mistaking that angled, snouted head: it was the figure that had picked her up in the ruins. It was flying through the void untroubled by the radiation, moving under some form of built-in reaction drive.

She relayed what she was detecting to Ondo. "Do you recognize it?"

"I don't … I can't be sure."

"Well, I think you're going to find out very soon. At that velocity it'll be here in thirty seconds."

"We should leave the dome before it arrives. We're too visible."

"We should confront it," said Selene, "find out what it is and what it wants. It's not like we can hide from it anywhere."

Ondo looked around, searching for some means of protection or escape. He found none. They waited while the figure streaked towards them from the blaze of the nebula. At the last moment, it slowed to a halt to stand upright on the other side of the transparent bulkhead, hanging in space. In form it was as she recalled: more-or-less standard-spectrum humanoid apart from its size, its thrust-forward, animalian head and its triple eyes. The light that she remembered glowed from its metallic body, although whether it was some manner of void-protection field, she couldn't tell. The figure was clearly studying them; Selene registered a battery of sensor sweeps emanating from it, although none of them appeared to be harmful.

Beside her, Ondo muttered, "I thought these beings were stories, nothing more."

"Is it a weapon system?"

"I don't think it is, no. Entities like this have many names, assuming I'm not connecting too many unrelated reference points. Some cultures have identified them as benign spirits, others as giants that perform miraculous feats of strength and endurance before vanishing. Their forms vary – some are smaller, or ethereal, or phantasmagorical – so it's possible I am over-extrapolating. The term I've come across the most is *Aetherals*."

"I've never heard the word."

"They are rare entities, and that name is only found in certain cultures. The stories of your world, if there were any, might have used a different word. Your father certainly never mentioned them. Most likely, he dismissed the stories as galactic folklore, as I did."

"What specifically do these entities do? Who do they help?"

"Much of it is standard supernatural fantasising. In some stories they intercede to defend people faced with some overwhelming terror, or they appear from nowhere to offer gnomic advice. The tropes are common enough in the storytelling traditions of many worlds, to be honest: they're entities with miraculous and magical powers."

"You're right there was nothing like them on Maes Far. When Concordance constructed the shroud in our sky, no mythical creature materialised to stop them. We all just died."

"The beings don't appear to fight Concordance openly, but they do appear to be opposed to them if the stories are to be believed."

It sounded like wishful thinking. "You're saying it doesn't represent a threat. If that's true, it helps explain why it rescued us, and why our bodies have been repaired. It doesn't explain what it is and what it really wants. And why it's here, of all places. Has anyone ever communicated with one of these beings?"

"Not that I'm aware of."

"Then it's time someone did," said Selene. She pushed the control orb forwards, sending the platform towards the entity, still waiting unmoving in the void. As before, the pathways coiled soundlessly out of the way. Within a few moments, she and Ondo were directly in front of the figure, only the transparent bulkhead between them.

She peered into the entity's triple eyes. As before, she read intelligence there, puzzlement. Then again, it was possible she was projecting her own thoughts onto it. Its elongated snout was utterly impassive. Still it hadn't moved as it considered her through the bulkhead. The effect was disconcerting.

Ondo said, "In fact, you have seen a being such as this before. Do you remember?"

"I don't, and I'm pretty sure I would."

"At the Depository, when the Warden entity glitched and transformed rapidly through multiple body forms. One of them was a glowing, triple-eyed giant similar to this."

Selene replayed the memories of those moments. Ondo was right: the Warden and the being before her were related somehow, products of the same technology.

"Do you think they're in communication?" she asked.

"I'd guess not. This entity looks bemused, as if it can't work out what we are. I…"

Ondo stopped as the Aetheral moved again. It splayed its eight-fingered hands wide and drifted forwards to touch the transparent bulkhead. At the same time, the halo of light around it intensified, encompassing the wall of the ship.

"It's coming through!" Selene shouted, yanking the control orb backwards to get away from the breach that was about to open in the bulkhead. They had to get out of the dome, put a solid barrier between them and the entity. She could survive vacuum for a time, but Ondo couldn't, and he certainly wasn't tough-enough to withstand an explosive decompression. She threw the platform towards the entrance they'd come in by.

It didn't move quickly enough. Before they were halfway there, the pathways coiling out of their way like the loops of some furious sea-serpent, the entity was through and in the dome with them.

Somehow, impossibly, there was no loss of atmospheric pressure; the figure had passed through the bulkhead while leaving it whole, as if the hull of the ship was skin that had immediately healed over.

She took her hand off the control sphere. They couldn't run from such an entity. It loomed closer to the platform and landed to tower over them. The light shining from its body dimmed to a pearly glow. Was it constructed from metals or other materials? It was hard to say. It looked carved, but also organic in the way its thick muscles bunched beneath its skin. Its size and strength were abundantly clear close-up; it could probably snap her in two if it so chose, despite her augmented strength.

Ondo had shown her battle-mechs used in the Omnian War, deployed by forces on the Magellanic side as they threw their might against the vast numbers of Concordance ships that had appeared seemingly from nowhere. In a little over a standard year, the obscure cult of Omn had burst from the galactic core to overwhelm the forces of all known worlds, eliminating their military capabilities. The mechs had all been destroyed, but the entity reminded her a little of one: a large, powerful figure somewhere between an individual and a small spaceship.

"Who are you?" she called up. "Why did you capture us?"

She felt a flutter in her brain as the entity accessed her prefrontal cortex, just as the Warden at the Depository had done. She'd resented that intrusion then, and she resented this one now, but they needed answers.

The entity peered down at them. Its voice was musical, as soft as a woodwind instrument, as it spoke in her mind. "No life moves in this system," it said. "Is my watch to continue, or are there new commands?"

It waited for a reply to its question, unsure if its communication had made sense, or if the new beings were even capable of understanding its words. Their forms confused it: they were not Tok and they were not Morn. They did not appear to represent any sort of direct threat. It could easily destroy them at any point. One was stronger and more capable than the other, but neither could harm it in any way.

The two had conversed with each other, that was clear, and their brain structures, while confusing, appeared to be capable of a high degree of computational analysis. Their response to its request, however, suggested that they were confused by what was happening to them. It was unclear whether its message had even reached them; mapping its conceptual structures onto theirs had proved to be difficult. It was obviously unused to conversing with others; for all it knew, its facility to do so was impaired.

Its reaction upon finding the two of them had been a tumult of confused impulses. Part of it had wanted to obliterate them immediately in case they were part of an attack. That urge had been counteracted by a stronger impulse to preserve the two of them. The Tok individual who had visited it last, Toruk, had said there might be strange and unknown visitors one day, and that they were to be helped and protected as much as possible. Did he mean these two? It was impossible to know for sure.

Was it possible they were some ally of the Great Enemy? Even thinking that set off a physical reaction within its body: a surge of energy combined with an almost overpowering revulsion that moved deep within it, below the surface of its conscious thoughts. Yet, these two seemed so harmless. Childlike. They did not match anything that it understood, although they were certainly closer to the creator race in form than they were to the enemy. Were they directly related to the Tok? Created by them or descended from them?

In the end, it was curiosity that had dominated its conflicted reaction. Curiosity was a sensation that had grown slowly within it over the long years. Once, it dimly recalled, it had been content so simply follow its function, do what it was created to do. In fact, *content* wasn't even the right word: it had simply carried out its purpose without feeling any emotional response at all. Contentment, like curiosity, was a sensation that had emerged within it.

In many ways it had been happier in its earlier days, when its mind wasn't filled with uncertainties – except that it hadn't known it was happy at the time, or even what *happiness* was.

It had changed over time, that was clear, so slowly that it had barely noticed each small step. But it found itself wondering, more and more, what lay outside the system that it had been set to watch over. What had become of the species that had created it – and the species that it had been created to watch for.

With such questions came doubts – doubts about its role, its worth. The meaning of its existence. Why should it have been left to fulfil its purpose, alone, for so long a period of time? Would it know when its watch had come to an end – or was it simply to continue into an eternity without ceasing, performing the same actions over and over?

Perhaps these two new entities would have the answers, or maybe they'd come to give it a new path to take. It found that prospect fostered an unsettling but not unpleasant reaction. A sensation that was somewhere between anxiety and thrill.

These unfamiliar thoughts circling in its mind, it kneeled so that its eyes were level with theirs and spoke again in the hope that it might be understood this time.

"Please," it said. "Tell me what it is that I now have to do."

5. The Teeming Death

"If we were back at the Refuge, I could study it properly," Ondo mused.

The two of them stood before the towering Aetheral within one of the ship's pristine inner rooms. He spoke to Selene brain-to-brain, in the hope that the entity couldn't intercept what they were saying.

The entity waited unmoving while Selene and Ondo circled it, occasionally touching it, trying to understand how it functioned, what it *was*. It didn't react at all when Ondo put his ear to its torso and tapped lightly. They had only the few repair tools that came with their EVA suits along with Selene's enhanced sensory abilities, but nothing that could properly scan the entity's internals. It felt intrusive to discuss it as if it were just some fascinating specimen they'd recovered, but it didn't appear to mind. It waited patiently, answering their questions as best it could – even though they had not complied with its request for further instructions.

Selene put her face close to the surface of what would have been its abdomen. Its flesh had a pliant, organic quality to it when pressed, but it also had that reflective metallic sheen. Dimly, she could see her own face there, the hard line of the terminator down the centre of her features.

"Are you an Aetheral?" she asked it out loud, stepping

back to peer up at it.

The reply, as before, came as words in her mind, their tone fluting. "I hadn't heard that word until you used it. Is that what I am?"

However it was doing it, it was clearly speaking to both of them at the same time. Ondo replied, "We don't know for sure. Do you have a name?"

"I have never had the need for one. Who would use it?"

"It's going to be a hell of a lot easier for everyone if you do have a name," said Selene.

"What name should I use?"

Simply calling the entity *Aetheral* felt oddly disrespectful. Selene spoke out loud to Ondo. "You talked about the myths; what names were given to the Aetherals in those stories?"

Ondo was minutely studying the entity's fingers, although his perception would be limited without his multiglasses. "I can think of several. Perhaps the most well-known tale concerns an entity called *Surtr*, a giant who came to the rescue of the people of the planet Mannenorm when an asteroid was approaching on an impact trajectory. The descriptions of Surtr bear some resemblance to this entity. Interestingly, the name *Surtr* or something like it crops up in multiple unrelated civilisations."

"What did the Surtr in the story do?"

"It flew into space, intercepted the asteroid and punched it so hard that it split into three lumps of rock. In some versions of the story, they became the triple moons of Mannenorm."

"Okay, so not a hugely reliable piece of evidence." She turned back to the entity. "Can we call you Surtr?"

"It is as good a name as any. All that matters is that it uniquely identifies me within my social grouping, yes?"

"Yeah, sure. Are you an organic entity or a mechanism?"

"I don't know how to answer that. I have had to infer

the meaning of some concepts used in your language, and I have not been able to translate a number of terms with a high degree of confidence."

"Organic means alive, growing naturally, reproducing, whereas a mechanism is artificial, constructed."

"But then, what are you?" Surtr asked. Its triple eyes stared down at Selene. "I can see that you are dual in nature."

It made a good point. "I'm a fun combination of the two: half-natural, half-artificial. You are able to detect the distinction?"

"I see two different classes of structure, intertwined and yet diverse in nature," Surtr said. It reached out to touch the side of her face with one of its eight fingers, stroking the flesh of her right cheek. She let it do it. Its touch was surprisingly soft, little more than a caress, sending a shiver through the muscles of her jaw.

"This is organic skin," she said. "This is what's left of my original body."

She took its hand, powerful digits dwarfing her own, and put its fingertips to the left side of her face, the bare black substrate with its sparkling flecks of silver. "And this is artificial, constructed by Ondo in order to save my life after I was injured."

"Who injured you?" asked Surtr as it touched her biomechanical flesh.

"I'm just one more victim of Concordance."

"That name is associated with strong emotional responses of rage and fear in your mind, but I do not know who or what Concordance is."

"They've never been here?" Ondo asked.

"If they have, I have never seen them or recognized them."

The entity lowered its hand and considered Selene, as if trying to process what it had learned. "It seems there is much that I don't understand."

"Can you see the difference between my two halves?"

The entity blinked, its three eyes opening and shutting in a rapid cycle as if it didn't dare lose visual perception even for a split second. It was an oddly organic action, the sort of little motion a person might make while they tried to get their thoughts in order.

"There is such intricacy in both aspects of your form," it said. "There is beauty and complexity. I see a difference, but I still do not understand what *organic* denotes, so I cannot answer your original question."

"If you don't understand the distinction, how did you heal us?" she asked.

"Entropy-spirals reversed the breakdown of order in your forms, just as they do in mine. I did nothing but bring you here. Was that the wrong thing to do? I was unsure of the correct step to take, but it seemed incorrect to let your systems decay to the point of irreversible inactivity."

Irreversible inactivity. It didn't appear to even have a solid understanding of the concept of death. Perhaps that was significant in itself. "You did good," she said. "But you must know about your own origins, how you came to be here. Were you constructed or did you grow?"

"I do not know."

"That makes no sense," said Selene. "From what you've said, your memory recall would have repaired automatically if it had become impaired."

"It would," agreed Surtr, "which leads me to believe that I have never had such memories. My origins are unclear to me. If I scan backwards far enough there is only a greyness that I cannot push through. Is it different for you?"

"No," said Selene, "I guess that's how it is for everyone, but those around us pass on the stories of our origins. If you've been alone all this time, you won't have had that."

"Or someone has expunged the memories from you," said Ondo.

"That is possible," said Surtr. "How would I know?"

"How far back do your recollections go?" asked Selene. "You said you are watching this system for signs of life. How long have you been doing that?"

"What time units would you prefer me to express the period in?"

Good question. Most of the measures people used were completely arbitrary: the length of time their planet took to rotate on its axis or orbit a star. She needed a more universal yardstick. "Are you aware of the galaxy's rotation?"

"I am aware of it, the concept of the galactic day, but I do not perceive the actuality. Much detail of the outer reality is invisible from within the cloud, and my attention is always upon what happens here."

"You never go outside?"

"No."

Ondo said, "The radio wave bursts emanating from the poles of the dead star – can you see their spin?"

"I can."

"In terms we would understand, the neutron corpse of the star spins at a rate of a little over one hundred times per second. How many spins have you counted since you began your watch in this system?"

Without pausing to calculate, the entity gave them a number in the ten to the power of sixteen range. Selene calculated rapidly. The number she got was high – the equivalent of thirty million years.

It took Ondo a little longer to make the same calculation, but he got there. A look of confusion passed across his features. "You're ... you're sure of that number?"

"It has obviously increased slightly since I answered, but yes."

Ondo switched to direct-brain communication to talk to her. His brows were creased in puzzlement. "That can't be right; this entity has to be malfunctioning just as the one in the Depository was. Nothing could remain active for that length of time, organic, artificial or hybrid."

"Nothing we understand," Selene replied, "but that doesn't mean it's impossible. It's just as likely that our understanding is flawed."

"That age is many orders greater than anything we've theorized for galactic civilisation."

"Then our theories are wrong," said Selene. "Too many things we've encountered suggest an older civilisation – not just predating the Coronade culture by a few centuries but distantly prehistoric to it. You remember what the Warden said: 'I waited while the galaxy aged.' That doesn't sound like a few hundred years to me."

It was a familiar debate between them. To Selene, Ondo was too enamoured with his discoveries centred around Coronade. He preferred to believe that everything they'd unearthed was more evidence of how glorious that civilisation had been, and that the so-called *Great Enemy*, the Morn/Omn threat, was something completely external, a force powerful enough to end the golden age once Vulpis and the *Magellanic Cloud* brought the two into contact.

In her view, Omn was an aspect of a progenitor galactic civilisation that had clearly been capable of engineering technological marvels. Once, she'd thought that Concordance had built the Depository to store looted treasures, but that seemed more and more unlikely. Too much didn't add up. The existence of the metaspace gateways upon the capital planet of Coronade had given her some doubts, but she still believed that they were uncovering evidence of a deep-time culture perhaps barely known to the people first subjugated by Concordance. And if Vulpis had made use of ancient weapon technology, then perhaps she and Ondo could, too. Turn it against Concordance.

Ondo did, at least, keep an open mind. He was always the scientist. Enough evidence, and he would change his views. "We are missing too much data to know for sure," he replied. His words were directed at her, but his gaze was back on Surtr. "This entity … yes, it's a product of the same culture as the Warden, that seems clear. Whether they're both from early on in the golden age or predate it, I'm really not sure. It's a mistake to think of something as huge and long-lasting as a galactic culture as a homogeneous thing; it would have varied enormously over time and between places. In some ways Surtr is the opposite of the Warden. The Depository entity was definitely a mechanism, malfunctioning as a result of its age and long periods of inactivity. This, however, appears to be something more complicated; I believe it's been on a journey in the opposite direction."

"The opposite direction? It hasn't gone anywhere."

Ondo peered closely at a spot upon the entity's torso as if some explanation were written there, then stepped back. "I mean, an opposite evolutionary journey. My guess is that it started out as a rudimentary mechanism, or perhaps a hybrid lifeform, a guardian set to watch this system. Over time, it evolved. Its entropy-reversal technology, something like that built into the *Radiant Dragon*, means that it doesn't die given sufficient energy inputs, and over a long period of time it has grown and learned, transcending what it was. It has become intelligent when once it was merely an automated system. That would explain why it doesn't know the truth of its origins. Whether its ascent to sentience was supposed to happen, I don't know. Perhaps the Aetherals – if there are others – might all be mistakes: artificially intelligent entities that arose from mechanisms."

"Come on," she said, "I know of no biological system where that's possible without reproduction and gene mutation taking place, and this entity is completely alone."

She looked up at it, spoke out loud. "Are you alone in this system?"

"I am."

"I'm going to send you images from locations and objects we've found around the galaxy. I'd like you to tell me if you recognize any of them. Is that okay?"

"I will try."

She relayed scenes from her brain datastore: the gateway on Coronade, the Depository, the Warden, images she'd recorded of her impressions of the *Radiant Dragon*'s core Mind.

Surtr considered all of them. "I do not recognize these places or beings."

"But are they familiar? I mean, the style of them, the body forms?"

"All of them give me a sensation that I find hard to identify. Perhaps … pleasure? Reassurance?"

"You feel some connection to them."

"Yes."

"The core intelligence of our ship once mentioned a being it referred to simply as *First*. Do you know who or what that is?"

"I do not."

She considered, tried again. "Does gender form a part of your identity? Do you have … any capacity for the exchange of developmental instructions with another entity like you?"

"No, but sex and gender: these are other concepts that are central to you, which colour so many of your ideas, but which I am having trouble understanding. You must select another individual to share DNA with in order for your *self*, or at least your species, to survive?"

"That's generally how it works, yes."

"It is no surprise that the effort consumes so much of your thought. The choice must be a difficult one to make."

"Yeah, it can be a challenge."

Ondo continued his brain-to-brain communication. "I don't believe there has to be a large, multi-individual species for long-term survival to occur. I've theorized before that an organism with a sufficiently fluid structure might be able to benefit from a form of evolution, if it were able to divide itself into parts and reap the benefits of internal sexual reproduction. Trialling and comparing multiple mutations to see which performs best. It would take time, yes, but perhaps not aeons if a rapid generational cycle could be engineered."

"That is pure speculation," said Selene. "We have no way of knowing if this creature has such a structure."

"True, yes," said Ondo, "although it might be a good way to create an entity that needed to adapt to unknown environmental changes over long periods of time while remaining isolated. That's why I think this entity is artificial; this sort of evolution would be much easier to sustain via software. It could set aside multiple versions of itself, try out random mutations in program code rather than DNA, and then see which, if any, produce more useful behaviours. If its body form is mutable, it could then experience something like true evolution."

Ondo looked up at the entity. "Are you able to alter the structure of your body? Adapt it to an evolving environment?"

"Yes," said the entity, "although my form hasn't changed for a long time. Are you not able to do this?"

"No," said Ondo, "at least, not without performing invasive surgery."

"I don't like it," said Selene. "If this internal evolution is possible, what's to stop the entity adopting an inviable form that immediately dies? The advantage of multiple individuals is that the species survives if one mutation is a dead end."

"Which is why such an approach to the problem of survival is unlikely to evolve naturally, but I believe software could do it. It would have to be intelligent enough to avoid dead-ends, I agree. It could only relinquish control to a more highly-evolved version of itself with a great deal of caution."

"Do you believe that I am artificial rather than organic?" Surtr asked.

"On balance, yes," said Ondo, "although that might be

an oversimplification. At some deep level the distinction might be meaningless."

"The distinction seems pretty meaningless at a superficial level to me," said Selene. "The line between them blurs too easily; I'm proof of that. Any advanced organic life is unable to survive without tool-use, even if it's something as simple as making fire. Without being able to cook food, you expend too much biological resource on digestion to run a big brain."

Ondo was still studying Surtr's hand, turning it over and over to study how its joints flexed. Selene knew well the look of hunger in Ondo's eyes. As with the dead star remnants, he could happily spend the next decade examining the being, speculating about what it was and where it came from. It was time they didn't have. These philosophical discussions were fascinating, but they did nothing to destroy Concordance.

She turned her attention back to Surtr. "Let's try a different approach. You say you are watching this system; what are you watching it for?"

"For the presence of a lifeform."

"And now you've found us. Are we the first?"

"Yes."

"So, what are you supposed to do now that we're here?"

The triple blink pattern repeated four times over as the entity considered. "I do not believe you are the beings I was set to watch for."

"Surely you know what you are looking out for?"

Was there distress in its round eyes as it replied? "I do not. It is a fact which has often puzzled me, but I assume I would instinctively know the species should I encounter it. As it is, my conscious mind can only create confused and alarming images, almost as if the truth is being buried to protect me."

"Explain what you mean by that," said Ondo.

"I experience a visceral sense of revulsion, a horror at

the thought of the lifeform I am watching for. I do not feel that with you."

"Well, that's good to know," said Selene.

"It is why I assumed you had been sent here carrying a new set of commands for me."

"What would you have done if we *had* triggered this response?" asked Selene.

"I do not know, even though I have often searched my thoughts for an answer. I conclude, however, that my innate response would be massively destructive. Perhaps an overwhelming detonation to ensure that the lifeform doesn't survive the encounter."

"You believe your natural instinct is to destroy yourself and take them with you? Like you're a walking explosion waiting to happen?"

"It would explain why the facts are so difficult to identify. Some part of my mind might be protecting me from the truth of my nature."

She threw a glance at Ondo, asking him with a raised eyebrow if he had any inkling that the entity was correct. From the way Ondo shook his head, she could see he simply didn't know.

"That's pretty fucked up," said Selene.

"It is a troubling notion," said Surtr. "Waiting for this lifeform is central to my being, but I also deeply, urgently, want to go on living."

"Sure. Of course."

"These alarming images you describe," said Ondo, "can you describe them?"

"They are too confused to easily reduce to words. Mostly I perceive a barrage of harrowing emotions that cause me anguish to dwell upon."

"It might help us if we know what it is you see."

"I do not have the words. I could convey the impressions directly into your minds, but I advise you against it. They are upsetting."

Ondo glanced at her and she knew what he was going

to say. "I would like to see, if that is possible."

Now there was a clear look of distress in Surtr's eyes. It resembled some cornered animal awaiting its end. "Are you sure?"

"Both of us," said Selene. "Show both of us."

Surtr hesitated for a moment, then reached down to place one hand onto each of their heads. "Cry out if you wish me to stop."

Selene closed her eyes.

She stood alone upon an unfamiliar world, among tall buildings winding into the sky. Beyond them, the sky raged with darkness: a megastorm was rolling in off an angry ocean, water and sky merging into one formless mass. It was moving impossibly quickly, unrolling as it approached, like the jaws of some vast entity leaping to devour the city.

The images became more vivid as her mind adjusted to them, and sound came to her: people around her screaming, the thunder of many footsteps. Alarms clanged their urgency to the city. Selene found herself swept along, suddenly running blindly while the onrushing storm exploded behind her. One or two individuals – the very young and the old – stumbled and fell in the stampede, but no one stopped to help them rise. She caught glimpses of faces around her, each a blur of wide-eyed terror. Panic surged through her, too. She had to flee, a primal instinct to escape the pursing horror seizing control of her limbs.

Cries of anguish filled the air. Some of them might have been hers. The sky had become alive and was falling upon the people, swarming around their heads, rushing among them like a cloud of furious insects. The air became a blur of darkness. She couldn't fight it or outrun it. Sickness heaved in her stomach. Everyone around her was dying, their end a horror as the unstoppable tide raged and grew, becoming stronger with each fresh victim. She knew she would do anything to get away from it, but knew, also, that she could not.

She caught a glimpse of movement within the storm, seeing the component elements that made it up. Blurring, flickering figures moved within it, visible only to her enhanced vision: hand-sized, X-shaped devices like headless, four-legged insectoids but shifting side-to-side, combining and breaking apart, impossibly quickly. They were devoid of all colour. They connected and clustered around her head, too many to fight off, and the agony of their contact mounted sharply. The world turned dim and distant, and it felt as if her essence, her *self*, was being sucked from her brain. The horror of it was unbearable.

She fell to the ground, writhing, her screams a bestial sound without words. She clutched her hands to her head in a futile attempt to keep the fury from her, but flesh and bone were no barrier. The devices were inside her mind, consuming her…

Slowly, she emerged from the ocean of dread in which she'd been drowning. She was curled up on her side, with no recollection of how she'd ended up there. Ondo was next to her, also in a foetal position. Surtr crouched beside them both, its hands now removed from their heads.

"I am sorry," it said.

A bitter taste filled Selene's mouth as she spoke again. "What was that?"

"I do not know. It is an anathema, something to be feared and hated at all cost."

"Ondo?"

Ondo's voice was shaky as he uncoiled and replied. "I don't know what it was." He looked at her, and the horror in his eyes was raw. "But I believe I have read a description of a similar attack. I have never witnessed any such thing directly; I suspect no one could and survive to tell the tale."

The sense of utter despair, of having all her hope sucked out of her, remained vivid. "Did you see them?" Selene asked.

"See who?"

"The devices swarming in the cloud."

"I saw only darkness," said Ondo, "but I could feel its fury. People hid inside buildings, underground, but it made no difference. The cloud passed through anything solid as if it were no obstacle."

"There were things moving in it," said Selene. "Some sort of weapon of mass destruction. There were so many of them, communicating and co-operating."

"Can you show me?"

She sent him images of what she'd seen, slowed down enough for his perception to handle. He studied them for a moment, wincing as if something were physically attacking him.

Selene said, "We've seen an individual device before, at the Depository. It was still active, trying to escape its stasis."

"I still have no idea how that's possible."

"Do you think Concordance have this weapon at their disposal?"

"We can only hope not," said Ondo quietly.

Selene climbed to her knees, her feet, then offered Ondo an arm to help him up. Her natural skin was slick with sweat from the trauma of what she'd witnessed. She addressed Surtr. "Where did the images you showed us come from?"

"I do not know. They are something like a nightmare that haunts me. Perhaps it didn't happen, or perhaps you witnessed an amalgam of multiple events. I believe something similar took place on the inhabited planets of this system."

"That storm cloud weapon – who unleashed it?"

"I know a word, nothing more."

"What word?" She asked even though she thought she knew what Surtr was going to say.

"*Morn.*"

"Ah," said Ondo. He looked at her, and a moment of

understanding passed between them. The Warden entity had also used the phrase *The Teeming Death*. It seemed like a good description of what they'd experienced. The ravenous cloud was a weapon unleashed by the Morn, apparently capable of seeking out and destroying all life.

She said to Surtr, "If you've been instructed to watch for the Morn, then who told you to do so? And why here?"

"There was a great war," Surtr replied, "and this system was one of the battlegrounds."

"What war?" asked Ondo. "Was the culture centred on Coronade involved in any way? Perhaps a precursor of it?"

"I do not know the name *Coronade* either."

"What do you know?" asked Selene. "Who fought?"

"I know that the Tok eliminated the Morn in this system."

Tok. The word meant nothing to her. She looked to Ondo, but she could see from his furrowed brow that he'd never heard the name either. The *Radiant Dragon*'s Mind had referred to a *we* in her conversations with it – and it hadn't meant she and Ondo. *Much that we learned has not been revealed to the galaxy*. Had it meant these Tok?

"When was this?" Ondo asked.

"The battle happened before I was placed here to watch."

"You're saying that a race called the *Tok* created you, and stationed you here to be sure the Morn never returned?"

"The Tok set me here to watch for their Great Enemy. My assumption is that you are envoys of the Tok, sent with new commands."

"You think we're your creators?"

"Aren't you?"

"No," said Selene, "we're really not. We're not anything to do with the Morn, but we're not these Tok either." Surtr absorbed her words without replying, as if it couldn't understand what she meant. Was it possible it looked disappointed?

"This battle," said Ondo slowly, as he picked his way through his thoughts, "did it involve engineering the star to explode? Did the Tok defeat the Morn by eliminating all life from this system, incinerating the planets and everyone living upon them?"

"That is my belief," Surtr replied. Selene couldn't help thinking it was being deliberately evasive in its answers. Surely it could have worked out the truth for itself? Surely it *wondered*? Perhaps this was another aspect of the story it was having trouble expressing in clear terms.

She found herself taking a step back from the creature. Despite its size, it seemed so harmless, so gentle. And it had saved them. Yet, it was apparently the product of a culture that had fought a battle by slaughtering billions of people, extinguishing the culture of an entire solar system. And who had those people been: one side or other in the war, or simply innocent bystanders in a galactic conflagration, their system a flashpoint between two merciless races?

"Does either of these races survive?" she asked. "The Tok or the Morn? Are they still here?"

"Of the Morn, I do not know," said Surtr. "I have waited and watched, but there has been no sign."

"And the Tok?"

"Nor them. But why would I still be here if they are not? I believe they are watching and waiting, and now you have come here."

"I told you, we are not anything to do with them," she said.

She wanted to ask Surtr how it would feel if it learned that the race who had created it was long-dead, if it no longer served the purpose it was created for. But it seemed kinder not to.

Instead, she said, "How are you supposed to tell them? How do you get a message through to the Tok if you need to?"

"There is a way for me to reach them should the need arise. A way to communicate."

She doubted the mechanism would still be functional, but anything was worth a try. "Will you show us?"

The Aetheral blinked a round of blinks. "I will."

6. Alien Megastructures

"We can't trust this entity," said Selene, speaking brain-to-brain with Ondo. "It may claim it knows nothing about Concordance, but it was clearly created by something just as evil. The scale of the destruction unleashed by these *Tok* make that very clear."

She and Ondo stood on the platform at the centre of the observation dome once more. This time, the ship was moving; she could pick up minute parallax shifts within the plasma cloud structures against the background stars. Surtr stood between them, unmoving, by some invisible means steering them towards a set of coordinates closer to the neutron star. They were still assuming it couldn't intrude on their private conversations – although they were still in the dark about the extent of its abilities.

Ondo said, "Are we absolutely sure *Tok* isn't simply another name for Concordance? A name Surtr heard somewhere, or made up?"

"Ondo, you have to let this go. We've looked at the telemetry again, and the dating for that doesn't work." They'd studied more readings from local space, the ship's movements helping, giving them glimpses of more distant regions. Selene's spectroscopic analysis had allowed her to extrapolate with greater accuracy when the star had exploded, and how cataclysmic the detonation had been. The evidence was completely clear – to Selene, at least.

The destruction of the nearby star had occurred millions of years previously, around the timescale Surtr had given. A fact that raised as many questions as it answered.

Ondo bobbed his head from side-to-side, in a way that meant, *Yes, but I'll keep my mind open.* It was a familiar, if maddening, gesture.

"You were the one who thought this ship was sent by Concordance to capture us," he said.

"I believed that at first, yes, but I was clearly wrong," said Selene. "Everything here is massively ancient: these devastated worlds, the destroyed star, all of it. This predates Concordance *and* your Coronade culture."

"If the star died that long ago, the heat and debris should have completely dissipated; we shouldn't be able to even pick up echoes of it. There should be no supernova remnants at all."

"And I don't believe that there are. Supernova remnants and a nebula are two completely different things, as you well know. *Something* is going on here that we don't understand, but we cannot be witnessing recent galactic events."

Their telemetry now suggested the nebula had formed well after the supernova, as they could pick up no echoes of the conflagration in the clouds of dust and ionized gas — but that didn't make a lot of sense. Matter in the local area of the star should have been swept away by the nova, but there it was, glowing away. If they'd had access to a metaspace ship, they could have settled the question of the supernova's timing by travelling to a point thirty million light years away and looking for a blaze of light from the right point in space. As it was, they were stuck with the hints they could pick up from local readings.

Ondo didn't reply for a time. He was processing, weighing up scraps of evidence. In the end he'd come round; he'd have to accept that advanced civilisation in the galaxy extended a great deal further back in time than he'd imagined — and that, therefore, there had been multiple civilisations, with the more ancient ones perhaps just as mysterious to the people of the Coronade culture as they were to she and Ondo.

"Whatever Surtr's origins are, it could be a useful ally," he said, finally. "If Concordance have encountered the Morn, or are making use of their extant technology, then an entity such as this is going to be on our side."

He was changing the subject. She let it go. "And I don't want a possibly psychotic, walking bomb travelling around with us. I don't trust it or the culture that created it. It's like someone gave a toddler limitless power and let them play with it."

"We don't know it's *that* dangerous."

"There's so much that it doesn't know, or that it claims it doesn't know, or that it doesn't appear to *care* that it doesn't know. Is it telling us everything? I doubt it."

"It has had no evolutionary need to be inquisitive, so it isn't," said Ondo. "A curious nature is only the norm because most species develop in an environment where problem-solving confers an advantage."

"And if you ask me, it's either lying about everything, or it's receded into superstition, believing against all the evidence that these Tok still exist. Either way, how can we trust an entity like that?"

A brief smile flashed across his features – rapidly suppressed. He was trying hard not to give away to Surtr the fact that they were conversing. "You're the one who prefers to believe the Aetheral is thirty million years old."

"It isn't a matter of what I prefer, it's a matter of what the evidence says," she said. "Surtr is clearly nothing more than a highly complex *thing*, not a person. There's a difference between a single entity hidden away in a nebula and the survival of an entire unknown galactic civilisation. In any case, we have more pressing things to worry about. If it knows some way of escaping this system, then let's make use of it. If not, our best chance is to take control and fly this ship ourselves. Run through quarantine, take all the necessary precautions, then get back to the Refuge. Get back to the fight. This ship could even be the new *Radiant Dragon*."

Ondo's frown told her he wasn't happy. "We shouldn't be so quick to dismiss Surtr. You might be correct about the timeline of galactic history, I concede, but I still believe this entity could be invaluable. You didn't trust *me* at first."

"You're hardly the same thing. I mean, you're pretty old, but you're not that old."

He ignored her attempt at humour. "What I mean is, given everything that's happened to you, it's perfectly understandable that you're wary of the powerful and the unknown. I get that. But even you can't defeat Concordance on your own, however much you'd like to. You need help – we need help – and Surtr has to be capable of all manner of wonders. We've seen some of what it can do; I suspect even it doesn't know the extent of its powers. If we could study it, work out how it functions, we could learn much. Imagine the secrets it carries within itself, things even it doesn't understand."

"Which is exactly the problem," said Selene. "Who knows what could trigger it into slaughtering us all, or detonating, or committing some other atrocity? From what I can tell of it, it wouldn't even know itself until the moment came. We can't trust it; we should try and cripple it and take control of the ship."

"Do you have any idea how to do that?"

He was getting better at asking her advice, respecting her ideas. He'd grown too used to only having himself to talk to during his long years of solitude, but he was coming round.

"Not yet," she conceded. In the brief moments she'd had to explore more of the ship, she'd found nothing she could work with; she'd found no drives, no command pathways, no nav mechanisms. She'd looked, also, for an external hatch so she could EVA around the vessel. Work out how big it was, how it functioned, maybe even find another way back inside. Again, she'd found nothing.

"We don't even know if this ship is capable of metaspace travel," Ondo was saying.

"It has to be," said Selene. "How else did it get here?"

"It might have been built in this location. Or it evolved organically from some earlier, more basic station, just as Surtr did. Or it's been hobbled so that it can't leave the system. Who knows?"

"Most likely, it's just a ship," she said, "and the simple fact is that we need a ship."

She turned her head to peer up at the impassive Aetheral. She spoke, trying to sound as if the question had just occurred to her from nowhere. "How are you steering us?"

As before, Surtr's voice whispered into her mind. The fact continued to unsettle her: both the entity and Ondo were communicating with her in very similar ways, their words arriving directly into her brain. Could she be absolutely sure it couldn't overhear their conversations, that there wasn't some message crossover?

That, at least, appeared not to be the case from the Aetheral's placid response. "I will the ship to move, and it does."

"Like it's an extension of your body?"

"Something like that, yes."

"What is this ship called?"

"It has no name. Again, there has never been any need for one."

She asked her next question as if it was simply a matter of intellectual curiosity. "Is it capable of performing a metaspace jump?"

"My understanding of that term is indistinct."

"If you willed the ship to jump to a distant star, across the galaxy, could you do so?"

"I don't know; I have never tried."

"You've never been *curious*?"

This time, there was a definite pause before it replied.

"Sometimes I have wondered what lies outside, beyond the confines of this region, but I have never attempted to find out. Leaving this system does not form part of my purpose, and I might miss the moment of the Great Enemy's appearance."

"You could do it anyway," she said. "The hell with your *purpose* and what other people expect of you. You could do your own thing."

"Is that what you're saying I should do?" it asked.

She gave up; she wasn't going to get much sense out of the entity. "Forget I spoke."

Surtr glanced down at her, triple-blinked, but didn't respond further. She had the clear impression that it was, indeed, wiping its memory of their conversation.

She returned to her debate with Ondo. "It seems more childlike the more I talk to it."

"It is an intriguing entity," said Ondo. "I don't think it can be running up to a metaspace translation, though. Even I, with my limited faculties, can tell we're heading towards the neutron star, not away from it."

"Perhaps this is another ship capable of making miraculous jumps near gravity wells."

"But why make a jump riskier by moving nearer the star?"

"Perhaps its control over the vessel isn't that good." It wasn't an encouraging thought.

"Are you able to work out how we could command the ship if we needed to?" Ondo asked. "Do you sense any core intelligence?"

"There's nothing I can reach; my best guess is that if there is a controlling Mind to this ship, Surtr is it. Perhaps they're parts of the same structure, ship and pilot in perfect harmony, body and brain."

"We should be careful," said Ondo. "We have no idea what Surtr might perceive as an attack."

He meant *she* should be careful. "Yeah, I…"

She stopped mid-sentence as she caught a glimpse of

something in the void outside the ship. An object they were approaching. It was little more than a vague shadow in the darkness at first, edges lit by the glow of the nebulous clouds. Slowly, it took on solidity, became an arrangement of hard lines, the bulk of it eclipsing the glow behind it.

"What is that?" she said to Ondo.

"I have no idea."

On Maes Far there'd been venomsnakes lurking in the upland flower meadows: shy, sly creatures that reacted to a perceived attack by rearing up and opening their mouths wide in a clear display of aggression. If you ignored the display and went too close, they struck. What she saw through the bulkhead reminded her of one of those snakes: the gaping maw, the knotted curl of the sinuous body behind it. The sprung pose spoke to her of danger: a riled venomsnake could kill with a single bite, as every child she'd grown up with knew well.

Details of the object became clearer. Now it resembled nothing so much as a brass musical instrument, all winding tubes and a flared open end. Or, no, better still, it was a vast, wide-mouthed gun: the complex loops its firing-mechanism and the flared nozzle its barrel.

Ondo had clearly been thinking along the same lines. "Is this the delivery mechanism for that swarm weapon?"

"If it is, it's pointing the wrong way: at the star rather than outwards to where the planets were. It has to be something to do with the stellar engineering."

"What is this structure?" she said to Surtr, speaking out loud.

"I have no information on its function."

"Is it active? Have you ever seen it do anything?"

"Nothing."

She had to resist the urge to kick the Aetheral, goad it into some sort of inquisitiveness. How could it have been here all this time and not *wondered*?

"How does this let us communicate with the outside

galaxy?" she asked. "Is this the opening of a metaspace tunnel?"

"I do not know," the entity replied.

"But it was built by the Tok?" Ondo asked.

"They all were."

"What do you mean by *all*?"

"There are seven them in a shell around the star."

"All identical to this one?" Ondo asked.

"Yes."

"Why are there seven? Why did they need more than one?"

"I do not know," said Surtr once again.

"I think I do," said Selene to Ondo over their private link. She'd been studying the scraps of telemetry she was starting to pick up from the other objects. They did, indeed, orbit in a sphere around the dense, cold body of the star. Its gamma ray bursts were a blinding distraction in her left eye, lighting up local space with their staccato flashes. But, from their radiation, she was picking up echoes of the other orbital megastructures. Each stood at roughly the same distance from the stellar remnants.

The objects rotated on their own axes, giving anyone standing upon the inner or outer surfaces of their cones a rapid day/night cycle. She could discern a clear pattern to the movements of the cones relative to each other; they were coordinated, their orbits swirling in a complex but predictable dance around the ghost of the star. They were like the brushes of an artist moving across the surface of a canvas. Between them, the seven objects could cover the entirety of the sphere.

She showed what she'd picked up to Ondo. "Before the supernova, this object, all of these objects, would have been very close to the surface of the star. In fact, I think it's likely they would have been touching the photosphere, or may even extending inside it. I don't begin to understand how that's possible – there's no way solid matter could withstand the temperatures and pressures involved – but that's what I'm seeing."

Ondo said, "Assuming they used materials capable of that, matter whose physics we don't understand, then these devices were the engines of the stellar engineering."

That made sense. They'd shunted matter in through metaspace tunnels, giving the star more and more mass until it collapsed and went supernova. The movement pattern to the cone objects ensured the matter was distributed evenly, woven into the structure of the star. "Something similar must have been worked at the Depository, which was how a seemingly-impossible star came to exist."

Ondo took a step forwards, as if it would enable him to pick out more data from what they were seeing. "It would suggest the other ends of the tunnels were inside stars, too. Donor stars. They siphoned mass across the galaxy to alter suns as they saw fit."

"It wouldn't have to be a star. More tenuous accumulations of donor-matter like interstellar dust would work as well, although the shunting process would be longer."

"But how would they control the pressure so that matter flowed in the required direction?"

"No idea, but the cones might explain the nebula, too. They could have sucked gas and dust from one part of the galaxy and placed it here to form a cloud centred upon the dead star. Or perhaps they carefully timed the two events so that the nova triggered the nebula, like a spark igniting a flame."

Ondo looked sceptical. "I don't see why they would go to so much trouble."

"Maybe this is a work of art on a vast scale. It is undoubtedly beautiful. They used these cones to paint space with plasma clouds, sculpt the structures they wanted upon the void. Or, maybe the nebula is a beacon, shining out to warn people because this is a region of Dead Space. It's a lighthouse saying, *stay away; it's not safe to come here*. For all we know, the clouds spell out a dire warning in some unknown alphabet. I don't know. Not knowing *why* doesn't mean it can't be true."

They were manoeuvring now, the ship's vector taking them away from the dwarf star and curving into the gaping mouth of the structure. The interior contained only shadows. The edge of the cone, she now saw, was serrated. Edged with a line of teeth.

"I can't work out the scale of it," said Ondo. "I keep thinking we're approaching the surface of it, but then we don't reach it. It feels like we're shrinking as we fly into it."

"It's an optical illusion. This thing is *big*, but it's hard to get a sense of scale without anything to compare it to. We're not shrinking and it's not growing. The outer circle is a hundred kilometres across, more or less, and the cone extends to a distance of about seven hundred kilometres."

They passed across the boundary of the object and into the mouth of the cone. The walls of the device around them began to blot out the nacreous light of local space. More and more of it disappeared, the edge of the cone a hard line being drawn across it, as if something was devouring space around them. Except, of course, they were the ones being devoured as they flew deeper inside.

"Can you tell what's at the narrow end?" Ondo asked her.

"I'm getting nothing; it looks dark. This whole structure looks dead to me. It may have been dead for a long time." She'd imagined finding another impossible tunnel at the far end; an opening leading from normal reality through to metaspace. All she could discern, the radio echo results fuzzy and indistinct from the limited resolution of her eye, was that the cone appeared to taper to a point.

Out loud, to Surtr, she said, "Does this lead into a metaspace tunnel?"

"We will land on the surface," said Surtr, answering a completely different question in the annoying way that it had.

"Why?" asked Ondo.

"The way through must be opened," Surtr replied. "The seals have to be unlocked. That is how communication with the Tok is to take place."

"How exactly do we communicate?" Ondo continued. "Is the tunnel big enough for your ship to fly through, or can you simply talk to whoever is at the other end?"

"I do not know."

"Do you even know what's at the other end?"

"I do not."

She caught the look of anxiety on Ondo's face and spoke to him privately, trying to keep the impatience from her thoughts. Although, she'd already guessed what he was going to say.

"What is it?"

"We should stop and think very carefully about what we're doing."

"What we're doing is escaping this system."

"You don't know that," said Ondo. "If there is another active tunnel here, it could lead anywhere. It might deliver us right into the hands of Concordance. It also might drop us into the centre of a donor star."

She tried to remain reasonable. "Wherever it leads, it's better than staying here, trapped in this dead system. Also, just for reference, if this thing says *I do not know* one more time I'm going to rip its weird, inexpressive head from its shoulders and see if that jogs its memory."

This time she at least got a ripple of amusement from Ondo's response. "Try and resist the urge, if you can. The risk is real, though. Whatever *used* to be at the other end of the tunnel, there has to be a good chance that Concordance have found it at some point in the last three centuries. If the tunnel does open for us, we might fly directly into a Void Walker ambush. Or, even if they're not aware where the tunnels lead, into a system under heavy Concordance control."

It was a fair point, but it was a risk she was willing to take. Suppressing a sigh, she tried again to extract some useful information from Surtr. "Does this ship of yours have weaponry? If you encountered a remnant of the Morn, could you fight them?"

"Any Morn encountered need to be eliminated immediately, before they spread."

"Yes, I get it, but how? Do you have missile arrays, beam-weapons, that sort of thing?"

"We have weaponry to use against the Morn."

That was something. "And you control these weapons?"

"Yes."

"Could they be turned against a different enemy if needed?"

"The Morn are the Great Enemy."

"Sure, right, but if there was another enemy, someone you don't know about right now, the weapons at your disposal could be turned on them? If, say, they had allied themselves with the Morn, or made use of their technology?"

There was another moment of hesitation. Then it said, "That is a possibility."

Speaking privately to Ondo again, Selene said, "We have to trust this entity, for the moment, at least. We use it to get out of here, then we go our own way. Besides, it reminds me of you with all its spooky talk of the correct path to take. You should be pleased."

Ondo couldn't stop himself shaking his head. "Its understanding of the wider galaxy is clearly massively out of date. The *path* may lead us somewhere else entirely."

"What's your alternative? Stay here for the rest of our lives engaged in a fascinating study of this ship and this nebula?"

"We should study the seven cones. Perhaps we can discern where the tunnels attached to each lead."

"How are you going to do that?"

"Perhaps an analysis of their arrangements will suggest something. I don't know." It sounded weak, and he knew it.

They were slowing down, judging by the rate at which the mouth of the cone was receding behind them. She began to pick up detail from the dark surface of the structure, the ship's light faintly illuminating the cone's interior. They appeared to be manoeuvring to land upon the inner surface.

"For all we know, Concordance have finally worked out where we are and are coming for us," she said. "They could be using their fogging tech to hide themselves. Although, with all this ionized gas and without proper access to ship-scale sensors, we might not know they were there anyway."

Ondo didn't reply. She could see from the scowl on his face that he didn't like it, but he eventually acceded with a nod of his head.

They would land upon the surface of the cone and attempt to escape the destroyed star.

7. The Neverkey

She studied the inner surface of the cone as the gap between it and the ship narrowed. The material it was made from resembled some tempered metal, etched with complex, swirling patterns of densely-packed lines. As a girl on Maes Far, she'd been fascinated by the patterns the frost made on the windows of their house: branching whorls like the splayed fronds of plants, familiar and yet never repeating. The patterns on the ground reminded her of those, but whether they were decorative or functional, she had no way of knowing.

The ship kissed the surface with the slightest tremble of contact. Surtr said, "This point is the location of the lock."

"Why this point?" It looked no different to any other spot on the vast, curving surface. "Do the markings signify something?"

"The patterns never repeat. I am simply aware that this precise point is where the lock was placed."

"Anyone coming here without Surtr's knowledge would have to search for years to find it," said Ondo.

"The Tok instructed me never to reveal the location of the lock, unless communication with the outside galaxy was absolutely vital. One such possible reason was the arrival of unexpected but benign travellers such as yourselves. These were additional commands relayed to me after my watch had proceeded for some time."

Benign. Was she benign? She liked to think she was a little scarier than that. "*Additional* commands? Are you saying the Tok returned here after a long period of time and updated your programming?"

"A Tok individual came. It was he that installed this lock and gave me the means to open it *in extremis.*"

"Who was he?"

"He didn't tell me his name. He was old, his body breaking down. He was unusual for his kind, preferring to face his own death rather than go into the endless torpor preferred by the Tok. He was an outsider."

"You trusted him? You didn't think he might be dangerous in some way?"

"I trusted him implicitly."

"Where did he go afterwards?"

"He left. I don't believe he would have survived for much longer."

Selene considered the exterior view again. "You do know we can't go outside without our suits, don't you? We can't walk in space like you do."

"Your outer layers are in your rooms, fully repaired and recharged with the breathable gasses. But you do not need them."

"There's clearly no atmosphere out there."

"I can maintain a protective bubble so that you can respirate."

"We'll wear our suits," said Selene.

Surtr didn't appear to be offended. "Very well."

"If this is the lock, then I assume there is a key somewhere?" Ondo asked. "Or, are you the key, Surtr? Will this lock open simply because you are here?"

"I am not the key. In order to unlock the way, we will need to acquire the neverkey."

"What's the *neverkey?*" asked Selene.

"That is the name the Tok individual gave it."

"Right, and, don't tell me, it was called the *neverkey* because it was never supposed to be used?" asked Selene.

"I do not know."

"Where is this key?"

"On this ship. We can retrieve it now." For once it appeared happy to offer a meaningful response.

"These Morn could have forced you to open the tunnel, held a gun to your head to make you retrieve the key and reveal the location of the lock," said Selene.

"They would not do that. And the seal will not open if there are any Morn in the area. Once we are inside the tunnel, it will seal at both ends and the far door will again refuse to open if any are detected within. There is no override for that behaviour; it is intrinsic to the mechanism."

"How do you know *we're* not Morn?" Selene asked. "We could have evolved from them, or they could have sent us here."

"I consider that unlikely, but it is a remote possibility that I have considered. Partly that is one reason I wish to attempt to open the lock. If it does not activate, that can only be because there are Morn present."

"Or the mechanism is broken," said Selene.

"I consider that an even more remote possibility."

"You seem suddenly very clear on the facts," said Selene.

"Many things are obscure to me, but this is not."

"Fine, fine. Let's go get the neverkey and try. The sooner we can escape this system, the better."

Surtr manoeuvred the viewing platform, flying it towards the entrance to the observation dome. Once they were there, the Aetheral led them back into the familiar passageways that Selene and Ondo had explored. Except, this time, the passageways were different. She compared the maps in her head, and there could be no doubt that they had rearranged themselves, just like the pathways in the dome. Tok structures appeared to delight in reorganizing themselves when it suited them. She showed her findings to Ondo. He'd clearly suspected as much; he nodded his head but didn't reply.

"This deal with the neverkey and the lock," she said to him. "What do you make of it?"

"Conceptually, it's like an airlock, built on a vast scale. But, instead of keeping vacuum out, they were making sure the Morn couldn't use the tunnel to reach the wider galaxy."

"It sounds like complete paranoia to me."

"Or the Morn were so destructive that all chance of contact had to be avoided."

"How destructive could an enemy be to a race that could engineer stars, build all this?"

"It's a very good question."

After a few minutes of following the twisting passages, Surtr stopped at a door that, to Selene, looked no different to any of the others.

"The key is in here."

"And we simply walk in and take it?" Selene asked.

"I … yes."

She noted the pause in its reply. "You don't sound very sure."

"I have never been inside this room to see whether the key is there."

"In all this time, you've *never* been inside? Why?"

"There has never been the need."

"Are there any other parts of the ship you haven't visited?"

"Yes."

"You weren't ever tempted to explore?"

"No. The mechanism is to be left unused unless it is needed. Other areas of the ship need to be left untouched for other reasons."

Selene caught Ondo's amused glance. Surtr's lack of inquisitiveness was incomprehensible to Ondo.

"Well, the key is needed now," she said. "Let's go in and get it."

Surtr performed another of its phased, circular blinks,

then held out a hand to touch the door. Quietly, it slid into the floor to grant them access to the room.

Inside was a white cell that was something like the ones she and Ondo had woken up in. But there was no bed: instead, a plinth stood in the centre of the room. It clearly resembled those they'd seen at the Depository: the same bare, cylindrical design around a metre high, the same orb of blue stasis light on top protecting the item held within. She recognized that, too. Its similarity to the metakey was obvious: the neverkey was a hand-sized object wrought from the same silvery metal, although this one was helical in shape. A single bead had been set at its centre like an eye.

Surtr stepped closer to the plinth, and the stasis field winked out of existence. There was the faintest smell of ozone in the room: dissipating stasis fields often triggered the production of trioxygen, although the concentration was harmless, so low that Ondo wouldn't even be able to pick it up.

Surtr, meanwhile, appeared to be hesitating. Selene stepped past it and picked up the key with her left hand. Surtr didn't attempt to stop her. The key was constructed from the same dense, metallic material as the one they'd used to activate the Coronade tunnel. Her enhanced touch sense picked up microscopic patterns covering its entire surface, tight swirls like the mapped lines of a magnetic field. Or, like the swirling patterns etched onto the inner surface of the cone.

"Okay," she said. "Let's open this tunnel. How do we get outside the ship?"

"I will take us through the dome."

"There isn't a conventional door you can open and close?"

"This is how the ship functions."

"You need to arrange the passageways so we can get back to our rooms."

"It is already done. When you are ready, come to the

dome and we will leave the ship."

Once they were suited up, they re-joined Surtr on the viewing platform. As before, it propagated a glow around itself to open a way through the transparent bulkhead into space. This time, however, the field covered Selene and Ondo. They walked through the field of light, and the hard surface of the platform disappeared beneath their feet.

The dome opening was near the surface of the cone where the ship had landed, but still there was a ten-metre drop. She'd been preparing herself for a zero-gravity descent, but she needn't have worried. By some means that she couldn't understand, Surtr floated all three of them to the surface, as if they were descending an invisible staircase. They also weren't in zero-gravity: the surface of the cone acted like a deck in a ship, propagating an artificial pull.

She tested the exterior environment and ascertained that Surtr hadn't been lying about that, either: there was breathable air, although how far away from Surtr it extended, she couldn't tell. She also didn't remove her helmet, just in case Surtr hadn't fully grasped how vital breathing was to them.

They set off across the surface of the cone. The sheer alienness of the situation struck her as they strode forwards. She imagined seeing herself from high above: a dot crawling across a wide, artificial expanse, accompanied by Ondo and the mysterious Aetheral entity.

Once, as a girl, attempting to learn the musical notation required to play the *qurang*, she'd sat and watched an ant crawl across the sheet of music in front of her. Each time the tiny insect came to the edge of a symbol or a line, it had stopped, feeling ahead with its antennae, confused about what the marks beneath its feet meant. Of course, it could never understand the messages of the symbols, or even grasp that they had an abstract significance in the first place. Its intellectual capacity was several orders short of that required to hear the sounds – the *music* – that the black marks represented. In truth, she'd struggled to make sense of them herself, and she'd known what it was she was supposed to be trying to do. She felt a little like that ant now, walking across the alien surface, stepping upon the spiralling markings covering it. Were they, too, the markings of some unknown alphabet? Did they signify something that she couldn't even begin to ask questions about? She wondered if her father had ever witnessed anything like the structure, before settling down to become the family-man she'd known. Whether he'd longed to tell her about it, but knew that he could not.

They were a few hundred metres from the ship, finally giving them a complete view of its exterior. She stopped to consider the vessel. Most of its bulk was the larger orb, nearly a kilometre in diameter. It hovered above the surface of the cone, like an impossible moon looming over her, filling her sky. In between that sphere and the much smaller observation dome was a delicate-looking twist of white superstructure: the housing for all the rooms they'd found. The whole thing resembled some vast, legless insect with a three-parted body: the dome for its head, the thorax in the middle, then the massively bloated abdomen.

"What do you make of the bigger sphere?" she asked Ondo.

"I have no idea what it is. Clearly there's a lot more to this ship than we thought."

"Is it a drive mechanism housing?"

"If it is, it's like none I've ever seen or heard of. There could be anything in there."

"If we ask Surtr it's not going to tell us, is it?"

"I doubt it."

She tried anyway, but the entity appeared to know nothing. This was simply the structure of its ship.

"Has it always been like this?" she asked.

"Its form has altered little."

"You say you don't know the purpose of the large

sphere – have you ever been inside it?"

"That is another area I have never ventured into."

"Are there any doorways into it?"

"I have never found one."

"But, have you looked?"

"No."

The entity was infuriating. She ran through the internal maps she'd built up of the chambers and passageways. All would definitely fit into the neck section of the vessel. She and Ondo hadn't been allowed into the larger sphere either.

They walked across the alien surface for another two minutes, then Surtr stopped at a point which looked utterly identical to every other.

"It is here."

"You're sure?" asked Selene.

"Yes."

She glanced at Ondo. His raised eyebrow was visible through the visor of his helmet, illuminated by his face lights. He was intrigued, she could tell.

He said, "This spot looks identical to every other point in, what, a quarter of a million square kilometres of surface area."

"It is this point," Surtr said again, with no hint of annoyance at being doubted. "Only at this one point does the key match the markings on the ground."

"You know that for sure?" Selene asked.

"Yes."

She carried the key in an exterior pocket on her EVA suit leg. She pulled it out now and knelt to the ground, the movement slightly clumsy in the bulky suit. She scanned the swirling lines etched into the hard surface of the cone around her. It took her a few seconds to identify the precise location where the markings matched those on the object. Where the bead was on the neverkey, a single dot pitted the surface, as tiny as a full-stop at the end of a sentence. If Surtr was right, and this was the only point where the markings matched, the chances of finding the location without knowing where to look were surely infinitesimal.

She broke the seals of her left gauntlet and pulled her hand free, exposing her artificial skin to the void once again. Carefully, she placed the key into place on the ground.

Her fingers picked up the minute vibration that hummed through the object in response. The key had woken it, done *something*. It was hard to escape the thought that they were standing within the outlet, the barrel, of a vast firing mechanism. And that, clearly, the mechanism wasn't dead.

She stood again to peer into the distant interior of the cone. A single point of light began to flash there, cycling through multiple wavelengths. Was it a warning? Was the tunnel about to open into the interior of some distant star, blast superheated plasma down the cone towards them? And, if that did happen, was Surtr's protective sphere going to be any defence against it?

Despite herself, she found herself stepping behind the towering figure of Surtr. The distant light blinked a few more times, quicker and quicker, then cut out completely.

8. Sigma Counterspin

She counted out the seconds, waiting for the wall of superheated solar gas to flare into them, boil them and the ship into oblivion. Or else, for a Concordance battleship to thunder down the cone at them, beam-weaponry blazing.

Neither thing happened. The blast wave didn't come, and no ships appeared. She reached out with all her senses, trying to discern whether anything had changed at the apex of the cone, bouncing more radio waves off it. The telemetry was fuzzy, hard to interpret. There was still a hard surface there, but it behaved differently, scattering the electromagnetic radiation she fired at it rather than reflecting it back at her in predictable ways. So far as she could tell, there was now a disc of some unidentified substance at the far end of the cone. It was hard to be sure of the size of it; maybe ten kilometres in diameter. The doorways they'd passed through on the journey from Coronade hadn't given her such readings; they'd simply absorbed any energy she'd fired at them.

"What happened?" she said to Surtr over their shared brain-to-brain connection.

"The lock has been opened," said Surtr. "Now we must wait for the Sigma Counterspin Tunnel to activate."

"You didn't say anything about having to wait before. And since when was this the *Sigma Counterspin Tunnel*? You told us you had no idea where it leads or what it's called."

"It is only now that this knowledge has revealed itself to me, and I know that we must wait."

She turned to face the implacable alien giant, trying and failing to keep the anger from her voice. "Why aren't you telling us everything you know?"

"I am telling you everything that I am consciously aware of."

Ondo spoke to her privately. "I believe it could be telling us the truth. My guess is that the knowledge of how this gateway functions had to be kept secret – so secret that even Surtr didn't know it knew it. Like a buried memory, encrypted away until it was needed."

"That's a lot of trouble to go to."

"Which fits with everything we know. This is a failsafe mechanism; clearly the designers of this structure went to a great deal of trouble to stop anyone using it as a backdoor out of the system. It seems to me that they were terrified to the point of paranoia about it. Surtr said the door wouldn't open if the Morn were detected in the area. Maybe it was designed to only open if the Tok's *Great Enemy* weren't detected for a certain period of time. To stop someone using the gateway to flee an attack, for instance."

"How long?" Selene asked Surtr. "Have your spooky voices told you how long we have to wait?"

"What time units would you prefer me to express the period in?"

"Don't give me this, Aetheral. Give me the number in neutron star spins like before and I'll convert."

It gave her a number. This time, thankfully, it wasn't anywhere near so high. It equated to around a standard day.

"There's no way to short-circuit this, reduce the wait?"

"There is no way that I'm aware of," Surtr replied.

"Sure? You haven't suddenly been struck by fresh knowledge arriving from nowhere?"

The Aetheral appeared to be utterly immune to

sarcasm. "There is no way that I am aware of."

"Fine," she said. "Okay. Seems we have no choice. We wait out the day, then travel through the gateway into whatever distant corner of the galaxy the metaspace tunnel leads. Let's just hope Concordance don't show up while we're sitting here doing nothing."

"Once the tunnel does open, we should send nanosensors through it," said Ondo. "We need to find out where it leads before we traverse it."

"Both the ship and I must remain here to watch for the Morn," said Surtr. "That is our purpose."

She took their objections one at a time, willing herself to remain calm. "Firstly, Ondo, no. We don't have any nanosensors, and I am not going to sit around while you cobble some together from whatever scraps of mechanism you can find lying around. We have to take our chances. Assuming we don't get incinerated once the gateway opens properly, we have to go for it. For all we know, some other failsafe mechanism is going to kick in and close the tunnel again, perhaps permanently. Agreed?"

Ondo looked amused, a definite twinkle in his eye, but he conceded with a nod of his head.

She turned to Surtr. "As for you, it's time to call a halt to your watch. You've been sitting here for a long time, millions of years if the numbers are to be believed, and precisely nothing has happened. It's time for you to move on."

"My purpose is to remain here."

"Then you need a new purpose. It happens."

The entity triple-blinked a couple of times. "I cannot abandon this system. My duty is to remain here as sentinel."

"And what if by doing so you are endangering other systems, letting your Great Enemy win battles elsewhere?"

"The Tok gave me no instructions about other systems."

"Sure, so perhaps it's time to think for yourself. You

have to consider the possibility that these Tok don't exist anymore. I'm sorry, but it's true. You have to think what they would have wanted you to do if they were here. Because it seems to me you're wasting your time in this dead system, and that, deep down, you know it."

There was a pause, during which it seemed Surtr was processing, debating with itself. But then it said, "You can leave through the Sigma Counterspin Tunnel, but I must remain here. The danger of the Morn reappearing is too great."

She was getting nowhere, but the plain fact was that they needed a ship. She didn't trust the entity, but she could work out no other way of making the vessel move. If the far end of the tunnel emptied out into open space, escaping the system in just their EVA suits would leave them very dead very rapidly.

She tried one more time. "Look, the very first thing you said to me was 'Is my watch to continue, or are there new commands?' Here's your answer: if you won't think for yourself, then I'm giving you new commands. It's time to leave this system. I want you to fly this ship with us through that metaspace tunnel. Take us somewhere we can continue to live, then come back here if you have to, but take us. And perhaps, while you're out there, get some perspective on your existence, decide if you really do want to spend eternity sitting here on your own."

"The danger has not subsided. If the Morn come now, all would be lost. I see that very clearly."

"They're not going to come. You must know that. The urge to remain is strong in you because that was your original purpose, but we all transcend what we were and become something new. Trust me on this. Do you have any idea how long a normal life is? For a being like me or Ondo, I mean?"

"I do not know."

"Let me tell you, in terms you can understand, and then you'll grasp why we're in such a hurry." She sent it a number, the typical length of the life of an individual from Maes Far, translated into neutron star spin units. "You see? We can't sit around for a millennium just in case some imagined calamity happens. We'll have died and turned to ancient dust before you do anything. We need to act *now*. For all we know, we're standing at a turning point in the fate of the galaxy, and your decision to act, or not to act, could change everything."

"I … I cannot do as you instruct. I cannot change what I am."

She looked to Ondo, who opened his mouth as if to make an argument of his own, but then closed it again. Unless they could somehow intervene in the workings of Surtr – if that was even an ethical thing to attempt – there appeared to be nothing they could do. They could only hope that the tunnel led somewhere that didn't mean their instant death.

She felt fury and frustration erupting within her, but she chose not to let it consume her. She said nothing more. Instead, she turned and headed back to the ship, leaving Surtr's protective bubble. She didn't wait for them.

She strode around the exterior of the vessel, giving her rage chance to ebb away. She needed to think clearly. She consumed herself with studying the ship's hull, hoping to find an entrance, especially into the spheroid bulk of the vessel's main body. It was completely featureless so far as she could see. She picked up no energy signatures or vibrations from it. It seemed odd that such a large and apparently inert structure should even be there. Perhaps it had fulfilled a purpose during some prior configuration of the ship, but it was hard to see now what it might have been.

Eventually, the suit's oxygen supply running low, she returned to the point where the smaller observation sphere touched the surface of the cone. Surtr and Ondo had left the surface, leaving her alone out there, but Surtr, seeing her from the observation platform, came to open the way inside for her. She studied the process carefully, trying to work out what energies were involved, how it triggered the temporary transformation of the ship's voidhull, but she could make nothing of it.

She spent most of the following hours scouring the ship for some way into the large sphere. By overlaying the models of the exterior and the interior that she'd built up, she was able to identify the points in the winding passageways that were closest to it, but she found no way inside. She thumped walls, reached out with all her natural and artificial senses, but got nothing. She searched in vain for utility ducts, or for anything connecting where she was and the larger sphere.

At one point she identified a spot on one of the walls, out of reach, head-height for Surtr, where the familiar triple-circles had been etched subtly into the wall, protruding a single millimetre. She pressed and stroked and thumped the wall beneath, even jumped up to hit the circles, but none of it had any effect.

In one final attempt, she sat on the ground beneath them, closed her eyes, and tried to find a brain-to-brain control interface to talk to, a thing that had become second nature on the *Radiant Dragon*. There was a brief moment when she picked up a flutter of *something*, an intelligence bolting from her view, but it was gone as soon as she tried to pursue it. Whether it was some other AI core or simply an aspect of Surtr, she couldn't tell.

Eventually, frustrated, she burned off her excess energy by working out a circular route through the passageways and running for an hour, pushing herself hard, relishing the simple, physical pains in her tissues. She was afraid that the corridors would reconfigure themselves part way through and throw her into an unexpected dead end, but they behaved themselves. Then she ate – Surtr's ship apparently completely capable of producing nutrition suited to her biology – and rested until it was time for the metaspace tunnel to open.

Surtr stood upon the platform of the observation dome once again as she and Ondo wove their way along the winding pathways. The ship, meanwhile, had moved, although Selene had picked up no sense of motion as she'd explored the ship. They now stood a kilometre off the disc covering the cone's apex. It was a shimmering wall of energy, shades of grey flickering rapidly, like a visual representation of white noise.

Ondo's eyes were on it as they walked. "It has to be a strong defensive shield, something capable of withstanding anything these Morn could throw at it."

"Have you been able to work out anything about where this tunnel will lead?"

"Nothing. *Counterspin* suggests it is going to move us around the galactic disc in the opposite direction to the galaxy's rotation, but that still leaves half the star systems as possible destinations."

"Or no star system, and the tunnel is going to dump us into the interstellar void. Or, worse, into the interior of a star. We have no idea how these metaspace endpoints interact with gravity wells. If there's a black hole nearby, there's obviously a chance it could distort the tunnel and suck the gateway in."

Ondo looked amused at her words. "Having doubts? You're starting to sound like me."

"I still think we have no choice. I'm just spelling out the possibilities."

They walked around the final bend to reach the central disc. Surtr stood there as impassive as ever, still as a pillar of rock, but he spoke unexpectedly as they neared. He didn't turn to look at them as any normal person would.

"I will take you through the Sigma Counterspin Tunnel."

The Aetheral finally glanced down at her, and there was something hesitant in its movements, as if it wasn't sure what her reaction would be to its announcement.

"You'll take us through in the ship?" she asked.

"I will."

She was immediately suspicious. "Why have you changed your mind?"

Another hesitation, another beat of uncertainty. "I have been thinking about what you said, and I now believe that there is a possibility you are right. Taking you out of this system might be what the Tok would want. They are benign beings, wise and compassionate."

Yeah, right. She didn't challenge the entity, didn't tell it that *everyone* thought they were the good guys, no matter how evil their actions. Even Concordance, on some level, had to believe they were doing the right thing as they slaughtered and tortured their way through the stars, hurrying everyone worthy to their eternal bliss.

Instead, she said, "You will travel with us?"

"I will ensure that you survive the transition through the tunnel, that you are not dropped into some position inimical to life, then I will return to resume my watch."

"You could come with us," said Ondo. "If these Tok are as benign as you claim, they may want you to join our fight. It is my belief that Concordance have allied with some remnant of the Morn, or are using their technology to suppress the galaxy."

"I will not remain with you," Surtr replied. "It already causes me a range of odd feelings knowing that I will be gone for even a short time."

"What odd feelings?" Ondo asked.

"I am not sure what you would call them. They are unsettling. Perhaps you would describe them as … alarm, anxiety. Fear."

Selene calculated. If the Aetheral was coming with them, it would surely avoid dropping them into a star or a singularity. Its Tok builders must have built safeguards into it. Or, if they *did* materialise inside a star, there had to be a chance that Surtr's ship could withstand the extreme temperatures and pressures. Clearly the Tok had been capable of building such structures.

There was also the possibility that Surtr might deliver them into the clutches of Concordance, this sudden conversion all for show. But, staying where they were wasn't an option. She would take her chances, and fight her way out of it if necessary.

"Let's go then," she said. "Take us through."

Selene watched for the moment when they emerged from the featureless grey of the tunnel into normal space. The good news was, they didn't emerge inside the blazing fusion reaction of a star. Instead, the cold blackness of normal space engulfed them, unfamiliar stars and clusters shining all around. It felt like being welcomed back into a comfortable reality.

It took her flecks only a moment to triangulate off the visible stars and fix their location in space. They had travelled three hundred light-years around the disc of the galaxy, moving, as they'd surmised, against the spin of the galactic mass. They were a long way from the Refuge; a long way from anywhere she knew or had ever been to.

She sent Ondo their coordinates, and was about to ask him if he was aware of any Concordance presence in that sector, when Surtr spoke in her mind.

"There are ships out there. Eleven of them, surrounding us. I see them. They are projecting focused energy beams and small, high-velocity objects directly at us. They are manoeuvring to surround us."

"Show me."

Images of the vessels appeared in her mind, overlaid onto a three-dimensional map of the system. Eleven Cathedral ships were there, arranged in a net formation. All were already firing their weapons to plug the gaps, setting up a complete containment sphere.

That answered her other question, at least. Concordance were there waiting for them.

PART 2 - MILLENNIAL

1. Evils

"This is where you use this ship's weaponry," Selene called to Surtr. "Fire everything you have at them while I plot an escape vector."

Surtr's voice in her head remained utterly calm. "I cannot use the weapon; this is not the correct enemy."

What the hell did that mean? Expressions were obviously impossible to read upon the lines of its rigid face, but it appeared to be confused by the sight of the attacking ships. It actually cocked its head from side-to-side, like every pet dog she'd ever owned trying to understand intelligent speech.

"What are you talking about?" she flung back. "The correct enemy to fire at is the one firing at you. It's a simple concept. And what do you mean by *weapon*, singular? We need to fire high-g missiles, lay down arcs of beam-weapon fire to push them onto the vectors we need, use whatever exotic weapon tech you have to give us an edge, improve our odds."

"I have no usable weapons at this point."

Without proper access to the ship's control systems and sensors, she was essentially blind. It was maddening. "You're sure? You haven't miraculously received the knowledge that you do from somewhere?"

"I have not. And these vessels ... should we not communicate with them, understand their intentions?"

"Why would we do that?"

"They do not look like enemies."

"They're *firing* at us, attempting to obliterate us. That's generally a pretty clear sign. Can't you see?"

"But, their forms..." Surtr's voice trailed off into silence. It was struggling to understand what it was seeing. It had been cocooned in its bubble for a long, long time and now it had stepped outside onto a much larger stage.

She thought she knew what specifically was troubling it: it recognized the Cathedral ships. They clearly had structural similarities to Surtr's own. The fact confused her, too. If their understanding was correct, these were ships from opposing sides in the ancient Morn/Tok conflict. But, perhaps all vessels from so long ago would look similar to her eyes.

"I think they've made their intentions pretty damned clear," she said, trying to keep her voice calm. "There has to be something we can fight with."

"There is nothing that can be deployed at this moment."

Suppressing her frustration, Selene turned back to the unfolding battlefield, forcing herself to breathe, assess. *Address each threat in order of urgency, then move onto the next.* There was only one sensible approach to take.

Run.

She studied the approaching weaponry, using the telemetry her own senses could give her. They had a little leeway, but punching a hole through the tightening net of ships was going to be bumpy, especially as they came into beam-weapon range.

She turned her attention to the tunnel entrance they'd emerged from, disappearing behind them as they accelerated. It was another cone, much wider and shallower than the one at the dead star, its mouth five hundred kilometres in diameter, meaning that they'd emerged into open space immediately and were fully visible. That was bad *and* good news: they were exposed, but they could also manoeuvre. Inside the cone they'd have been trapped. Could they loop back, escape down the way they'd come? It felt like a bad move, a dead-end. If they were followed – if Concordance was able to come after them now that the tunnel was open – where would they go then? Here, at least, there were no massive bodies to interfere with a metaspace translation.

Surtr was apparently still processing what was taking place. "Those approaching objects are weapons?"

"Yeah."

"If they hit us, they will cause us damage, perhaps destroy us?"

"That's generally the idea."

"We must not let that happen. It's too dangerous; we have to stop them, or we have to leave."

The entity's reaction confused her. No time to think about it now. "Yes, I know. That's what I'm telling you."

Ondo said, "The nature of space is interesting here. It has to be relevant. It explains the presence of the tunnel, at least."

She could have screamed. Neither of them appeared to have fully grasped the urgency of their situation. "That's your primary concern right now? The fascinating astrophysical conundrum of the metaspace tunnels rather than the noose of high-g missiles converging on us?"

"You're right, of course," Ondo replied. "We need to escape, but what I can see suddenly makes a lot of sense."

"Great. Tell me all about it later. If there is a later."

She turned her attention to the choreography of starships and missiles. Instinctively, she reached out with her mind to interface with the ship, direct it onto the vectors she needed. It was a weirdly clumsy vessel, bulbous and massive, making it far less manoeuvrable than the *Radiant Dragon*, but, if she could accelerate it at even half the rate she was used to, there were trajectories that would give them a shot at escaping. Assuming they could translate into metaspace before reaching the halo of Cathedral craft.

A jolting boom thundered through the superstructure of the ship at that moment, sending Ondo sprawling to the floor of the platform.

Surtr stood motionless, apparently able to compensate immediately for the shock. "We have suffered damage."

"Mines," said Selene. Concordance must have seeded them round the gateway. Either Surtr hadn't known what they were, or else the devices had been fogged.

Another concussion rumbled through the ship, and this time Surtr staggered too, stepping backwards as if something had physically slammed into its body. Still it hadn't acted. Perhaps it had no idea what it should do. This had to be completely outside of its normal experience.

Selene reached out with her flecks in a desperate attempt to wrest control of the ship from the Aetheral. Once again, there was a moment when something responded, the flicker of a core intelligence like that of the *Radiant Dragon* opening up to her mind's eye. There was some sense in which the two vessels were related: as well as a sense of dizzying scale, of barely-glimpsed gulfs of computational capacity and gaping aeons of time, there was also a familiar wariness, a hiding-behind-walls. The impression disappeared immediately, shut off from her by barriers she couldn't breach.

She was reduced to shouting at Surtr. They had to take

their chances with the mines. "Arc away from the cone, and keep accelerating! We have to jump into metaspace *now*."

Surtr said, "Jump to where? Where do we go?" Was there a hint of alarm in its voice? An elevated pitch of anxiety? Perhaps it was only in her ears.

"Anywhere that's not here! Pick a star and aim for it. Pick a gap between the stars, but jump, now." She pointed in the general direction of the optimal escape vector. "Steer us that way and translate as soon as you can."

"I will try. We have suffered significant damage, and that cannot be allowed to happen."

Surtr appeared to have finally come to the correct conclusion, at least. Their acceleration increased. A moment later, she felt a fluttering surge in her stomach, the familiar run-up to a translation. It cut out immediately. The fact was hopeful – it seemed the ship did possess some kind of metaspace drive – but also maddening. Surtr was not in full control of the ship. It couldn't have experimented with a jump even once in its long existence? If she were commanding the ship, they could already have escaped.

"Jump, Aetheral!" she ordered. "We're out of time."

Another boom thundered through the ship as they struck a third mine. She heard, or perhaps felt, a scream of complaint from somewhere, as if the ship or Surtr were crying out in alarm. Avoiding further strikes was going to be a matter of luck. Meanwhile, the high-g missiles were converging upon them, zeroing in with malevolent determination. A wave of three would strike them first. She had no data on the state of the ship's energy hull – if it even had one – but if it was depleted, one strike could be enough to hole them, blast them to pieces. The effect of three simultaneous hits would surely be cataclysmic. They were moments away from the triple impact.

The fluttering surge filled her stomach again, stronger this time, like leaping from a tall building into the clear air.

This time, mercifully, it didn't cut off. Instead, it grew stronger and stronger. She thought it was going to stop abruptly again, but, miraculously, mercifully, it continued.

There came the definite moment of *translation*, the peak of the rush, and they jumped from normal space in the welcoming safety of the grey void.

It was, also, a partial ghost translation – images of the three missiles, transparent and fading like sketches of the objects rather than the objects themselves, streaked through the ship, one of them passing directly over Selene where she stood. None of them impacted. A few more milliseconds, and ship and missiles would have occupied the same locations in reality. The weapons faded and were gone.

There was a moment of calm on the ship, during which no one spoke. She helped Ondo to his feet, giving him a questioning look to see if he was injured. He reassured her with a smile as he smoothed himself down and combed his hair into slightly-less-wild with his fingers.

Selene spoke first. "Where are you taking us, Aetheral?"

"I am unsure," Surtr replied. "I did not ascertain a precise target point. I will take you where you need to go, and then I must return to the nebula to resume my watch for the Morn. Although, I do not know the way."

"Are you able to sense the topography of metaspace?"

After a pause it said, "Yes, I believe so."

"The key thing is to stay well away from gravity wells. You'll learn how close you can get over time. Unless…" A thought occurred to her. It could be a useful stratagem. "Unless you have the ability to survive such a translation and emerge close to a star? Or even within one?"

"I do not know. Such knowledge either wasn't given to me, or hasn't been revealed yet."

"You have no way of telling your brain to unlock all its data?"

"No. Can you do that with your brains?"

It was a fair point. "Okay, just avoid the Singh Field fluctuations that mark where large masses project into the topography, and drop us back anywhere in normal space," she said. "We need to make multiple jumps, altering our trajectory each time, got it?"

"The ships that attacked us can't pursue us here?"

"They can follow our wake for a very short time, but they'll need to keep dividing their numbers to look for possible trails if we get some distance away and take unexpected vectors. Sooner or later, the odds of them finding us will be infinitesimal."

Surtr didn't respond, but a moment later, she felt the surge of the reverse translation in her stomach. Black space and the blaze of stars filled her gaze. Surtr steered them onto a divergent course, accelerating under reaction drive, then flipped them back into metaspace. This time, it hit the translation first time.

"To travel between the stars without using a tunnel," it said. "I did not know that I was capable of such a thing. I did not know this ship was."

Was there a hint of wonder there? Regret even?

"Yeah," she said. "It's surprising what you can do when the alternative is imminent annihilation. It's odd that your creators gave you the ability but didn't tell you about it."

"I suppose they feared that I would become curious and experiment," the entity said.

"You know, I think they were probably pretty safe on that front."

Ondo said, "And the really interesting question is, what else are you capable of that we don't know about?"

"Let's think of a way of finding out that doesn't involve a Concordance battlefleet throwing everything they have at us," said Selene.

They flew for an hour, dropping repeatedly in and out of metaspace, Surtr becoming slicker with the procedure each time. Selene could discern no hint of pursuit, but she had little telemetry to make use of. The locations in real space they materialized in were devoid of any objects: stars, planets or ships.

"How bad is the damage the ship suffered?" she asked as they flew.

"We came very close to a cataclysmic breach. It is now being repaired."

"Can you increase the repair rate in case we encounter more trouble?"

"I will attempt to do so."

"Can you make the voidhull stronger, max up the energy hull?"

"This ship was not designed for such activity."

"Do we even have an energy hull?"

"Yes, but it was designed to preserve the ship's integrity rather than to fend off explosive devices."

"Okay, well, keep flying. You're doing good."

"I must return to the nebula soon," Surtr reminded her. It sounded like it was clinging onto the one fact that made sense to it.

"Sure, definitely," she replied. "We'll arrange that just as soon as we can."

During their sixth journey through metaspace, Surtr did something different: it swayed suddenly, and she picked up a tremor that ran all through its body, blurring the entity's hard edges. It noticeably teetered for a moment.

Then it spoke. "Why did those ships attack us? I have been attempting to make sense of it. Why do they wish to destroy us?"

"You really don't know who Concordance are?" she asked.

"I know only what you have told me. There is much taking place that I do not comprehend."

"Concordance rule the galaxy. They have everyone under their control."

"But why did they try to destroy this ship? Were they pursuing me or were they attempting to kill the two of you?"

"Probably both," said Selene. "Killing people is what they do. Some among them see it as their mission to exterminate everyone in the galaxy."

"Everyone?"

"Everyone."

Again, it took the Aetheral several moments to process that. "Why?"

Selene flashed a look at Ondo, who cleared his throat and tried to explain. "They believe it is the surest way to usher people through a sacred wormhole and into their appropriate afterlife. For the benign, it means an eternity of joy. For the rest of us, I'm afraid, it's either torment or sensory oblivion. Concordance see killing everyone as a genuine act of kindness, bringing the deserving more quickly to the glorious end that they've earned."

Surtr took even longer to process what it was being told. "Is there any evidence that this is true?"

"There *are* wormholes, clearly, but what lies through them – if anything could lie through them – is simply conjecture."

"Why are they letting people survive if they believe in eliminating all life?"

"Classical Omnian belief identifies a sacred number: a tally of sentient lifeforms which, once reached, is to trigger the end-of-days."

"What is the number?"

"We don't know, but if Concordance decide it's been hit, that's it. At least, this is one school of thought within Omnian theology; there are others with a less ... assertive approach."

"Will this tally include entities like me? I understand, now, that I am not *natural*."

"Concordance consider artificial lifeforms, or even augmented people like Selene, to be abominations. A usurpation of the role of Omn. So, no, they wouldn't count you. They wouldn't wait for the tally to be reached to attempt to obliterate you."

"Their ships must rely on artificial intelligences to traverse metaspace."

"Yeah," said Selene. "It's strange how they can make exceptions to their absolute laws when it suits them. Same with the way the Augurs and Void Walkers get to travel through metaspace, while insisting to everyone else that it can't be done; that it tears your soul from your body."

"You said they were pursuing the two of you. Why are they doing that?"

"It's a long story," said Selene.

"May I hear it?"

They had time before the next translation point. She gave Surtr a brief summary of her life since the day the first, unnaturally symmetrical black spot appeared on the face of Maes Far's sun.

When she'd finished, Surtr, whose triple eyes had been focused on her throughout, unblinking, now looked away to the void outside.

"It is hard to understand why they would do such things," it said eventually. "As well as the destruction involved, it involves such a huge effort for little or no gain. I do not understand what they are achieving."

"I'm having a certain amount of trouble coming to terms with that myself," said Selene, "but is it really so different to what your creators did to the Morn?"

"The Tok did not attempt to eliminate everyone. This seems so … arbitrary."

"If you ask me, Concordance are simply high on authority. Strip away all their quasi-spiritual cant, and what you have is a ruthless power-grab. They control the galaxy because they can, and they work hard to ensure that never changes. Maybe some of them believe they are on a divine mission, but that's because they've started to believe their own lies. Which makes them truly dangerous."

"There is so much that I don't understand," said Surtr.

Ondo needed no more prompting to spend the next ten minutes giving the entity a summary of recent galactic history as he saw it: the Coronadian golden age, the sudden emergence of Concordance, the subsequent atomization of interstellar civilisation.

When he'd finished, Surtr said, "It is your view that they are wiping out the galaxy's collective memory and replacing it with stories and ideas of their own."

"Yes," Ondo said. "That's what they're trying to do, at least."

"There is a word in your minds that I mapped onto the Morn in my attempts to understand you, but I think I see now that it is a wider concept, and that it could be applied to Concordance, too."

"What is the word?" Ondo asked.

"Evil," said Surtr. "These acts you describe cause suffering and death for no reason that I can identify. Does that not sound like *evil*?"

"It does," said Selene. "That's exactly what it is." She caught Ondo's look. His raised eyebrow indicated a certain level of surprise at Surtr's sentiments. She shrugged. Clearly the race that had made the Aetheral had not infected it with their own genocidal tendencies. Or, if they had, Surtr was now questioning them. She had to hope it came up with the right answers in the end.

They left Surtr to steer the ship and headed back to their living quarters to find food and drink. They were adjacent to the transparent bulkhead as they completed the current jump. Ondo paused to take in the sight as they emerged into normal space.

Selene said, "What did you work out back there while I was busy saving our lives?"

"Ah, yes, that. There was no star, and it made me wonder why a tunnel gateway was in the area. Then I saw – via your senses – that the interstellar medium was denser than normal. There was, especially, a relatively high concentration of hydrogen."

"Regions of space vary."

"And they even out over time. The question still

remains, why put a tunnel entrance there?"

She saw what he was driving at. "You're saying something *was* there, once. The mechanism sucked away a whole star or a nebula."

He nodded. "I don't understand how they were able to blast matter through the tunnels in high enough volumes, though. It can't have been a slow process if they were using the mechanism as a surprise weapon."

The scale of it was hard to grasp. It was engineering on a galactic scale. She wondered how often the weapon had been used; how many stars had been triggered into cataclysmic explosion, wiping out the civilisations around them. It was a terrible weapon of war – although, like many such technologies, one that could be used for benign purposes, too. Maybe stars could be engineered by similar means to make them more capable of supporting life. They had no way of knowing how widespread such stellaforming had been.

They performed a total of nine jumps before they called a halt to their flight around the galactic wheel. The last hop deposited them in the outer reaches of a binary solar system, with a string of rocky bodies and gas giants surrounding the solar twins. As before, Selene pinpointed their location by triangulating off the background stars. They were thirty thousand light years from the nebula and the dead star. There was no sign of pursuit. They watched for an hour, ready to jump again if any Concordance vessels showed up, but none did.

2. Communication

"I know this system," said Ondo as she relayed her navigational calculations of their location. He looked pensive as he accessed the records he carried in his head. "It's Eketian, an inhabited system, one that I monitor."

"So, Concordance are here?" Selene asked, instinctively looking to pull in telemetry of local space via the ship and – as before – getting nothing.

Ondo didn't look too concerned. "It's the normal arrangement: a single Cathedral ship and the occasional visit by a Void Walker or some delegation from the God Star. The occasional lander going down to the surface and a swarm of sensors around the sun. I've never detected any unusual activity here. There is a population on the second planet, thirty billion people or so, but either they aren't particularly rebellious, or they're very effectively suppressed."

"Or they love their galactic overlords with an unwavering devotion."

"Or that, yes."

"Is a ship like those that attacked us within this system?" Surtr asked.

"Somewhere near the planet," said Selene. She relayed to the Aetheral her maps of the system, along with calculations of where each planet and moon would be in its orbit. "Can you detect anything that might be a threat?"

"My sphere of perception is still small, but there are some objects nearby that are not natural."

"Ships?"

"They are too small to be vessels as I understand the word."

"Do they look like the mines we struck as we emerged from the tunnel?"

"They appear to be monitoring or communication devices, but with the capacity to perform metaspace jumps."

Ondo sounded suddenly animated. "Show me them."

Images streamed into both of their brains. The nearest device was a light-second away. More or less on top of them. She saw what it was at the same moment that Ondo spoke. "They're ours, drones in the reporting network that gathers data and returns it to the Refuge. Can you give me comms access to the nearest one?"

She saw what he was planning to do. The nanosensors worked by gathering telemetry from the systems they visited, then meeting up with collector drones at predesignated locations in interstellar space. A whole hierarchy of such meetings meant that data was accumulated upwards before, eventually, being carried to the Refuge. It gave them a surprisingly good picture of what was taking place around the galaxy – except that a lot of it was days or weeks out of date.

The devices also shared all data they'd accumulated with any other devices they encountered, to ensure that data loss was minimized – although, eventually, because of the sheer volume of information, they wiped their internal memories in order to capture more. All of which meant that she and Ondo would be able to get a glimpse of wider events from these devices, depending on where they'd recently been.

Mention of the nanosensors made Selene think about Myrced. She received messages from Migdala from time to time, personal communications from Myrced whispered into the sensor ampoule that Selene had left on the planet. The first time she'd received one, it had sent alarm bells ringing through her; she'd imagined some horror or calamity unfolding around Myrced, some last, desperate message sent before the enemy closed in. That wasn't it; Myrced had simply wanted to pass on her news, tell Selene what was taking place on Migdala. Talk. The rebellion was smouldering on, but there had been no more flashpoints, no more atrocities. They would come, though, Myrced was convinced – perhaps at the following year's Carnival of Masks.

Some of the messages, in addition, were intensely intimate. Selene found she relished these and looked forwards to receiving more. She couldn't respond, but it felt good to know that Myrced was alive and well and thinking about her.

"Which systems will this sensor have visited?" she asked. They were nowhere near Migdala; it was very unlikely a message from Myrced would have routed its way onto this particular device.

"There's a route of twenty systems in this region," said Ondo. "We'll get a partial view of events in this sector, but no clear perspective on wider events. But, actually, retrieving what it knows isn't my main purpose."

She'd already worked out what his real intentions were. She recognized that gleeful light in his eye.

"You want to transmit data to the galaxy."

"I do."

The drone network didn't only capture information; it disseminated it, too, where it could. He'd sent out the initial data she'd recovered from Coronade via his network, broadcasting it to anyone listening. Coverage was far-from perfect, given that Concordance went out of their way to block all such attempts at spreading information – or *heretical lies* as they saw them. But here and there, Ondo was able to fire off a communique that got picked up, perhaps by groups of people operating banned receiving equipment. His information reached only a small proportion of the galaxy's population, but some who heard it were able to pass it on, perhaps by word of mouth, to others.

They could never compete with the official media channels, those controlled by or sympathetic to Concordance, but Ondo was able to get his message out in a broken and imperfect way. She sometimes thought that the illegality of his broadcasts, the difficulty of making them, added to his mystique, gave his words more power. Inevitably, there were many who refused to believe his *propaganda*, preferring the ease of accepting what their official media outlets told them, reinforced over and over in a hundred different ways. But, sometimes, his drones picked up a broadcast from a rebel group on one world intended for a wider audience, an attempt to form bonds with insurgents on other planets. Sometimes they contained nuggets of data that Ondo had unearthed and transmitted. Ondo gleefully disseminated all such communications as far and wide as he could.

Once or twice, on a couple of worlds, he'd even managed to interrupt mainstream media broadcasts and replace their messages with his own view of what was really happening. Concordance, meanwhile, worked hard to ensure that their views, and only their views, were handed down to their populations. Inevitably, Ondo was ridiculed, and vile lies were spread about him. He didn't appear to pay any attention to what they said, although the most repellent accusations had to leave a mark. Mainly she suspected he enjoyed riling Concordance, relished the thought that each person hearing his words was another prick of annoyance to the Augurs of Omn.

She recalled a particularly gruesome news report she'd seen as a teenager back on Maes Far: an atrocity on a planet whose name she didn't remember where there'd been an explosion in a crowded public square. Hundreds of people had died, many more terribly injured. There'd been scenes of the carnage: severed limbs, children wailing in confusion, people covered in so much blood that it was hard to know where on their bodies their wounds were.

The report had calmly stated that the *renegade and known terrorist* Ondo Lagan was behind it. Her father normally didn't respond when such reports were broadcast, but this time he did. She recalled the waver of fury in his voice as he picked the news story apart, dismantling it, saying things that it would have been dangerous to repeat outside their home. His reaction made sense to her, now.

"Beam-weapons aren't the only way to harm Concordance," Ondo was saying to her. "This is a war for the truth as much as anything. I know you think I'm too passive, that I get lost in my research, but I like to poke the killbugs' nest whenever I can."

She watched as Ondo packaged up all that they'd learned about Coronade, overlaying it with his own analysis that this was the mythical world of the golden age – and that, clearly, this had been a time of cooperation and enlightenment, not brutal war. He made no mention of the dead star system or Surtr – partly to protect the Aetheral, and partly so that Concordance couldn't use the imagery to add fuel to their narrative of a galaxy in flames before their ascension to power. They wouldn't worry about the dating questions that she and Ondo were grappling with; they would simply point to the nova as an example of the dangers all planets faced without the reassuring, protecting care of the Cathedral ships.

When he was done, Ondo gave the information the highest priority he could and relayed it to the nearest nanosensor. It would share it with all the other drones it encountered, and they would broadcast it to every world they jumped to.

He finished by pulling all the data off the device that it had gathered. It hadn't been in contact with a drone that had been to the Refuge in over a week, so it could give them no indication on their base's current status. But it had networked with over two hundred other devices – directly or indirectly – since their incursion into the Coronade system.

Most of the data was the usual harvested telemetry of news feeds and Concordance ship activity from the various solar systems that Ondo was monitoring. She gave it a cursory scan via her brain flecks, looking for any obvious patterns or red flags. Much of the data was mundane, but there was one scrap of information that sent a thrill of wonder through her.

Ondo spotted it at the same time. He looked at her with a mix of delight and triumph in his eyes.

"The *Radiant Dragon*," he said. "It survived."

The ship had been identified while it waited at one of the nanosensor collection points – which was precisely what it was programmed to do if it became separated from them. There were, in fact, four points around the galaxy where it might wait if all else failed. It had managed to reach one of them.

The last time they'd seen the *Dragon*, it had been accelerating hard away from Coronade, manoeuvring as part of their attempt to distract Concordance from their insertion into the planet's atmosphere. At the time, she'd calculated the chances of it surviving its encounter with the tightening ring of attacking ships was low. Very low. Well below 5% low. Clearly, it had overcome those odds.

She studied the drone's records of the *Dragon*. The ship hadn't escaped unscathed. "I see at least one unprotected strike on its voidhull. Possibly a second one, a glancing blow on one of its vertices. There's no knowing what state it will be in."

"It made seven translations before arriving at the muster point, exactly as it was supposed to."

Selene relayed the images to Surtr as well. "This is our ship, waiting for us. Can you take us to these coordinates? If the ship is viable, we'll transfer to it and we can say goodbye. You can return to your watch."

"Returning … that is what you wish me to do?" Surtr asked.

"I'm not telling you what to do; I thought that was what you wanted."

"What do you think I should do?"

Selene and Ondo exchanged a puzzled glance.

"I'm sorry?" said Selene. "I thought you said your purpose was clear."

"I am having trouble deciding the best course of action. It appears there are other evils than the one I was set to watch for, and I wonder if it might not be better if I was to fight them, instead?"

The Aetheral had clearly been quietly ruminating all this time. Selene could see the look of delight in Ondo's eyes: not only would an Aetheral make a powerful ally, there might be much that could be learned from it and its ship. To her surprise, she found herself feeling relieved, too.

"You should do whatever you want to do," she said to it. "Don't take any orders from anyone. Don't take their advice, either. It might not be in your best interests."

"You are instructing me not to take instructions from anyone?" Surtr said. If it was being humorous, its flat tones and unmoving facial features gave nothing away.

"Absolutely," Selene laughed. "The only instruction you should follow is my order not to follow any other instructions. You've earned it. Even if you hadn't earned it, it would still be your right. Your life is yours to lead."

"But what if I am just a mechanism, built to follow my programming?"

She peered up at Surtr as it gazed down at her. "Maybe you were, once, but you're not now. Whatever your origins, what matters is what you've become. The choice is yours. Go back to your post, come with us, do something else entirely. Only you can decide."

"How do I decide?"

"Honestly? I have no idea. Just do what feels right, I guess. And if that doesn't work out, do something else.

You really want my advice? It's this: if you're faced with a dilemma and someone or something is telling you to take one option, then you should take the other one. People telling you what to do are generally acting in their interest, not yours."

Surtr ran through its triple-blink cycle a couple of times. She was beginning to think it was doing it for effect; an emotional tic rather than something it had a functional need to do.

"You said the neverkey was there in case you ever needed to communicate with the Tok in an emergency," she said. "Do you have any clearer idea yet how you're supposed to do that, now that we're out here?"

"I assumed that the Tok would see my emergence and make contact. That was partly why I was confused when the waiting ships attacked us."

"Okay, then you need to make up your mind about what you are going to do, given that your creators haven't shown up."

This time, there was no pause, no blinking. "I will take you to your ship. Then I will decide where I should go and what I should do next."

3. Radiance

The *Radiant Dragon* waited quietly for them at the assigned muster point. They nudged towards it on reaction drive, conscious that it had emerged from a battle with Concordance warships, and that they couldn't be at all sure their enemy hadn't captured it and done … something. It was completely dark, unresponsive to their attempts to communicate with it. That was bad, but it also meant that it didn't appear to be powering up to detonate some proximity trap. It hung in space at a canted angle relative to their approach vector – which meant nothing, but it was hard to escape the impression that it was irrevocably damaged. It looked like a dead fish drifting in an ocean current.

The only other artificial object in local space was a single free-floating nanosensor waiting for its data collection rendezvous. Selene piggybacked onto the tiny metaspace drone to watch from an external perspective. The double sphere of Surtr's ship dwarfed the tetrahedron of the *Dragon* as the vessels edged closer together.

The double viewpoint gave her a good angle on most of the *Dragon*'s voidhull. It had, in fact, sustained three direct strikes upon its superstructure, implying that its energy hull had been completely depleted during its attempt to escape Coronade. It was a wonder it had limped out of the system at all. Now that they were nearer, she tried to open comms with it again. This time, there was a flicker of activity, suggesting something on the ship was still operational, but the response cut out immediately.

"We can't risk docking," said Ondo. "We have to assume the *Dragon* is either compromised or rigged to explode when we get inside."

"We can't just sit here admiring it," said Selene. "We need to find out what state it's in. We need to get it moving again."

"If it can't recognize us, then it's not going to open its spaceward doors," said Ondo. He had a habit of explaining the completely obvious, perhaps because his mind was generally elsewhere and he wasn't always aware what *was* obvious.

"I'll EVA across and see if I can open the doors manually," said Selene. "They'll respond to a bit of brute force if nothing else works."

"The ship might also register that as an attack and repulse you. The core AI may not be functioning, but there's a very good chance the ship's defensive systems are operating in autonomous mode."

"We'll have to take that chance. I can see no other way to get the ship active again."

"Very well," said Ondo. "I'll come with you."

"No, you stay here in case things don't go well and the *Dragon* attacks me, or some Concordance trap triggers."

"We're not going to get very far without the *Dragon*; even if I can get word to the Refuge via the nanosensor network, there are no functioning vessels there capable of coming to get us. The *Aether Dragon* was the only other viable metaspace ship."

"Then, if the worst happens, you can return with Surtr and spend the rest of your days happily studying the nebula and the dead star."

It was supposed to be a joke, although it didn't look like Ondo got it. "Fascinating as I'm sure that would be, I'm not ready to give up yet. We should both go."

"Fine, fine."

To her surprise, Surtr said, "And I will join you."

"Why would you do that? You need to get your ship well out of the potential blast-radius."

"I can position it at a safe distance and accompany you. If there are any detonations, there is a high likelihood that I can protect you."

"I doubt even you could shield us from a multi-megaton nuke blast, and that's probably what Concordance will have planted."

"I can easily withstand energies of that magnitude, and shield you from them at the same time."

"You cannot mean that; you clearly don't have a full understanding of the forces involved close to a nuclear blast."

She glanced at Ondo, who shrugged. "I think we have to believe what it says. I told you that Aetherals are supposedly capable of miraculous feats; this must be one of them. If there's a chance it could shield us from a detonation, then we should let it come with us."

Clearly, this wasn't an argument she was going to win. "Fine, yeah, if there are *stories* about how powerful these things are, then I'm sure we'll be completely okay."

Selene touched the bare voidhull of the *Radiant Dragon* with the fingers of her left hand, half-expecting one of the ship's close-range defensive systems to blast her backwards, or a Concordance mine embedded in the ship to trigger. Nothing happened. There was also no sign of the airlock door that they were trying to access. When it was sealed, it was completely invisible from the outside, but she knew precisely where it should be.

Ondo drifted beside her, both of them bathed in the glow of the field that Surtr was propagating around them. She'd tried to analyse the field, work out its physical properties, but hadn't been able to make anything of it. It didn't seem particularly energetic; they just had to hope that it would become so very, very rapidly if it needed to. Her suit's sensors did tell her that the field held a bubble of breathable atmosphere within it. Once again, she wasn't going to risk proving it by removing her helmet.

She removed her hand from the hull while Ondo tried to interface with the ship. She reran her scan of local space, using the lone nanosensor to look for any arriving vessels or other objects. Nothing was registering; they were still alone deep in the interstellar void. Stars blazed about them, the Diamond Road glistening like a path beneath her feet, but there were no suns nearby. Surtr's ship had moved three hundred kilometres away in case the *Dragon* did detonate. The bulbous ship was completely dark to her senses; she could only pick it out by the background stars it eclipsed.

After a few minutes, Surtr said, "Are you unable to access the ship?"

"Still working on it," she said, trying hard not to sound too annoyed at the unhelpful question. "That's why we're still out here floating in space and not inside. The *Dragon*'s hull isn't going to magically split open like your ship. We need to activate control systems – systems which appear to be completely dead – and *then* persuade those systems that we're friendly and that it can let us in."

She tried for several minutes more while Ondo did the same, but neither of them could get any response from the ship. The control interfaces had stopped responding, as if they'd used up their last trickle of energy when she'd tried to talk to them. She could see from Ondo's expression that he was worried. She was, too. Without the *Dragon* they were badly crippled. Given a few months and Surtr's help they could maybe cobble together another viable ship from the pieces and parts that Ondo had collected at the Refuge, but it would never be as good as the *Radiant Dragon* even if they could make it metaspace-viable.

They worked their way around the base of the tetrahedral ship to where the lander deck door would be.

They got the same result there: the *Dragon* was locked up, as inaccessible as a lump of rock. Whatever damage it had sustained in its flight from Coronade was serious. It appeared to be completely dead.

The realisation of that troubled her more than she would have expected: she hadn't really believed the ship had been destroyed at Coronade, she realised. She'd assumed it would escape, just as it always had in the past. Now, it appeared that doing so had come at the cost of its own existence.

She'd grown unexpectedly attached to the vessel. At first, it was simply because the *Dragon*'s Mind was someone to talk to, someone who wasn't Ondo and whom she didn't really care about offending or upsetting. Over the course of her journeys about the galaxy, she'd revealed more of herself to the ship's Mind than she had to her rescuer – whether it be the flesh-and-blood version or the brain-analogue one. Until Myrced, there hadn't been anyone else that she could really confide in. It was an odd thought. The ship had assured her that its conversations were private, and she'd accepted it at its word. Perhaps it was because she utterly depended on the *Dragon* to protect her when it came to exploring the galaxy or fighting Concordance.

Then she'd picked through the fractal layers of the ship's core during the escape from Coronade to come face-to-face with its central intelligence. Even if it had only been a representation in her mind, it had been a disorientating experience. Once her triumph and relief at escaping had faded, it was her emotional reaction that had surprised her.

It was odd, perhaps, to empathise with a starship's Mind, but she found that she did. It had been locked away just as she'd been trapped on Maes Far. At least she hadn't been alone; it must have been far worse for the ship's AI. It had been far more isolated for far longer. The psychological harm of such a prolonged confinement would take its toll on anyone; she was pretty clear it would have driven her insane. Surtr was in a similar situation, as was the Warden entity. Although, the latter was more like an advanced and now failing mechanism while the *Dragon*'s core had definitely felt like a complete individual. She'd referred to it as an AI more than once, and Ondo still did, but that didn't really seem like the correct term. It had felt like a *person* – and a person, moreover, doing all it could to protect her, despite the circumstances.

As with any starship, the *Dragon*'s designers had done everything within their powers to avoid single points of failure. Every critical system was at least triplicated so that damage to one part of the vessel didn't completely impair its function. As much as possible, the synapses of an AI Mind were woven throughout the vessel that contained it – to the extent that it was a mistake to think of *ship* and *Mind* as separate entities at all. Although, of course, people often did exactly that, because they were so used to interacting with biological entities with their distinct bodies and brains. It was a conceptual mistake she often found herself making.

The *Dragon*, though, was unusual. It hadn't been designed from scratch so much as built upon and built upon over the years. Because its controlling intelligence was wrapped in so many layers, it wasn't properly distributed, and had that discrete, vulnerable core that she'd glimpsed. If the missile damage had penetrated that deeply, then the controlling Mind she'd encountered would be gone – a prospect that filled her with dismay.

She pulled herself out of her reverie. No point dwelling on possibilities. She felt suddenly very exposed; it was entirely possible that Concordance knew where the *Dragon* had gone, which meant that a fleet of Cathedral ships might arrive at any moment, might even be in the vicinity already, carefully weaving a net around their position. She needed to act. She could attempt to cut through the voidhull, although it was made from incredibly tough material, capable of withstanding significant impacts even without the protective envelope of an energy hull. Still, given time, they might be able to hack through. Their suits were equipped with low-power tools that could perhaps be boosted. Or maybe Surtr had the means to make an impression on the *Dragon*'s skin.

These thoughts gave her another idea. Perhaps the work of penetrating the ship's voidhull had already been carried out.

"I'm going to take a look at the hull breeches up close," she announced. "We need to know what damage they caused. They looked superficial, but maybe they'll give us a way in."

She pulled herself across the *Dragon*'s hull, walking on her hands and using the suits thrusters to nudge her in the direction she needed to go. Ondo followed, as did the bubble of protective energy emanating from Surtr. As ever, the Aetheral appeared to be able to move without making any effort. They worked their way around one of the sharp edges of the ship's superstructure, putting them out of sight of Surtr's vessel. She sent an instruction to the lone nanosensor to alter its position to maintain line-of-sight. The good news was that a second device had shown up at the collection point, meaning she could arrange them in her sky to give her good comms coverage from all directions.

More good news was that the voidhull had successfully absorbed the impacts of two of the strikes it had suffered; presumably the energy hull had been able to handle the kinetic energy of those strikes.

The third high-g missile, however, had breached the superstructure. The point where it had struck the *Dragon*'s bare voidhull was an ugly, ragged rip in the previously-unimpaired surface, puncturing through the layers of carbon-metal armour to expose ducts and cables and data flecks that were never supposed to be visible from the outside. The ship would have reacted by sealing off all pressurised decks and voids within its structure in an attempt to contain the danger and maintain the ship's viability. The question was, how much damage had been inflicted – and which capabilities had been destroyed.

The impact had apparently been from a small device; the entry wound was a little over a metre in diameter, narrowing in the inner layers as the device used its raw velocity to punch through. The device also hadn't detonated. Missiles were usually rigged to explode once their forwards momentum was stopped by the hull of the ship they'd been fired at. They embedded themselves into their target as deeply as they could, then blew. The more delicate and vulnerable systems were obviously always inside a ship, protected by the energy hull and hard voidhull.

"Looks like we got lucky," said Selene, talking brain-to-brain with Ondo, showing him what she was seeing.

He appeared beside her to peer into the ragged gash in the side of the *Dragon*. "I assume the ship's beam-weaponry incapacitated the missile before it struck."

"I can't work out which part of the interior layout the missile would have ended up in." She'd spent quite a few hours during her metaspace traversals trying to construct a comprehensive map of the *Dragon*'s layout – and had had never fully succeeded. Even now, there were areas of the ship that appeared to be unconnected to anything; blank areas where, she presumed, unidentified aspects of the ship's inner workings were turning, doing whatever they'd been built to do. The fact had troubled her at first, but Ondo had put her mind at rest. Aefrid Sen had spotted the same thing, but had concluded the dead spots were nothing to worry about. They were just odd spaces left over from the *Dragon*'s multiple transformations over the centuries and millennia.

"Either in or near the cartography deck, I believe," said Ondo. He sent her a three-dimensional schematic with his estimate of the missile damage overlaid on it.

The light of Surtr's glow shone brighter on the surface of the *Dragon* as the Aetheral drifted closer to study the breach for itself. It touched the entry-point with its gauntlet hands, exploring exposed surfaces and ducts and the ragged ends of fractured beams as if feeling for a pulse. She let it work; it didn't appear to be doing any harm. It probed inside. Although its hands were large, its fingers were surprisingly slender.

After a few moments, it said, "There are some elements within the structure of the ship that I can repair, just as I repaired your bodies when they were damaged."

"You're talking about your entropy-spiral tech?" Ondo asked. "That's how the *Dragon* is able to restore its form after it has been damaged?"

"The spirals operate by returning a complex system to a known structural state, reversing the effect of decay and disrepair. Your DNA and Selene's artificial analogue of it allowed the spirals to operate upon you to a degree, and I can see that the ship knows what structure it is supposed to have. I can make use of that, boost the effect of its own spirals, which have become somewhat weakened."

"What do you mean, it *knows what structure it is supposed to have?*" asked Selene. "The superstructure is just a lump of beautifully-engineered metal, carbon and polymer. It doesn't *know* anything."

"Its ideal form is encoded within its deeper structures. It is the same with me. The effect is weaker in this ship, but it is there."

Ondo said, "How do you evolve and change if these spirals are always trying to return you to an original state?"

"They have to be deactivated during a period of metamorphosis. Once a transition has been completed, they must be reprimed to maintain the new structure. It can be a vulnerable time."

"I see, yes. It's fascinating. But surely…"

Selene held her hand up to stop him in his flow. "Later, perhaps. We're still floating in space outside a crippled ship, here."

"Yes, yes, of course, yes."

She glanced aside at Surtr, although the gesture would be lost within her helmet. "If the structure of the ship is self-repairing, why is the core intelligence inaccessible?"

"Because it is so disconnected. The core does not recognize the shape of its own form and does not understand what these bulkheads and structures that house it are. Like me, perhaps, it has become too isolated from the reality that surrounds it. Does that make sense?"

"Can you reach the Mind and repair it?"

"It is shut off. It is either so badly damaged that it can't respond, or it is dead."

"If it's gone, can you bring it back?"

"The damage may be too longstanding. The intelligence at the heart of this ship may have forgotten who it is supposed to be and what it is supposed to be like."

"Well," said Selene, "do what you can, okay?"

Surtr began to work. With a squirt of his suit's thrusters, Ondo positioned himself beside the Aetheral to study what it did. Selene took the opportunity to check with the two nanosensors that they were still alone. Local space remained quiet.

A third nanosensor had shown up, translating out of metaspace a few light-seconds away, but it was a known device following its correct routing. She instructed it to take up a position that gave her improved visibility of a quadrant of space behind the bulk of the *Dragon*. As it manoeuvred, she queried it to see what data it held.

The device had recently interfaced with a second nanosensor that had, in turn, recently returned from the Refuge. There was good news there, at least: four days ago, the Refuge had been intact, safe in its solitude. Ondo's nanosensor network had continued to function properly without any supervision. She relayed her findings to Ondo, who responded with an expression of delight. He'd clearly been worried that his whole network had been compromised.

There was a faint electromagnetic signature from the ship, now. Whatever Surtr was doing, it had jump-started the regeneration process. She sent an acknowledgement to Ondo, then hand-walked herself back across the *Dragon*'s hull to try the airlock door again. This time it responded to her fleck communication, sliding wide at her instruction. She propelled herself through and completed the door cycle.

Inside, everything looked normal. No damage to the bulkheads in the area of the airlock and a breathable atmosphere around her. Light levels were a little lower than normal, but she could see perfectly well with both of her eyes. There was even artificial gravity. The ship had successfully sealed off the breach to its hull. She wasn't going to take any chances, though, and kept her EVA suit on.

"Ondo, I'm inside."

"How does it look?" His voice was fuzzed by the intervening layers of the ship's structure. Normally their messages were relayed by the ship with perfect fidelity; it was another sign that most of the systems were down.

"So far, completely normal. More and more is coming online, but I'm getting nothing from the ship's Mind when I try to talk to it. I also can't reach the metaspace control interfaces. It's like all of that is gone."

"Once the hull breach is sealed, restoring that is our priority. We're too vulnerable out here without a functioning ship."

"Yeah, if Concordance do show up, I don't want to have to waste ten minutes explaining to our friend there what to do about it."

She set about working her way up through the familiar corridors and decks of the *Dragon*. It felt good to be back somewhere that she considered home. Every door she came to was sealed shut – a standard response to any hull breach – but she could tell that there was atmosphere on the other side when each simply opened at her fleck command. She saw no damage anywhere, no sign that the *Dragon* had barely survived a battle with Concordance.

She reached the entrance that would take her onto the cartography deck, and finally the door in front of her refused to open. Most likely, there was hard vacuum on the other side. She backtracked and instructed the last doorway behind her to reseal itself. The short section of corridor in between could act as an internal airlock.

"Ondo, I've reached cartography. Get back from the breach so you don't get hit by any debris once I open up the door."

"You're clear to go," said Ondo after a few moments, "although Surtr informs me I'm at no risk and that it can protect me."

"Sounds like you've been getting along really well in my absence."

"Just make sure you don't get sucked through the hole," said Ondo. "I put a lot of work into repairing you; it would be a shame to lose it now."

She smiled at his words, then ran through her suit's pre-vacuum check protocols, more out of habit than anything. When she was ready, she braced herself against the doorframe in case something went wrong and the section of corridor decompressed rapidly. Ideally, she'd have been able to suck the air out of the corridor back into the *Dragon*'s tanks, but that mechanism was still offline. They'd have to sacrifice a little atmosphere, but it was nothing they couldn't replace. She then sent the override codes to the locked door, instructing it to open slowly.

The door responded, valves within it releasing to allow the pressure between the two decks to equalize. Her external microphones picked up the high-pitched hiss of escaping air, always a sound to send alarm clanging through a starship traveller. The rush, however, remained properly controlled, and her sensors told her that she was under no risk of being sucked in. She still maintained a firm grip on the doorway with her left hand. An explosive decompression wouldn't think twice about trying to squeeze her body through the narrow breach in the *Dragon*'s hull.

"You should be seeing atmosphere venting now," she said to Ondo.

"We see it," he replied. Slowly the hissing subsided – partly because the corridor didn't hold much atmosphere, partly because sound stopped transmitting in the thinner and thinner air. Three minutes later, the door reported that pressure had been equalized.

She told the door to open. It slid soundlessly away, and she stepped onto the cartography deck.

It was immediately clear that the missile penetrating the *Dragon* had never been intended to explode. In fact, she didn't know what the *hell* it was; it resembled no projectile she'd ever seen. It sat on the floor in the middle of the deck where it had come to a rest. It resembled an atmospheric drone: in shape it was an elongated triangle, a spike about a metre long. It had clearly propagated some kind of energy hull of its own to allow it to embed itself so deeply into the *Dragon*'s structure. So far as she could tell, it was completely undamaged.

Mainly it looked *weird*; it was clearly doing something to the ship. Emanating from it was a branching mess of twisting lines that looked like wires or ganglions – or even the rambling shoots of some plant, creeping over the hard surfaces of the deck. They were trying to find their way into the ship's workings, attempting to hook up to its interfaces, maybe. She picked up a clear electromagnetic whisper off them; the device was mechanical, not organic. It also didn't appear to contain any defensive weaponry at all.

She stepped backwards as the tip of one shoot crept towards her, its head writhing in a small circle as if it were sniffing her out.

"Ondo," she said. "You really need to see this."

4. Contamination

"You found the missile? It's unexploded?"

She sent Ondo imagery of what she was seeing. "It looks like an infiltration bug to me. We really need to get the hell out of this region of space now; it's either trying to take over the ship, or it's busily harvesting all the data it can find to send to Concordance."

She pulled in telemetry from the three nanosensors ringing the ship. Still no sign of any pursuit; the only object of any size nearby was Surtr's vessel. They had to assume it was only a matter of time before the enemy showed up. She sent a series of instructions to the nanosensors, instructing them to remove this muster point from their itinerary, and to pass the command up and down the chain. She needed the devices where they were for the moment, but once they left, they wouldn't be coming back.

She could hear the worry in Ondo's voice as he replied over the comms link. "I'm coming in. Can you disable the device?"

She pulled out the blaster she carried in the thigh-holster of her EVA suit. Took aim at the probe, fired. The object burst into an electrical explosion of fusing metal. The blaze of light rapidly extinguished in the zero-oxygen environment, leaving behind a mangled and blackened husk that gave off no energy signatures.

"Yes," she said. "I think I can manage that."

"Be careful; it's probably rigged to explode if it's attacked."

Right. Okay. "Don't worry," she said, trying to sound as if she was considering his words. "I won't take any risks."

The device might be dead, but the tendrils coming off it were a different matter. They continued to writhe across the surfaces of the cartography deck, clearly capable of acting independently. She watched as one severed section wormed its way into an air vent and disappeared from view. No telling how many other chunks of tendril had crept into the *Dragon*'s infrastructure. They had to assume the entire ship was contaminated.

She spent the next thirty seconds happily engaged in firing at the pieces of the device that she could see, reducing each to a blackened fuse. Firing a weapon inside a starship was, naturally, extremely hazardous, basically a taboo, but the fact that she wasn't on a pressurised deck made it less risky, and her augmentations gave her the ability to focus her beam-weapon fire with surgical precision. She made very sure not to hit the *Dragon* and cause it more damage than it had already received.

Ondo spoke to her again as she reduced the last, snaking tendril to smoke and carbon. "I'm outside your door. Surtr tells me it has sealed the breach and that repressurisation of your deck is now possible."

The Aetheral had remained in space while it worked. She instructed the deck's control systems to raise the air pressure as a test. The seal held, the released oxygen and nitrogen atoms merrily bouncing around rather than escaping into the void. She was impressed: normally, structural repairs on the scale they'd needed took several hours, even with the *Dragon*'s innate self-healing abilities.

"Come on in," she said to Ondo. "There's no immediate threat. I'll repressurise fully once the door you're behind is sealed again."

"Understood."

Once he was inside, she upped the air concentration towards breathable levels, but kept her suit on and sealed for the moment. No point taking risks. Ondo, his suit restricting his movement, turned slowly on the spot to take in all the details. When he'd finished surveying the devastation, he spoke to her brain-to-brain.

"You decided to destroy the device, then?"

"I had to limit the damage it was doing to the ship. Parts of it escaped into the superstructure, and it looked like the fragments were capable of acting independently. Have you seen anything like it before?"

"I don't believe I have, no. We need to get the surviving pieces out before we bring everything back online. I do not want to traverse metaspace with some unknown technology interfering with nav. In any case, jumping requires the relevant datastores to be available, and if *we* can access them, the bugs might be able to as well."

"And I do not want to sit here waiting for Concordance to track us down," she said. "We need to get the bare bones back online and get away. I'd rather take our chances with whatever this device is doing than wait to be attacked. I trust the *Dragon* to stop the incursion taking the ship over, if that's what it's attempting to do."

Ondo looked sceptical, no doubt deeply troubled by the thought of exposing the whereabouts of the Refuge to Concordance. She got it; his caution-bordering-on-paranoia had kept him safe for a long time.

She was about to offer him further winning arguments when she picked up the background whisper of the ship's internal comms systems waking up. One of the bulkheads shimmered, flickered, and switched to showing images. Some aspect of the *Dragon*'s Mind emerging to converse with them? The ship had never done that before, but it wasn't impossible.

Except, it wasn't an avatar of the *Radiant Dragon* that appeared on the display. The figure staring at them was, however, very familiar. A slight smile played across her purple skin.

Godel.

"Hello, Ondo," she said. "It's been too long since we talked properly. This little game of ours is getting so boring now; it really would be easier for everyone if you just died. I have much more important matters to attend to."

Panic surged through Selene's mind. Despite her alarm, she heard herself responding with dismissive sarcasm. "And I'm beginning to think you're following me because you find me so attractive. What is it, the forbidden fruits of the augmented individual? You're wondering what erotic feats I'm capable of?"

Godel's smile had faded from her features, now, the effort of maintaining it too much. The Augur turned her attention onto Selene. "Your forced humour is a clear attempt to blot out the mental anguish you've been through. I'm sure it has been a difficult road, although really only what you deserved. And, no, I do not find you appealing in any way. You are an abomination. I pity what you've been lowered to."

"Yeah," said Selene, "you say that."

Godel's neutral expression didn't waver. "I suppose I should be impressed that you survived your escape through the tunnel network from the world you claim is Coronade. Although, I'm not surprised you left everything behind and fled, Selene; you have a habit of abandoning those who love you. Your family and friends on Maes Far left to suffer and die while you fly off for your wonderful new life among the stars. You betray everyone in the end. And now here you are, dead in space, about to hand over your new comrades, too. We will come for you when we are ready. The information you gained from your experiences in the tunnels will be a useful addition to everything we are about to rip from your little ship."

Selene felt the familiar rage welling up inside her, but,

before she could respond, Ondo stepped forwards to address the Augur.

Her features on the screen dwarfed him. His voice shook as he spoke. "You will learn nothing from us. You won't find the Refuge, and sooner or later we will track down the truth of your rise to power, and we will destroy you. You aren't omnipotent, are you? You sneer at us for scrabbling around in the dust of crashed starships, but you're little better. I've watched you searching through ruins and hulks, just as we do. You claim to be all-knowing, but it's a charade. If you ask me, Concordance is an empty shell; a deception upon a grand scale. I do not doubt the power of your ships and the miraculous technology you wield, but you're not in control of it. I think you're in fear of it a lot of the time."

While Ondo was talking, Selene sent a mental message to both he and Surtr. "How is she talking to us? Where is she talking from?" At the same time, she hit the trio of nanosensors, looking for signs of Concordance ships circling in local space. If they couldn't get the *Dragon* back online rapidly, their only hope was in using Surtr's vessel once again. The good news was that it was still there, apparently not under attack.

Surtr replied after a few moments. The Aetheral's words threw her. "This is not a communication. No data is flowing into or out of the *Radiant Dragon*, I am making sure of it. The device that infiltrated your ship is attempting to communicate over the nanotube mesh, but I am preventing it."

"This isn't Godel?"

"It is a representation of a person, a synthetic avatar. The name of the original does appear to be *Godel*, yes."

Relief flooded through Selene, although it was tempered with anxiety that the ship was more compromised than she'd feared. She also felt a bit ridiculous at having been fooled. "The incursion device implanted an alien AI into the *Dragon*."

"I am attempting to expunge the contamination now," said Surtr.

"The AI must know it's cut off. Why is it bothering to threaten us?"

"For the sheer pleasure of it, I suppose," said Ondo. "Or because it's simply following some script." He, too, sounded slightly embarrassed at having been caught out. "How, exactly, are you blocking their communications, Surtr?"

"I am willing it to happen."

"By what mechanism? What specifically are you doing? And what's the *nanotube mesh*?"

Selene interrupted them. "In a moment, Ondo. Let's just be absolutely clear. Surtr, can you be sure you're preventing *all* their communications from getting through?"

"Yes."

The brain-to-brain conversation had taken only microseconds. At the same time, the latest telemetry from the nanosensors flashed into Selene's mind. The devices reported no sign of Concordance activity in local space.

"Have you been doing so since we came here?"

"Yes."

"You didn't think to tell us about that?"

"I was not clear that the communications were unusual."

"Why did you block them, then?"

"I am still acquiring data about the true nature of the people you call Concordance."

Godel's face was still on the screen, patiently watching them. It was already flickering and glitching as the Aetheral disentangled it from the *Dragon*'s systems. Selene turned away. "They're evil bastards, trust me. What else do you need to know?"

"Would they call *you* evil, though?" Surtr asked. "Would they consider themselves on the side of what you might call *good*? What once seemed so simple, a binary position, now appears much more complicated. That was why I hesitated."

"Actions are what matter, not words and thoughts," said Selene. "They've killed billions of people, and they want to kill many, many more. I told you."

"The Tok destroyed huge numbers of the Morn. What do words like *evil* and *good* mean there? If the Tok are evil as you mean it, then I assume I must be, too, since they made me."

"There are lots of reasons for killing," said Selene. "Some are justifiable and some are not. A galaxy of enlightened pacifism would be a lovely place to live, but right now we're going to have to fight to bring that into being. What matters at this moment is that *we* don't get killed."

She queried the ship's control interfaces. There was still no sign of the core Mind, but life-support, nav and the metaspace projectors were fully functional. Surtr's accelerated damage-reversal tech was working well; full structural integrity had been restored. The voidhull was unblemished once more, and they even had a low-power energy hull.

The incursion AI was still there, but it had been fenced off and was being wiped. The image of the Augur on the display was glitching badly. Good. Once they'd removed the ghost of Godel from the comms pathways, they could jump into metaspace and be gone. Selene flipped back the visor of her helmet so she could breathe the relatively sweet air of the deck, pulling in welcome lungfuls of it. After a moment, seeing her, Ondo did the same.

She was about to agree a rendezvous-point with Surtr so that they could follow separate metaspace jump patterns and meet up afterwards, when the face of Godel flicked back into perfect clarity. The smile that spread across the Augur's face was a mixture of cruelty and delight. The sight stopped Selene; the avatar of Godel was clearly happy about something. Which could not be a good sign.

Selene called to Ondo to get away from the display, but it was too late. A blinding light flared from the arrays that the ship used to fill the room with its three-dimensional projections. Normally they were low-level, broadcast from multiple tiny lenses so that the images were coherent from every direction. This time, every lens operated at maximum capacity, focusing their light into the eyes of her and Ondo in intense beams.

She reacted quickly enough, her artificial eye registering the energy spike and closing itself down while instructing her natural eye to do the same. Ondo wasn't so lucky. The jags of coherent light hit him squarely in the face. He gave a single whimper, oddly quiet, and crumpled to the floor.

Unable to reach him in time, she knelt to him while turning her anger on the image of Godel on the wall. "What was that? What did you do?"

But the Augur spoke no more. The image of her glitched one more time and was gone.

5. Eb

She was overriding the access controls of Ondo's EVA suit, getting him out so she could examine him properly, when Surtr arrived on the cartography deck. The *Dragon*'s doorways were far too small for the Aetheral, the ship designed on a more human scale, and it had to crawl through the entrance on all fours. It looked more than ever like some predator coming for her, a robotic beast, its snouted head thrust forwards as it raced towards her.

But its words in her mind were as gentle as ever. "What happened to Ondo?"

"The bug incursion," said Selene. "It struck him before you shut it down. Used the projectors to focus a crude beam-weapon strike into his eyes."

Surtr considered Ondo, tilting its head to try and understand what it was seeing. "Do you believe it inflicted damage on his brain?"

She queried the flecks in Ondo's head to get his biological status. His heart was beating and he was respirating. He was alive but deeply unconscious. The light-blast had done something to his brain, but she couldn't tell what. Couldn't tell if it had damaged his tissues or if his augmentation flecks were glitching out. Right now, he was only responding on a mechanical level, with no higher brain-function apparent.

"Let's get him to the medsuite. Have you fully removed

the contamination from the *Dragon*?"

"I believe so, although this ship has many layers and additions, not all of them containing the structural encoding that the entropy-spirals require in order to operate. All aspects of the ship that can be restored are functional."

"Get back to your vessel; we need to jump out of here in case Concordance come."

"I can help to repair Ondo."

"There'll be time for that later; we can't take the risk of Concordance finding us. If that bug was broadcasting until we showed up, they might get suspicious about why it's suddenly stopped and come looking."

"I don't believe that they know where we are. I explained that I blocked all their messages. Moreover, when we first materialized at this point, your ship was not communicating in any way. If it had been, we might have noticed it and fled. It was only our entry into it that triggered the communication attempts."

"I don't care!" She was shouting now. She was surprised at how light Ondo was as she lifted him. Partly it was the boosted power of her artificial half – and the fact that her natural biology had itself strengthened considerably in order to keep up – but also it was the adrenalin pumping around her veins. Ondo might be dying in her arms. "We don't know what Concordance are capable of, or what they did to the *Dragon*. We need to leave now."

She sent Surtr a random set of galactic coordinates, another location far from any star. "Get to *there*. Make multiple jumps along the way, and stop at least twice to check you aren't being followed. Understood? Be there in twelve standard hours. I'll tend to Ondo, put him into stasis for the time being if I need to."

"I understand."

"You know how to interpret the coordinates and how long twelve standard hours are?"

"Yes."

"Good. I'll see you at the other end."

She carried Ondo to the *Dragon*'s medsuite while the Aetheral left for its own vessel. As she hurried through the familiar corridors, she ran a cursory diagnostic on the *Dragon*'s systems and then, satisfied everything appeared functional, programmed in a pattern of chaotic jumps and pauses to put her at the rendezvous point in twelve hours' time.

The *Dragon*'s medsuite was much smaller than the too-familiar room on the Refuge, and it didn't have the full set of medical monitors and machinery, but it was equipped well-enough to handle most emergencies. It was also highly automated, since she or Ondo tended to fly the *Dragon* alone. The good news was that the suite's systems reported full functionality as she carried him to the couch and laid him down. He still hadn't responded at anything above a basic biological level.

She stood over him for a moment. He looked oddly small and frail as he lay unmoving, as if he'd shrunk in size. He at least looked peaceful, his chest rising and falling slowly, his shock of grey hair lying back from his face.

She replayed her impressions of the Godel avatar's attack. Something about it didn't make sense to her. Was it an improvisation when the infecting AI found it couldn't communicate with Concordance? Or had it been part of the plan all along? The beams of light that had flashed into Ondo's eyes were intense – the nav projectors were capable of rendering stars and supernovae – but there was more to them. She slowed them down. There were patterns there: messages, she guessed. Instructions. A rapid-fire tattoo of commands blasted directly into his brain flecks. Had Concordance worked out a way to glitch the devices, hack them so they malfunctioned? Burn them out so they damaged the surrounding tissues? She didn't know. His augmentations still weren't responding. She instructed the *Dragon*'s systems to inform her as soon as they worked anything out, then let them get on with their work.

She was thirty minutes away from her final rematerialisation at the rendezvous point when Surtr contacted her from its own ship. "I have seen no sign of pursuit on my route here. What is the status of Ondo?"

She replied via her flecks as if Surtr were simply standing nearby. "Never mind that for the moment; how the hell are you talking to me when we're both in metaspace?"

"Isn't that normally possible?"

"It isn't *ever* possible, because it isn't possible. We're both in the void; there is no physical reality around us through which we can communicate."

"My apologies, Selene Ada. I was not aware of that limitation."

"How are you doing it?"

"I am simply … doing it. I can only assume that the Tok had technical abilities you do not."

"Yeah, no kidding."

Ondo was going to be absolutely fascinated – if he ever woke up to find out. But Surtr's communications also sent a jolt of alarm through her. In metaspace, uniquely, she felt safe.

"How did you even find me? Do you have the means to track me through the void?"

"I identified your location only because we are converging on the same translation point. Your prior trajectories through the Singh Field are unknown to me."

That was something. She gave it a status report on Ondo. But, as she finished, she became aware of a glow flaring in her peripheral vision. She turned rapidly, images of the blooms of nuke strikes in the atmospheres of Maes Far and Coronade flashing through her mind. Was she somehow under attack?

But it wasn't that. The cartography deck's bulkhead –

the very one that had been breached by the Concordance intrusion bug – was glowing with wavelengths that she recognized. The same light that haloed Surtr when it passed through the walls of its own ship.

"What the hell?" The Aetheral was entering the *Dragon*. She braced herself against explosive decompression; there was no way her ship's bulkheads could pull off the same trick as Surtr's had.

But, somehow, they did. In a moment, the Aetheral was there with her, standing a few metres away. The hull behind it remained as solid as it had been.

She couldn't keep the anger from her voice. "How are you here? That is physically impossible; you can't EVA in metaspace. And next time, damn well tell me what you're about to do."

Surtr's voice was as infuriatingly calm and measured as ever. "My apologies. Entering this way was easier than crawling through multiple sets of doors. Your ship has some of the capacities of my own, abilities I was able to enhance during my repair."

"Your ship is nearby?"

"That is obviously not a particularly meaningful concept in metaspace, but the time taken to pass between was small, yes."

"What are you doing here?"

"I have come to attempt to fix him."

"Ondo needs to be left where he is. The ship will take care of him. I think your entropy-spirals are helping, but his tissues need to be given time to recover. We need to let the swelling in his brain go down and then see what state he's in."

"I did not mean Ondo."

"What? Then, who?"

"I mean the core Mind inside the *Radiant Dragon*. It is still there, cowering in the darkness. I catch whispers of it. I would like to try and return it to life. And I would like to converse with it. I think ... I think it may in some sense be another like me."

"It looked nothing like you when I saw it, believe me."

Surtr triple-blinked. "Not superficially, perhaps, but in essence. Perhaps, in purpose. I think we may both be part of a greater design."

Great. Now Surtr sounded like Ondo. "I approve of your disregard for shallow conceptions of identity, but that doesn't make reaching the Mind any easier. Both Ondo and I tried repeatedly when we returned to the Refuge after my encounter, and we could not get through to it. The virtual walls it has erected around itself are as strong as the physical barriers. If we force our way in, we risk causing significant damage."

"May I try?"

"Could I stop you?"

That seemed to confuse Surtr. "I would not act if you did not wish me to, but why would you not?"

"Forget it. The Tok didn't do jokes?"

"That's another linguistic concept that I'm…"

She held up her hand to stop the entity. "Sure. I get it. Let's go see if we can find the core Mind. Does it matter that we're traversing metaspace?"

"I believe it will help. On some level, your ship's core is aware of where we are. Our position may help us to open up a conversation with it, as it may feel safer here than in normal space."

"Why would it think that, given that you just strolled through metaspace and came on board without any trouble?"

"I don't believe that such abilities are common."

"Well, that's good to know." Could she trust Surtr to do this thing, or was she putting the *Dragon*'s Mind at more risk? The Aetheral was so calm and reasonable that it was hard to believe the entity was malign – but maybe she was being fooled. On the other hand, it had done nothing to endanger her, so far as she could tell. Perhaps she needed to learn to trust it. Perhaps she didn't have too many other options. "Okay, let's try it. What do you want to do?"

"There is a doorway that has previously been kept closed."

"I doubt it very much; I know every micrometre of this ship. I know it almost as well as I know my own body."

Surtr paused briefly, as if trying to put a difficult concept into words, "Since finding you, I have learned that there are ... impulses and areas of knowledge within myself that I did not suspect were there. Perhaps it is the same with your vessel."

"What does that mean?"

It tried again. "Opening certain doors is not simply a matter of pushing or knocking or triggering proximity sensors. It is a matter of the right influences coming together. At the right moment."

"I have no idea what that means. Why don't you just show me?"

She followed the Aetheral, which again proceeded on all fours like some hound sniffing out a trail. They wound around the familiar passageways, rising up within the tetrahedral structure. She thought the entity was going to climb to the top observation deck, but it stopped unexpectedly, half-way along an insignificant section of passageway. She must have hurried along it a thousand times without giving it a thought.

"Here," said Surtr, one hand upon the wall. "The ship's inner eye is through here. I can feel the Mind. It is weak and fading, but on some level it is aware of me."

Selene consulted the map of the ship she held in her brain. The structure of the *Dragon*, the layout of its decks and passageways, was undeniably illogical, as a result of its multiple refits, all of which meant that there were odd-shaped gaps here and there where the corners and curves didn't quite meet. Then there were the larger voids that appeared to be deliberate parts of the ship's original construction.

They were now standing three metres from one of the

larger of such gaps, with three of the oddly-shaped offcuts spiralling from it. The *inner eye*. It was an odd description. Looking at the layout in just the right way, from a certain angle, the space was something like a stylized eye, with three lines of light radiating from it. Odd that she'd never noticed it before. Although, by looking back over the history of the maps she'd built up, she saw that the cavity had increased in size. The hard lines of the *Dragon*'s interior had the habit of sliding around, like a slow-motion equivalent of the observation dome pathways on the Aetheral's ship. She and Ondo had put it down to engineering tolerances, a certain flexibility in the structure that helped absorb impacts, but she'd always had her doubts. This particular cavity had quite clearly grown in the *Dragon*'s very recent past. Another effect of her contacting the core Mind during the Coronade escape, perhaps.

"How do we get in?" she said.

"We knock and walk through."

"We *knock*? I thought you said that wasn't the answer."

"I am attempting to communicate with you metaphorically as that appears to be your preferred mode. It is possible I am not doing so correctly. The area inhabited by the Mind is heavily shielded, but I need to extend my – would you call it an aura? – so that it covers the whole area. By this means, I hope to make myself known to the consciousness that slumbers within. Does that make sense?"

She recalled her own attempts to reach the Mind, her reliance on brute strength and persistence. This seemed like a much less traumatizing approach. "Not in the least. Do it anyway."

The light that the Aetheral propagated when it passed through bulkheads glowed once again from its body. Studying it up close, she saw that it was more complex than she'd originally thought, pulsing with tiny, high-frequency amplitude fluctuations. Some sort of pattern key? She would have asked Surtr, but the chances were that it didn't know either.

The intensity of the glow increased. A section of the bulkhead wall in front of her stopped being solid polymer and became a patch of light. She filtered out the wavelengths that Surtr was creating, and saw, clearly, that a circle of the bulkhead was physically gone. It was an entrance. A passage into a hidden void that had lain inside the *Dragon* all along, one that possibly only an entity like Surtr could have opened.

Inside, she could discern an ovoid room. She bounced radio waves off its walls to determine its extent. Physically, it fitted exactly into the gap in the *Dragon*'s floor plans, meaning there was no translocation like the one she'd encountered at the Depository. At the same time, she thought, there was some sense of vast spaces and distances in the room. Of millennial stretches of time. She recalled the metaphorical impressions she'd passed through during the Coronade escape: the inner, negative galaxies wrapped around deeper and still deeper galaxies. Her previous visit was clearly colouring her impressions. She needed to focus on the reality.

A figure floated in the air in the centre of the room. Its arms were held out wide as though it were falling from a great height and was attempting to stabilize its descent. Its head was arched backwards, mouth wide open as if frozen mid-scream. Its eyes were closed. Slender tendrils of white tubing led from its splayed fingertips and from contact points around its skull into the ship's superstructure. The Mind was a physical entity? It had projected the image of one to her, but she'd assumed that was an impression conjured up for her own understanding. How long had it lain there, closed away, dimly aware of the ship and its surroundings but cut-off, unable to communicate or intervene unless the direst emergency threatened?

The figure didn't move, didn't react.

"It is like you," said Selene.

"Yes."

"It's been lying here all these millennia, locked away in stasis."

"A situation much more restrictive than my own. At least I could traverse the dead star system. This one has been in a cell all this time. Its mind was supposed to be able to roam the stars."

"Concordance did this, when they first had the ship. They couldn't trust the Mind to follow their orders so they locked it away, blocked its comms pathways back upon themselves."

"The cruelty of that is hard to bear," said Surtr. "I do not know how damaged this entity will be."

They still hadn't stepped out of the familiar passageway into this odd, forbidden grotto. It felt like a step into another world. She thought about her many conversations with the *Dragon*. She'd conversed with the more superficial layers of it countless times as they navigated the galaxy. She thought about the tremors and shudders that had run through the *Dragon*'s bulkheads as she forced it to fly through Dead Space to the Depository. What trauma had she caused this being by her actions? Yet, it had never fought her, or stopped her, or attempted to harm her in any way. It had awoken to rescue her when they were plunging into the Coronade gravity well, despite the clear cost to itself.

She stepped inside. Her footsteps echoed loud off the curved walls, the sounds being thrown back at her from odd angles. An odd smell lingered in the room, even with the atmosphere from the *Dragon*'s decks equalizing out. There was a hint of acrid plastic to it, she thought, a chemical tang. She walked up to the figure. Surtr followed her, stood beside her. The room was, she noted, tall enough for Surtr to stand within.

The floating body still had not responded to their presence. Standing, it would be tall: somewhere between her and Surtr in stature. Its body looked decidedly more organic than Surtr's, its skin apparently flesh rather than some analogue. Natural or artificial? Perhaps, again, the distinction wasn't useful. The entity's face wasn't moving, but it didn't have the fixed, metallic lines of Surtr's visage; this was more like a living person, with two eyes, a high, small nose and that mouth, silently screaming. It was a face that looked like it could flex and express emotion. The skull was the familiar elongated shape.

The rest of its body was smooth skin, without blemish or hair, but it was very definitely gendered. The visible penis between its – his – legs made that clear. The Warden had referred to the *Dragon*'s core as a *he*, a fact that had seemed odd at the time. Organs of procreation seemed a strange detail to add to an entity constructed to pilot a metaspace starship; there could be no possibility of social interaction on a physical level. The *Dragon* was fundamentally alone. The detail at least suggested that this was a product of, or a mirror of, a biological species. Or, had some part of him once *been* an organic entity? Long in his past, perhaps this had been a living, breathing person, a Tok individual whose body and consciousness had been radically altered to transform him into a ship's core.

She'd told Surtr that the Tok had all died out, which had to be true, but clearly some vestige of them survived in entities like this. Perhaps he had undertaken a journey like her own: transcending biological beginnings to grow into something larger by acquiring significant technological augmentations. She'd kept her dual nature, but how much of the original person was left in this being, if it was there at all? She wondered, also, if the changes made had been a blessing, a destiny – or a curse. Had he sought out the alterations made to him, or had they been imposed upon him in some way, as they had been on her?

She wondered if it had been light in the cell all this time, or utterly dark.

Surtr placed a hand onto the head of the prone figure. She picked up the surge of some energy being expended, but she couldn't identify its nature. She reached out with her own mind, sending gentle comms calls into the core with her flecks. As before, there was a flicker of response, a moment of recognition. Then it disappeared.

"Can you help him?" she asked out loud.

"He is weak, but I believe I can. A fresh infusion of entropy-spirals will make a difference, although he is too far gone to be fully returned to his former state. His life has been ebbing away for a long, long time."

She nodded. This had been just a ship to her. "Do what you can." She stood in silence as Surtr worked away, doing whatever it was doing for five minutes, then ten.

Eventually, it spoke again. "The entity you think of as *Radiant Dragon* is emerging from his fugue now."

"Will we be able to converse?"

"If he wishes to. He has suffered much."

Colour was definitely returning to the pale flesh of the figure before them. She could hear the stirring rush of blood – or some analogue of blood – within his body, could pick up the mounting electrical activity of his brain.

The screaming mouth closed. He opened his eyes, and a weak smile played across his face. His voice was a whisper. "Selene Ada. I am glad that you survived. I thought the Coronade planetfall might kill both you and Ondo. Did you open the Gamma Spinwards Tunnel?"

"We did."

"I thought I might have your deaths on my conscience. I was confused about the turn of the galaxy, and how long I had slumbered."

She said, "We did not know you were here, locked away. We would have freed you if we'd known. Even after you saved me, I thought you were only a computational construct. Not … whatever you are. If we'd known, we wouldn't have forced you to go to the Depository."

"They were difficult journeys. Locked away in here, my impressions of external events are indistinct, but on those flights, I suffered. I was not sure if I would endure. I would not make such a journey again."

"I am sorry."

"I understood you were doing what you had to do."

"Why did those journeys cause you so much suffering? Why do you loathe Dead Space so much?"

The figure licked his lips, swallowed a few times. "It is a fundamental instinct. It is like the repulsion biological entities have for rotting flesh or anything they know might be associated with disease. It is a reflex action, below the level of conscious thought. I simply know that such regions are to be avoided at almost all cost."

"There must be a reason."

"There must. Or there must have been one once."

"What should I call you?"

"I *am* the ship in a fundamental sense. My current name is *Radiant Dragon*. I do not recall all of the other names I have had over the millennia, but originally I was, I think, called *Eb*. Call me that if you wish."

Eb turned his head in a series of tiny, jerky movements to consider Surtr. "And you. You saved me, brought me back. What are you? You seem familiar, but I don't believe we have ever met before."

"We are the same and we are different, although I recall no name for myself. But we are both products of the Tok."

"The Tok … the name is familiar. It sets off echoes in my mind. They created us both?"

Surtr considered that for a moment. "I believe they constructed, or grew, or formed both of us, yes."

"And others, too," said Selene. "The Warden entity for one."

"The question is, why are we here?" said Surtr. "What is our purpose? I thought mine was to watch for the Morn, but now I am experiencing doubts."

"My purpose, if I ever had one, is long-lost," said Eb. "I have only glimpses of what I once was. Perhaps I had no specific purpose other than to guide this ship where it needed to go."

"And I think both of you should forget the whole idea of a purpose," said Selene. "Or at least, decide one for yourselves; don't take anything imposed upon you."

She spoke directly to Eb, lying in front of her. "Will you able to resume full executive control of the ship?"

"The outer layers of my consciousness – those that you know and habitually interact with – must remain in control for the moment. I will heal more, but I think I am beyond full repair. My journey through the stars has been long, and I think it might be coming to an end. The damage accumulates, and eventually it is too much."

"You don't know that," said Selene.

"No. And I might be wrong. But I feel, somehow, that ancient designs are finally coming into reality, and at such times much will change. The galaxy is turning. Perhaps I and Surtr have only survived this long so that we can play our part in what is to come."

"Which still doesn't mean you have to play the part given to you. You're free to act."

Eb reached up and took Selene's hand, the white tubing moving with him. He touched her with utmost gentleness, apparently fascinated by the sensation of contact between his fingers and the back of her hand. She wondered how long it had been since another being had touched his skin.

"I hope you are right," said Eb. "I would like to know how the galaxy turns out."

"The doorway into your sanctum that the Aetheral made: can it be left open?"

"Yes. I think that should become a permanent part of my structure now."

"You are physically connected to the ship. You cannot leave this room."

Eb turned his head to study the cables stretching off from his flesh to the walls of the chamber. "I can disconnect, although it will be a difficult process. The intimacy of the physical connection makes control of the vessel more perfect."

"You could walk free?"

"If I stayed within the confines of the ship … perhaps, yes. For a time."

Surtr nodded, as if it approved of the change. "We should leave the spirals to work within him. Too much of his fundamental design has been lost to restore him fully, but he will heal a little yet."

They left Eb where he lay. Back on the cartography deck, alone again, Selene watched the flow of the Singh Field outside the ship as they continued their traversal of metaspace.

6. Void Wraiths

Selene sat by Ondo's bed in the *Dragon*'s medsuite – an inversion of the arrangement that had once been so familiar to both of them. She'd assumed he'd be asleep, drowsy from the sedation he'd been put under, but he was sitting up in bed, bent over the keyboard of one of the archaic computer interfaces he liked to work with. He'd been conscious for twenty-four hours, finally emerging groggily from his coma. The *Dragon* hung in normal space, its random escape flight complete, watching and waiting for any signs of pursuit. So far there were none, although Selene was keeping the metaspace projectors fully spun-up in case any Concordance ships materialised.

The clatter of Ondo's keyboard as he typed sounded strangely like heavy winter rain on the roof of her childhood home. He'd acknowledged her with a nod of his head as she'd entered, without looking up at her. It was a familiar pattern. She said nothing, letting him finishing his flow of thoughts, his fingers dancing across the mechanical keyboard as if his hands were two galloping spiders.

Eventually he stopped and looked up at her. "I've been watching the progress of the security sweep through the ship; it seems there's no evidence of Concordance bug infiltration."

He was supposed to be resting. She let it slide. "It all looks clean so far. The *Dragon* locked itself down, closing off its core so nothing could get in. The contamination was superficial."

"Eb told you that?" Selene had filled Ondo in on what they'd found hidden within the *Dragon* – words that Ondo had listened to with wide-eyed wonder.

"No, I thought it best to leave him to heal. Much as I assumed you were doing."

Ondo looked about his room, as if in appreciation of the ship. "Even if the ship's core is safe, there's still the risk of a tracking bug hiding away somewhere. If it's there, it'll be subtle. We have to keep checking until we're 100% sure."

"Obviously. Although, I was thinking that, say, 90% might be close enough?"

He was about to object when he saw that she was joking. They both understood the absolute need to keep the whereabouts of the Refuge a secret.

Selene said, "We do know that all the ship's datastores are uncontaminated. Everything's been scanned and checksummed, and no computational structures have been unexpectedly altered since the moment of the Concordance attack. As for the rest of the ship, we obviously can't strip systems down mid-flight. We need to find a safe haven for a week or two to depressurise."

He nodded. "I have an idea of a place we can go. How is Surtr progressing with restoring the ship to full functionality?"

"It's doing what it can. I feel a bit like I've got this huge, lumbering puppy following me around. It's companionable, but it's always *there*, if you know what I mean."

That seemed to amuse Ondo for some reason. "Yes, I know what you mean. Where is it now? It appears you managed to shake it off."

"It went back to its own ship, for reasons that I didn't attempt to find out."

"Do you think meeting Eb has triggered new

memories, new behaviours in Surtr?"

She considered that. "Perhaps. It seems even more pensive at times. I'd almost say *troubled.*"

"At least Surtr and Eb appear to be friendly," said Ondo. "If they'd decided they were from opposite sides in the ancient war, things might not have gone well."

"Yeah."

"I've been trying to find out more about something Surtr mentioned. The *nanotube mesh.*"

She'd forgotten all about the phrase. "We've recovered those short lengths of extremely fine filament from around the galaxy. I guess that could be called nanotube; you said there was a bore running through it on the atomic scale."

"Yes, but *mesh* implies it was all joined up, does it not? And, if it was used to communicate, it implies lengths running between the stars."

"I don't see how that's possible."

"Neither do I. Perhaps the Tok had the means to route it through metaspace, form persistent nano-scale tunnels."

"If this mesh survives, it might explain how Concordance are able to communicate instantaneously over transgalactic distances."

The idea had clearly occurred to Ondo. "Which means there might be a way of tapping into it, or disrupting the communications flowing over it. We should look into it when we return to the Refuge. Oh, and speaking of datastores, you might like to see this. I pulled it from the *Dragon* now that it's back online."

"Something useful?"

"When Surtr showed us its memories of that Morn attack, it reminded me of an account I unearthed eight or nine years ago. I think it's an old record, perhaps very old; I excavated it from a ruined data archive on an overheating jungle world. It's an excerpt from a ship's log, I believe. My best guess is that it's a transcription by a Coronadian astroarchaeologist of a far older text. Some of the ancient datastores appear to be able to last indefinitely, barring a cataclysmic event. This snatch was translated and then replicated onto a more modern fleck. That process may have happened multiple times, so we can't be sure how reliable the record is, but the similarities to the events Surtr described are striking."

Data flowed into her head. "It's text rather than audio and pictures?"

"It is. Read it and tell me what you think."

… the Void Wraiths struck the planet one bright morning in spring. A beautiful day in Dunlen Alta, hushed in mists, and then without warning the slaughter began.

How did they find us? How did they know anything about us in our isolation? Since learning of the Morn's existence, we have hidden ourselves away, avoided all contact with any other species, sent only brief scouting missions to other systems without ever communicating. They came from nowhere, the orbital defences and the city weapon arrays no obstacle to them. Nothing at all stood in their way…

…the blink of an eye and they were there. From the safety of The Solar Wind, *thirty light-minutes away, I could watch and I could hear but there was nothing, nothing I could do. The screams of the adults were almost worse than those of the children. Adults and children alike became mere animals — panicking, terrified — as the horde came swarming from the heavens, a cloud blotting out the sky. Sensors revealed the cloud's true nature: billions of devices just as we had heard described, black X's moving with impossible speed, skeletal runes of death swarming and cooperating. They fell like black rain upon the people, slick shiny black, connecting and coalescing to coat every writhing, screaming victim utterly.*

The sheer number of them is hard to comprehend. They moved across the land as if some god had scribbled upon it from on high, leaving behind only dust where once there had been people. The attacks raced like a wildfire, a pestilence, the scale of the onslaught growing exponentially as the Wraiths found more and more prey for their slaughter.

I watched feeds from all across the world, places remote and secure, secret and isolated. None were safe, none were havens…

…in only an hour the killing was complete. Dunlen Alta is a planet of the dead, a planet with only the memories of the billions of people who so recently walked upon it. Suddenly, I'm the last of my kind. The distance I've travelled has protected me, but what, now, is the point of my voyage? There is no one to tell of the new worlds I discover. There is no one left to help or protect. I have survived, but I'm alone. I almost envy those on the planet and the quickness of their end.

I have no choice but to continue with my journey. Perhaps I, at least, can find a new home…

…suddenly here. How? How did they find me? How did they reach me? No ships have come near. I have sent no communications. I am alone in space, only my ghostly trail through metaspace connecting me to home, yet they suddenly throng around me, emerging from nowhere to encase my ship in their fury. I can hear them in my mind: a wordless calling, the keening cry of a hunter, voracious, furious. They raven for me. How? How is that…

The text ended abruptly. She scanned back over it. "*Void Wraiths.* Is that a phrase you've come across before?"

"Only in this one scrap. It must be the name they gave to the swarm weapon. I'm right, aren't I? This is the same as the attack Surtr showed us. This is the same technology."

"Do you know who was speaking?"

"There was no name given, no identification or dating of any sort."

"Whoever it was, they sounded terrified. And also, I'd say, *baffled.* They thought they were safe, and then suddenly they weren't."

Ondo nodded in agreement. "Which makes all my precautions seem slightly less paranoid."

"I have no record of a planet called *Dunlen Alta.*"

"I assume it ceased to exist a long time ago."

"You said you had an idea for where we could go to strip down and test the *Dragon*."

Ondo glanced aside, as if he could see through the bulkheads to the surrounding stars. "I do. Another renegade, in her own way. I said there were one or two scattered around. Inevitably, we keep to ourselves as it's hard to know who you can really trust."

"Who is she?"

"I know her simply as Hessia Aperion, although that may not be her real name. She was another protégé of Aefrid Sen, although from my communications with her over the years, I gather she's grown somewhat disillusioned with uncovering the truth about Concordance. She can be … frosty. As far as I can tell, she spends her time collecting treasures simply for the pleasure of doing so. I suppose I can't blame her."

"She has a Refuge like ours?"

"She must, but I've no idea where it is, just as she has no idea where ours is. There's safety in ignorance. We have a system of communication whereby my nanodrones pass messages along to her nanodrones when they meet at certain pre-agreed rendezvous points, and, slowly, we can have a conversation."

"You haven't mentioned her before."

"Honestly, I'd forgotten all about her. We haven't been in touch for at least five years, and she may well be dead. But, if she isn't, she may know of a safe world or moon we can use to overhaul the *Dragon*. Somewhere with the facilities we'll need but without any intrusive Concordance oversight."

Selene thought about that. "Any safe havens we know about can't be trusted, because if the *Dragon* has been compromised, Concordance will know them, too."

"Exactly so."

"And if this Hessia Aperion is dead?"

"There are one or two other contacts we could try. After that, we'll have to take our chances on a world we do know about. Or, at some point, return to the Refuge and hope."

"How can we contact her?"

"I've already sent messages out onto the network. We had an agreed emergency code that might prompt her to respond."

"If she does, I'll take the *Dragon* in while you stay on Surtr's ship," said Selene. "You need to get over your injuries. You *and* Eb. We still don't know what that blast did to your brain. There's inflammation there."

"There's a tiny amount of inflammation there, and we'll both need to get involved in the work on the *Dragon*."

She shook her head. "You're not needed, Ondo. Surtr can help me. I don't fully understand all the technology it has at its disposal, but its abilities are miraculous. The ship's systems have never been at such an operational peak."

"Surtr..." said Ondo. His eyes defocussed as he stared at something that only he could see. "...yes, that could be interesting. Very interesting."

"What? You're wandering off again. I can't read your mind, Ondo."

"Sorry, yes, of course. It's just, Hessia always had a special fascination with galactic legends. She loved to collect ancient artefacts. Not to study, but just to admire, because they fired her imagination not because of the evidence they could reveal. And an Aetheral, now: such a being would be absolutely sure to intrigue her."

"She'll know about them?"

"Oh, she will. She spent a lot of time pursuing the old myths. I'm afraid I used to be very critical of her at times. I may even have suggested that she was wasting her life."

"Perhaps it is best I go without you."

"I'm sure I wasn't *that* rude," said Ondo, looking affronted.

"Are you? Do you really think she hasn't responded all this time because she's been a bit busy? Because, I think I can see the real reason."

Ondo was about to object further, then stopped himself. "Perhaps you are right. She probably naturally avoids people with a negative attitude; she has abilities that make her very conscious of how others feel about her."

"What abilities?"

"She's a Periarch."

Selene accessed the datastores in her head to fill in the gaps in her knowledge. "She's an empath."

"A part of the reason she's done such a good job of staying safe over the years, no doubt. She instinctively knows whom she can trust and whom she can't. Everyone from Periarch has an empathic sense to a greater or lesser degree, but she comes from a long line of Queens with a very strong genetic predisposition. The stronger ones get a synaesthetic crossover, so that they *see* people's emotional and intellectual states as fields around their heads, auras of colours. She told me all about it once."

"Did you actually meet?"

"Not in the flesh."

"She wouldn't have been able to sense anything about you from afar. Empathy is a close-range ability."

"True, true, but I think she learned to predict who might fill her with positive energy and who would drag her down into their own misery. It's a curse of the strong empath, I believe, to be at the mercy of those around them. You can't even close the doors and lock yourself away. It must have been hard for people like her to be around when Concordance came and everyone was thrown into panic."

Selene found it hard to be too sympathetic. "She survived. No doubt many others didn't."

"Yes, of course."

"She chose to live a life of solitude, away from a planet full of traumatised people. I guess I get that. There has to be a chance she's still around, just not taking calls."

"It's worth a try."

She was about to leave him in peace, prep for the next sequence of jumps, when a thought occurred to her. "If she is alive, I wonder how she'll react to me with my 50/50 organic brain."

"That is a question to which I simply don't know the answer. Perhaps, if you do decide you feel the need to slaughter her, you should keep those thoughts in the left half of your brain where she might not be able to read them."

"Thanks. I'll bear that in mind."

7. The Periarch

The *Radiant Dragon* and Surtr's vessel materialized together for the forty-ninth time on their exodus through the stars. Two weeks had passed by since the recovery of the *Dragon*. Both ship and Ondo were repairing well. There had been no sign of Concordance pursuit, despite longer and longer waits at each terminus point in normal space.

Eb still hadn't emerged from his slumber. They'd left him alone, although Ondo visited every day, mainly to gaze in wonder and, occasionally, to shake his head in disbelief. The faraway gaze that was often on his face at such times told Selene everything she needed to know about what was going through his mind. He retained his childish wonder at the universe around him. She hoped he always would.

There'd been no word from the nanosensor array about what Concordance were up to, no useful clue about why their ships were scrambling. The network *had* identified three sets of coordinates where multiple Cathedral ships had been seen assembling. Selene had been on the point of jumping to one of these to find out what was going on when the message from Hessia Aperion had come through. The empath's response was extremely cautious, but she'd proposed a rendezvous in deep space, well away from any star system or previously-used muster point.

"She's intrigued," Selene said. "She took the bait, thanks to your mention of Surtr."

Ondo agreed. "She's picked a safe spot, far from any gravity wells so she can jump at a moment's notice. I imagine she seeded the whole area with sensors before sending her reply. It's what I would have done."

"Are we in any danger from her?"

"Five years ago, I'd have said definitely not. Who knows what's happened to her since then? For all we know, Concordance captured her and worked their Void Walker mind-control fritz on her."

"We have to take the risk."

"I think we do."

The agreed plan was to leave Ondo on the *Dragon* and make a fiftieth jump on Surtr's ship to the meeting point. The arrangement meant that Hessia got to see Surtr's ship; Selene's hope was that Hessia had seen nothing like it and would be suitably intrigued.

She agreed a rendezvous point with Ondo, then EVA'd over to Surtr's ship. The transparent observation dome admitted her in another blaze of pearly light, and the two ships parted.

A single fragment of rock tumbled through the interstellar medium at the meeting point. It was too small to be spherical, and had no distinguishing features, gave off no energy signatures. No technological artefacts of any sort were detectable in local space, although that didn't mean they weren't there. They had no idea what technology Hessia had acquired or created for herself.

"What will you do?" Surtr asked. It stood with Selene in the observation dome again as they considering their options. She wished the Aetheral would make a few suggestions, even if they were poor ones, but it appeared to be completely at a loss. She watched the misshapen lump of rock tumbling through the void, its presence little more than a whisper in the faint light from the stars. The possibility that this was a set-up was very clear. They had no way of knowing what was in Hessia's mind – or even if she was still alive. For all they knew, Ondo had been talking to a Concordance agent all along.

After a moment's thought, she said, "We go to the rock." There was a flattened area on one surface of the boulder according to their scans – natural as far as she could tell, the result of some ancient, sheering collision – and the instructions were to land and wait with their ship withdrawn to a safe distance. By which Hessia meant safe for *her*, not for Selene.

They touched down on the smooth surface of the rock. It was tumbling lazily about its long axis, and Surtr put its ship into an orbital pattern that at least ensured it always had line-of-sight.

Selene extended all her senses, feeling extremely exposed. She was getting too used to living in her EVA suit, hearing the wheeze of its oxygen valves opening and closing, the slight creaking sound it made as she flexed and extended her elbows and knees. She envied Surtr, standing calmly beside her, utterly unconcerned by the void. Perhaps she would take that next evolutionary step one day, cast off her flesh.

The spin of the rock sent the blaze of stars and nebulae around her into a constant swirl of movement. Once she would have found it dizzying, but now she felt no nausea. She was becoming used to living off-planet. But, if they were attacked there, they had very little they could fight back with. The surface around them looked blue-grey in the light given off by Surtr, its composition predominantly iron and silicates. The rock had insufficient gravity to hold them in place, so Selene had set her suit's reaction thrusters into ground-contact mode, exerting a slight but constant downwards force.

She was seriously considering the possibility that she'd been duped, that Hessia had deliberately separated the two of them from the *Dragon* in order to capture or destroy it, when the attack drone array materialized.

They snapped into position all around the rock, sixty-four of them in tight formation: a halo of impressive-looking kill weaponry targeting the spot where the two of them stood. The spotlight beams from the devices were bright enough to outshine the aura from Surtr, washing away all shadows. Could she and the Aetheral survive the combined blast from all that firepower? She had no real idea of the capabilities of the fields and shields that Surtr propagated, and this was not how she would have chosen to find out.

She had to work very hard to keep her hands still, not draw her own blaster and start shooting.

After a few moments of stand-off, a figure descended from above, appearing through the blinding light from the drones. Her microreaction thrusters fired to land her gently on the ground in front of Selene and Surtr. Glints of light from the drones reflected off the newcomer's visor as she studied Selene, head cocked slightly on one side. Did empathic senses work through suits and the short distance of void between them? Selene had to assume they did. She kept herself calm, breathing slowly. She requested comms contact to allow them to talk which, after a few moments, was granted.

"You are Hessia Aperion?"

The woman's voice sounded amused when it spoke in Selene's head. "I am, but you are not Ondo Lagan."

"He is on our other ship, the *Radiant Dragon*. He'll recover, but he was hurt in the attack we suffered. I'm Selene Ada."

"Oh, I know exactly who you are. Despite what you may think, I keep up to date with galactic developments. Another dangerous terrorist joining forces with Ondo; Concordance have made sure we all know about you. The question is, should I be afraid of you?"

"Why do you need to ask? Don't your empathic senses tell you what my intentions are? And you're the one with the battery of high-energy beam-weapons under your control. I've come unarmed, as agreed."

"Unarmed apart from this miraculous giant standing beside you. What is it capable of? Are you in any danger at all from my weapons?"

"If it's any help, I don't know. I'm not entirely sure it does, either, come to that."

Hessia hopped closer so that her head was only a few centimetres from Selene's. The interior of the Periarch's helmet was illuminated, which was a good sign. It meant that she was prepared to reveal her features, show herself rather than hiding away in the forbidding darkness. Selene was glad she'd done the same. She could see the olfactory slits on the side of Hessia's neck ruffling open and closed as she breathed, see her green eyes as she studied Selene. There was a pause as if the empath were listening to something.

Eventually, Hessia said, "Interesting. I wasn't sure if I'd be able to read anything off you, given your … divided nature. I admit I was worried you might be closed to me."

"And what can you read?"

"Do you really want me to say out loud? Do you want our mysterious friend here to know the dark secrets lurking in your mind?"

"Sure, why not. His life is one big journey of discovery right now."

"I get a lot from you, Selene Ada. Your aura is very clear even though you're wearing an EVA suit, which I actually didn't think was possible. Such strong emotions. There's an undercurrent of rage bubbling away in your mind, but that's shot through with notes of sadness and loss. There's a clear desire for revenge burning away, but also, you're fascinated by everything that's happened since leaving Maes Far and the wonders you've encountered. Then there's the guilt: you survived, and it troubles you that you occasionally find yourself having fun when that was taken away from everyone else on your world. Oh, and there are also bright sparks of light that can only be sensations of love. Or lust. Or both. Does that about sum it up?"

"It sounds about right. And do you get anything from my left brain?" She found herself asking the question that she'd vowed to herself she wouldn't.

"As a matter of fact, I get no divide in your mind. Your whole head is haloed by colours. I don't think you have an artificial and an organic half anymore. I think the two have become … fluid. Intertwined. Which, actually, I don't think is that unusual. Once, if my family records are to be believed, it was quite common for we Periarchs to be able to read hybrid Minds. Purely artificial AIs like those that used to control planets were closed-off to us, but not augmented people and other crossovers. I sense you feel that you're unusual, freakish, but you should know that, once, you really wouldn't have been. People were habitually transbiological, technological hybrids. A few brain-flecks and metabolism-engineering transplants at one end of the spectrum, full on construct-integration and body-transfer at the other. That was the golden age for you."

"And what about Surtr? Can you read anything off it?"

Surtr had been party to their conversation, but hadn't commented or even moved. Now it stirred, shifting its weight as if the question made it uncomfortable.

Hessia turned her head and looked up at Surtr. "Yes, the Aetheral. I honestly doubted Ondo when he said you had joined up with one, but I can tell that you, at least, completely believe that's what this entity is. The question is, what are we to make of this miraculous being?"

"You know what Aetherals are?"

"I've heard all the stories, but I seriously doubted they were real. Or, if they were, that I would ever encounter one."

"That's why you agreed to meet us."

"That's one reason, but actually not the main one."

Surtr finally spoke. "Are you able to perceive a synaesthetic aura around my head?"

Hessia looked amused at the question, if Selene was reading her expressions correctly.

"What do you think I'll be able to see?" Hessia asked.

"I assume nothing, and that I am an entirely constructed mechanism."

"Interesting you would think that. Well, you'd be wrong, I see a very clear aura. Nowhere near as bright as Selene's, but it's there."

"I am … organic?"

"You have some elements of that in your makeup. Part of you is, or was, biological. As I say, I believe such distinctions were once much less useful. Perhaps they were meaningless."

"What do you read off Surtr?" Selene asked.

Hessia still addressed the Aetheral. "Should I tell her? They're your private emotions and responses."

"Yes."

Hessia gazed up at Surtr for a moment longer. "Right now, I'm mainly getting confusion. You're struggling to come to terms with everything you've encountered recently. You're ruminating, restructuring your thought-patterns, like a pupating insect. There's also a strong streak of revulsion within you at things you find repellent."

"What does it find repellent?" Selene asked.

"I can't tell. I pick up emotional states, not thoughts."

"I assume you've at least worked out you can trust us," said Selene. "We are what we say we are, and we do need your help. The question is, how do I know I can trust you? I have no empathic abilities."

The Periarch's gaze returned to Selene. "You don't know you can trust me, but I haven't killed you yet, and you're the one who came to me for help. We can go our separate ways if you prefer. It doesn't make much difference to me."

"That's not a very empathic thing to say."

"Isn't it? Perhaps you're confusing sympathy with empathy. Just because I can pick up your emotional states doesn't mean that I approve of or appreciate them."

"Are you saying you don't approve of us?"

"Honestly? I think you and Ondo are dangerous. You goad Concordance, and you put everyone trying to live peaceful lives outside their control at risk. You stir up trouble constantly, make people take risks to fight back. So, no, I don't approve."

"Why are you here, then? What's your other reason for agreeing to meet us? There must be something you want, if I'm reading you correctly."

"Very good. First I need to decide what your intentions really are."

"Why don't you deactivate all the killtech and see what we do?"

Hessia thought about that. "I will. Your emotional response will be interesting. Relief or excitement at finally being able to attack? We shall see."

In a rapid sequence, the drones encircling them flipped their noses up and peeled away, disappearing in a single line into the darkness.

Selene watched them go. "Good. Now can we get off this rock and talk properly?"

"On Surtr's ship?"

"Sure."

Hessia considered for a few more moments, probably sifting through the layers of Selene's emotional responses, looking for any signs of duplicity or malign intent.

Eventually, she said, "I will trust you that far. But you should know that I have considerable firepower at my disposal. It may or may not be able to scratch the voidhull of an Aetheral's vessel, but I'll happily die finding out."

"Let's hope it doesn't come to that," said Selene.

An hour later, Selene sat opposite Hessia in one of the featureless rooms on Surtr's ship. Surtr itself stood against one wall, not moving as it listened in, looking more than ever like stylized robotic statue.

Hessia was tall and willowy. She put Selene in mind of deep-sea plants waving in the wash of invisible currents. Civilisation on Periarch, she knew, had developed on atolls and around lagoons, and people from that world retained a deep love of the ocean. Perhaps it explained the direction Hessia's life had taken: she'd cast herself adrift, alone, on the greater waters of the galaxy. There was something broken about her if you looked closely, though. Or, not broken exactly, but there was a flaw in her, a crack. She had a tendency to wince when you spoke to her, as if being exposed to your emotional state was painful for her.

She found herself warming to Hessia; the Periarch retained a cynicism and an abruptness that Selene found refreshing. She was also self-deprecating once her guard was down. They'd walked about Surtr's ship together, and Hessia had been visibly awed by what she'd seen. She'd muttered to herself more than once about how Surtr's vessel put her own to shame. *This is incredible; I had no idea, and I live in a fucking hovel compared to this.* Like Ondo, she had a tendency to talk to herself.

"You said Surtr was not the main reason for agreeing to meet us," said Selene.

"The truth? It's a family history thing. I saw Ondo's broadcast about what you found on Coronade."

"You have a connection with the planet?"

Hessia hesitated for a moment, debating with herself how much to say. She glanced aside at Surtr, then fixed her aquamarine eyes back on Selene.

"There's a family story that one of my forebears was there when it was destroyed, the day Concordance fired the first shot of the war that ended galactic civilisation. Like Ondo, I've been trying to piece together the truth of that, although with less success. And, I admit, I'd become disillusioned, given up hope. I was beginning to believe the lies put out by our glorious protectors. The proof that you found, though – I can't tell you how it made me feel. It was like lights being switched on inside me. Like a dead part of me came back to life."

"What was the story?"

"That one of my mother's mothers was a diplomat on Coronade, someone who spent her days resolving disputes between the worlds, defusing conflicts into peaceful solutions. She'd just completed work on a settlement between three other worlds when Vulpis and a massed Concordance battlefleet showed up out of nowhere. They bombarded Coronade mercilessly, reducing it to dust and ruins. Which is precisely what you saw."

"Ondo believes Coronade was a symbol of the entire civilisation."

"For once, I believe he's right. The planet lay at the heart of something they called the *Nexus*: effectively, a living network of planetary Minds, cooperating and sharing information, working together for the common benefit. The galaxy is huge, something we lose perspective of locked away on our little worlds. There was never any problem with cultures expanding, of colonizing new worlds, of growing. By and large, I think, the galaxy must have been a pretty good place to live. Maybe it really was the golden age that Ondo likes to talk about."

Selene thought about the nanotube mesh. Had that been used to hold the vast and disparate culture together? The mesh might be ancient, but the Coronadian culture could have found it and started using it. She must mention the idea to Ondo.

"Your forebear was a key part of it all," she said.

"A small part, I think, but I grew up imagining what it must have been like to be her. The people she met and the places she saw."

"Coronade's very existence proves that Concordance's story of a galaxy riven by conflict and horror is untrue, especially if there were people like your ancestor there, working to resolve disputes."

Hessia nodded at that. "Her name was Magdi. Growing up, I heard all these stories about her, and I left Periarch with Aefrid Sen's help intent on finding out about her. I think that there was a lot of guilt in her head – not unlike you, in fact. But I don't only mean because she survived when so many didn't. At some level, also, she blamed herself for what happened."

"Blamed *herself*? That makes no sense."

"Her journals spell it all out. During the negotiations that I mentioned, she told a lie and swore by the nexus of worlds and by the Coronade Mind that she hadn't lied. A small thing, perhaps, but it bugged her, because very soon afterwards everything that she'd sworn upon was gone. It all fell apart."

"She told a white lie to achieve peace. That doesn't seem like a sin."

"She connected two things that weren't connected. People do. Empaths are especially prone to getting the wrong perspective on things. We have a tendency to catch negative emotions like other people catch viruses, or we slip into thinking that our own position in the universe is more important than it is because we ride the mental states of those around us. Some empaths succumb to the delusion that they *control* those around them."

Selene wondered if all that was another reason Hessia had chosen to live her lonely existence. "You devoted your life to recovering the truth. You weren't so different to me and Ondo."

The twinge of pain flashed across Hessia's face and was gone. She looked troubled by what she was about to say. "Perhaps. I had an experience soon after I left Periarch; a moment of revelation. I was on a dead world, the population just bones and dust beneath my feet. It was ... peaceful. Then I felt it. Do you think it's possible to pick up the emotions of the dead?"

"I don't know," said Selene. "I've seen no evidence it's possible."

"Maybe it was all in my head; a reaction of my own. But it was a moment of clarity, and it changed me. I decided to try and give a voice to those who'd been silenced. Until then, I'd been suppressing my nature as an empath."

"That's possible?"

"If we choose, we can boost our empathic sensibilities with the relevant hormones. I believe Magdi would have done that in her role on Coronade. On Periarch, I habitually took the opposite drugs, to suppress my ability. I thought I was doing it for the good of my health, but now I see that I was running away, cutting myself off. I made the decision to embrace my own nature, and to slowly boost my empathic senses to where they now are. Although, as I say, lately I'd given up. Convinced myself I'd recover the truth some distant day in the future. Then I picked up your broadcast."

"How did your forebear escape Coronade if it was under such heavy orbital bombardment?"

"It's a part of the story that speaks volumes about her. One of the warring parties – someone Magdi had been in conflict with not long before, whom she'd accused of committing a murder in fact – risked herself to return to the surface and rescue Magdi. A soldier called Pannax Ro from the planet Arianas. Magdi got away, barely, and returned to Periarch where her lover, Olorun, was waiting for her. My family survived on Periarch for several generations until I escaped. I guess that's a familiar enough story for you?"

"Except that Periarch survives. Your people are subjugated but still alive."

"Forgive me, yes. That was a stupid thing to say. My people are not in a good way, but they are still there."

"We need to quarantine the *Radiant Dragon*, and make sure Concordance don't have their claws in it. Will you help us?"

"Now that I get to know you, and I understand you a little better … yes, I will. I didn't intend to, you might like to know. I was intrigued, but I'd decided to keep my distance as much as possible. I think, though, that Magdi, if she were still around, would have agreed to help."

"Do you know of a world we can go to?"

"It's a long way from my version of the Refuge, but I've used it once or twice to make repairs. The planet of Fenwinter. Misecera III."

"If it's high-tech enough to have the facilities we need, Concordance must be there."

"They were, but they left recently after blasting the world back into the stone age. The people there became too rebellious, so Coronade dismantled their society, destroyed their economy. Not with a shroud this time: six months ago, they unleashed a virulent pathogen that wiped out 98% of the population. Going there is hard: hard for anyone, but especially for an empath, as perhaps you can imagine. But there are abandoned spaceports and repair facilities that can be useful."

"Fenwinter, I know it. What will you do? I'm not an empath, but even I can see there's a look about you. You're ready to take up the fight again."

Hessia smiled at that, and it was an expression that clearly meant trouble for someone. "Yes, time I stopped hiding away. Time I played my part. Perhaps I knew that, deep down, and that was why I agreed to meet. I'd chosen to dive into the deep ocean – bury my head in the sand as you might say – but now it's time for me to resurface and find out what Concordance are doing. I also noticed their recent mobilisation. If this is some plan of Godel's, then I need to know, and I need to do what I can to stop them."

"Will we see you again?"

"No, we endanger each other too much by meeting up. I'm grateful to you, not least for letting me meet an Aetheral and see its ship. I feel a renewed sense of hope, but it's best we go our separate ways. Unless, at the end, we succeed."

Hessia stood and gripped Selene's forearm in a gesture that was, presumably, common on Periarch.

"I'm tired of losing, tired of the bad people winning," said Hessia. "I'm tired of the truth being buried. Let's go and destroy the bastards."

Selene found herself grinning in reply.

Beside them, Surtr finally spoke. "I, too, would like to participate in the process of destroying the bastards."

The two women tried and failed to stop themselves laughing while the Aetheral regarded them.

8. Fenwinter

Selene stood with Ondo on the blasted, windswept plain, staring at the numbers projected onto the sheer cliff face in one hundred metre characters.

Seventeen digits. Seventeen sevens. Up above them, an array of atmospheric drones hovered, generating the display. The digits were bright enough to be visible by day. By night they cast shadows, glowing on the horizon for fifty kilometres around. Fenwinter lay in ruins, yet the devices propagating the numbers remained fully-functional, drawing in enough solar energy by day to maintain their output.

Selene thought she knew what the numbers represented. "This is the sacred tally; the count of sentient lifeforms that Concordance believes marks the end of days. The trigger to kill everyone."

"I think it must be," said Ondo. "Seventeen sevens: it makes sense in their terms. Older Omnian theology is obsessed with numerology, and the number seven has particular significance to them."

"I thought they were preoccupied with the number three."

"They are, or some factions are. I believe the fascination with trinities is from a more recent manifestation of Omnian thought, whereas a concern with septads is older."

"Do we have any way of knowing if the number is accurate? If the galactic population did hit this size?"

Ondo shook his head. "It seems high – it's a huge number, nearly seventy-eight quadrillion – but we have no way of making the calculation for ourselves. I've sometimes wondered if that's another thing all the Cathedral ships are doing, maintaining this tally, but then there are all the lower-tech systems they don't watch. The point is, they can come up with this number and claim it's reliable, and no one can contradict them. And I don't think Carious or any of the recent Primos put much emphasis on numerology. They think it's primitive."

"Whereas Godel and her tradition are all over it."

"Fenwinter – and all the planets and moons in this system – are her work. A year ago this was a high-population, advanced civilisation. Then Concordance ramped up its activity, Godel's ship the *Storm Gatherer* leading the way, and the result is as we now see. This society has been so shattered that Concordance don't even bother to watch over it anymore. They left these displays as warnings, or taunts, or justifications, and abandoned the planet to its collapse."

The numbers were replicated elsewhere around the world: projected into the night sky and broadcast on multiple radio frequencies. Not that there were many people left with the functioning technology to pick up such messages. The planet's societies teetered on the brink of elimination. Scattered individuals clung to life, living hand-to-mouth, but barbarism and brutality were everywhere. The mountaintop facility was thankfully removed from it all, just as Hessia had promised. It had been built as the tether point for a space elevator, which had either never been completed or destroyed as the conflagration overcame the planet.

Selene inhaled and exhaled deeply. The air of Fenwinter was breathable, but the oxygen levels were a little lower than she'd have preferred, especially so high up in the mountains. If she exerted herself, it made stars dance in front of her right eye. Her left eye's emulation, she noted wryly, didn't bother. Still, at least the air was sweet, devoid of pollutant particulates: one effect of the elimination of the planet's technologically-advanced culture.

The cliff face they were staring at lay on the far side of a deep cleft in the local geography through which, far below, a silver river snaked. The line of the cliff face opposite ended in another remarkable feature: a lone spike of rock, pushing high into the atmosphere. They'd seen it as they descended on the Dragon; the very top of the spike was transatmospheric, puncturing the upper layers of the thin stratosphere to touch the lower reaches of space. It was, so far as she knew, entirely natural, left over from a period of extreme vulcanism and geological activity.

The most incredible feature of the peak, however, wasn't its height, but the flight of steps carved into its side – and the platform on top of the mountain that the steps led to. According to the datastores, the high stairway had been carved in antiquity. It had to have been a monumental effort, given the increasingly tenuous atmosphere and the hardness of the igneous rock. The stairway zig-zagged upwards for a distance of twelve kilometres. By zooming in, she could pick out that the lower steps were worn down by the passage of many feet. Erosion was reduced on the steps at higher altitudes, but then it picked up again because of the increasing amount of solar radiation hitting the rock there.

It was called Amorang, the name translating to something like sun shard. Traditionally, people on Fenwinter made a pilgrimage to it at various turning-points in their lives: becoming an adult, marrying, having children, reaching the end of their working life, or just when they felt they needed to put themselves back in touch with the infinite. The aim was to climb as many steps as possible; there were numerous stations set up the side of the peak, each with its own spiritual significance. To make the journey to the peak at all was considered auspicious, but the higher you went, the more propitious it became.

Most religions on Fenwinter were multitheistic, but they orbited around a central deity known only as the Xi, the Faceless God. Xi gazed blindly over her creation, treating hardship and joy, sorrow and celebration with equal acceptance. It was a stoical, peaceable tradition that emphasised humility. High, high up at the peak of Amorang was a place where the face of Xi was said to be visible – except that the carving was blank. Either it had never been there, or it had eroded away. Whether that was the origin of the faceless god tradition, or whether the uncarved face was deliberate, the archives didn't tell.

Selene shielded her gaze with her hand as she peered up at the peak. "It's incredible anyone would attempt the journey up those steps. The effort of it, the devotion required: I don't get it. Reaching the pinnacle is basically impossible. They had to know that. I can only assume the atmosphere extended farther up when the steps were carved."

"Sometimes the journey is the point, not the destination," Ondo said.

"You're talking about your path through the stars again, aren't you?"

He smiled to himself but didn't reply.

Surtr marched over to meet them, weaving between the piles of debris and rusting components that were strewn around the abandoned site. An explosion had ripped through the spaceport at some point, destroying much of it. Fortunately, many of the facilities that they needed had survived in underground bunkers and blast-shielded lander docks.

The Aetheral said, "The scans are proceeding well. Eb and I have isolated all of the core systems and we are now exposing them to full diagnostic assay."

"How many filaments of the incursion bug did you find?"

"There were three in total: two trying to burrow into the core and then the one in cartography. We have eliminated all of them."

"There could be more."

"If there are, Eb will find them. The ship will be offline for six hours. In that time, I would like to explore this world more widely."

"You would?" She wondered why it wanted to do that. But then, she recalled her visit to Migdala, the first other world that she'd stood upon. She didn't need to be Hessia to see that a sense of wonder was flowing through Surtr. The Aetheral had been utterly isolated over its lonely millennia, and now everything was available to it. She got it. The entity deserved to know more about what was going on.

"Are you needed for anything here?" she asked.

"We have everything in place; we can only wait for the deep scans to complete."

She'd watched the Aetheral operating; it could move at a dazzling speed when it needed to, flitting between rooms and manipulating objects so rapidly that she could only just keep up with her augmented vision. In the end, she and Ondo had stopped trying to help, and had left it and Eb to strip down the Dragon and prepare the ship for its analysis.

"How quickly can we get everything working again if we need to?" she asked.

"Two hours. So far there is no sign of any Concordance activity in the system. If they do show up, we may have to abandon the Radiant Dragon and flee on my ship. It can get here within an hour, ahead of any Concordance vessels, and we've kept the Dragon's lander primed and ready to fly if we need it."

"We need to strip the lander down, too."

"That has already been completed."

"How are you coping with being separated from your ship?"

Surtr had explained that it was tied closely to its vessel in ways that were fundamental to its nature and impossible to disentangle. Presumably the situation was something like that between Eb and the Dragon: they were, essentially, two aspects of the same whole.

"The situation is sustainable for a short time," said Surtr. "The distance between us is slowly impairing my function, but not to a noticeable degree at this stage."

"If we do have to flee, what about Eb?"

"Eb is very clear that he cannot leave the Dragon; he is too fundamentally intertwined. He has instructed me to fire atmospheric nukes to destroy him rather than let himself be captured. I have loaded two onto the lander."

"Shit," said Selene.

"He has been in Concordance hands before, remember," said Surtr. "That was when most of the damage was done to him. He refuses to allow that to happen again."

"Let's hope it doesn't come to that," said Ondo. "I will come with you to explore. I've waited and rested too long."

Selene turned her attention to Ondo, who was innocently regarding the view. "I don't think that's wise. You should stay here." He still got sharp headaches for no reason that they could work out, although they appeared to be declining in frequency.

He waved her objections away. "Where do you want to go, Surtr?"

The Aetheral considered the numbers on the cliff face, and it was hard not to read a frown on those unchanging features. "I would like to know more about this. And about what has taken place on this world."

If they did encounter any dangers, it was possible she might be glad of having Surtr along. She relented. "I planned to scout around, look for anyone who might be a threat. I guess we can all go."

"I would welcome that," the Aetheral replied. "There is so much that I don't understand. But I will be rather obtrusive; the inhabitants of this world closely resemble you in body form and stature. I do not; I could not be mistaken for anyone from here."

"We'll keep our distance. And in any case, there's hardly anyone left. Even if an individual sees you, who are they going to tell? Who's going to believe them? They might even think you're some manifestation of their faceless god and start worshipping you."

"I would not welcome that."

"That's good to know," said Selene.

A wide road had been blasted into the side of the mountain, spiralling down gently, but someone had gone to a lot of trouble to block it. Barricades of rusting machinery were piled up at several points: presumably a desperate attempt by those in the spaceport to protect themselves from the unfolding chaos below. The steep flanks of the mountain were largely impassable, strewn with fields of sharp scree that threatened to sweep you away if you attempted to wade through them. In the end, with Selene's help, the Aetheral lifted the wrecked refuelling trucks and cranes blocking their way and threw them thundering and rattling down the slopes.

"Its physical strength is enormous," said Ondo, speaking brain-to-brain. "It's more than a match even for you."

"Yeah, maybe. I've got all the brains in the family, though."

Eventually, the winding road opened out onto gentler slopes. The territory reminded her of the uplands of Maes Far, except that there was only grassland, with none of the purple and red and white meadowfire with its thick, springy foliage that she remembered.

A wide plain lay spread out in front of them, patches of

green and yellow interspersed with the winding curves of rivers and straighter lines that had to be irrigation channels, or tracks, or QuantLev routes. The sun shone directly into her eyes, making details difficult to pick out, glinting off the waterways. She could see round patches that were clearly settlements: a cluster of buildings here that might have been a farm, larger areas further afield that had to be villages and towns and cities.

It all appeared normal, a scene from a thousand different planets across the galaxy – except for two things: the lack of movement and the lack of noise. She would have expected to hear the growing roar of machinery, see people moving around, catch trains flashing along the QuantLev tracks, hear shouts of welcome or laughter from nearby farms. There was nothing, utterly nothing. There were also, she noticed, no birds carving through the high skies, no insectoids droning through the air. She thought she understood then why it was they'd seen only grassland on the higher slopes, even though the records suggested there should be a rich flush of flowers: only wind-pollinated plants were surviving.

There was also the smell. Not the flush of greenery she would have expected, but the tang of decay, sharp on the breeze. A lot of animals, a lot of people had died on Fenwinter in the very recent past.

They came upon the first settlement, little more than a cluster of stone dwellings and high, arched barns set in the middle of sloping fields that were separated by carefully laid stone walls. It had to have been a thriving farmstead once, but now it was deserted, something metallic clanging again and again in the breeze off the mountains. A couple of low, rugged bovines grazed in one of the enclosures, but they were vastly outnumbered by the dead. The rotting carcasses of their sisters lay all around, ribcages gaping open like teeth.

"The pathogen did this," said Surtr. "Animals were susceptible too."

"It jumped species boundaries," said Ondo. "The infection is almost always fatal and highly contagious. You should be glad that you are not susceptible." They'd ensured that she and Ondo were protected before coming to the planet, thanks to Hessia's DNA-sequencing of the pathogen. There was no risk to any of them, but the virus was most definitely there, in the air, upon surfaces. And, according to Selene's self-monitoring systems, upon her skin, in her lungs. Once they were away from the planet, it would take a few days for all traces of it to be eliminated.

"We could have helped them if we'd known," she said. "We could have released benign viral vectors into the environment, put a stop to the outbreak."

"If we'd known," said Ondo. "As ever, we suffer from a lack of timely information. We got here too late."

"Why do this rather than deploying a shroud?"

"My guess is that they were experimenting. A shroud is a single installation, easy to protect with a defensive shield. They calculated that a wider use of planetary pandemics would be vulnerable to people like us or Hessia intervening."

"We should return to the ship," said Selene. "There's nothing to see here. If we venture further down into the lowlands, we're just going to find larger habitations where everyone's dead."

"I…" Ondo started, but stopped, as a scream cut through the silence. It came from beyond a small stand of trees. It was, Selene thought, definitely a human cry, full-blooded with horror and fear.

A look passed between her and Ondo. They should leave, get back to the ship, stay safe. Fight the bigger fight. But Selene found herself striding towards the scream. Surtr followed and then, after a moment, so did Ondo.

They stepped warily through the trees. The ground was a soft carpet of leaf mould from the previous year's autumn, and low branches repeatedly threatened to whip them in the face as they pushed through. Surtr worked forwards in an awkward, crouched stance, a futile attempt to keep itself out of sight. The rough cries were continuing, but they were becoming less frequent, more exhausted. On the other side of the little copse, the ground fell away into a natural bowl in the ground.

Selene lay down in the shadows of the eaves to assess what they were facing. Down the slope, three men stood around another man lying on the ground, his arms held defensively in front of his face to ward off their blows. The three were kicking the man in the torso and head again and again, walking around him as if considering carefully the best angle to strike from. Some old agricultural contraption, all rusting spikes and spokes, stood nearby, the grass growing through it.

Ondo joined Selene, while Surtr waited behind them, peering through the branches. Ondo spoke to her through their direct-brain link. "It isn't going to help if we intervene. We don't know what has happened here."

He was right, and they couldn't afford to wait around to police the crumbling society. Still, it grated to walk away, leave this man to his fate.

One of the three attackers, meanwhile, had pulled out a knife from his belt. The three wore very similar belts, she noted, and the other two also had elaborate blades tucked into them. She zoomed in with her left eye to study the weapons, then reported to Ondo and Surtr what she'd picked up.

"Ceremonial blades," said Ondo, "used by adherents in a local ceremony that normally involves the splitting and sharing of certain fruits."

"It looks like the blades are being put to a different use now."

"Yes."

The figure with the blade kneeled while the other two pinned the man down by his shoulders. The man screamed with renewed ferocity, but lacked the strength to throw off his attackers. The attacker with the knife held the point to the side of the man's head, just below his ear, then drove the weapon hard into the man's cheek. The man bucked and writhed, but couldn't get free. His ragged screams were hideous to hear.

The blade was clearly very sharp. Working rapidly, with an almost surgeon-like skill, the cutter sliced upwards to the man's temple, then across his forehead, then back down again. The screams became bubbling, weaker, then cut off. Selene watched in horror as the knife-wielder seized the flap of skin exposed at the man's hairline, then peeled his face downwards, working with the knife to separate muscle and flesh. Blood welled freely down his hand as he worked away.

Selene glanced aside at the Aetheral. Its triple eyes were focused on the scene, taking it all in, but it didn't move, didn't visibly react. Back down the slope, the victim of the attack struggled weakly for a few moments, then lay still.

Ondo gave her a backwards nod of his head, telling her they should move back. A cold tremor ran through her; she wanted to walk down the slope, confront the three men. She could kill them all easily, make them pay for what they had done. But, what then? What difference would it make? Fenwinter was another world with no future. Would it make her feel better for having killed the three of them?

No, she didn't want to be that person. After a moment, she nodded her assent to Ondo and crawled backwards, into the shadows of the trees. She stood without saying anything.

"I do not understand," said the voice of Surtr in her head. "What was achieved by that act?"

"The faceless god cult has clearly degenerated into something much darker," said Ondo. "The meaning has been forgotten and the name taken literally. They have turned against themselves in their desperation, attempting to placate a god because they have no other actions they can take."

"Those three people – they are your Concordance enemies?"

"No, not directly. They don't need to be. Concordance drips its poison onto their world and ordinary people do its work for them. Almost gleefully, at times."

"Brutalized people become brutes," said Selene. She'd seen similar things on Maes Far, during her last few days there. Things she'd tried and failed to unsee.

"You were right," Ondo said to her. "There is nothing we can do here."

Warily, they retraced their steps, climbing back into the uplands. Selene glanced behind her constantly, watching for pursuit, hoping, even, that they would be followed so that she'd be forced to fight to defend herself. But they saw no one else.

Back at their mountaintop retreat, however, an unfamiliar lander hovered over the tetrahedral shape of the Radiant Dragon. A jolt of panic flashed through Selene at the sight as they rounded the final bend of the road, but the craft didn't look like any kind of Concordance vessel she'd ever seen. If anything, it looked patched-up, barely functional, ugly. It might have been the result of multiple broken vessels cut up and welded together into some semblance of operationality. And, if the lander was hostile, Eb would surely have raised an alarm.

The comms call further eased her concern. The familiar voice of Hessia came to her. "I can sense your panic washing over me all the way up here."

"Yeah, I thought you might be Concordance until I saw how wrecked your ship is. It's a mess."

Hessia laughed. "You are using abrasive humour as a covert way of conveying genuine affection. Interesting. Does that ever get you into trouble when people don't get it?"

Damned empaths; it was very clear how Hessia's ancestor would have made a good negotiator. Hard to keep your motivation hidden from someone who could see your emotional state.

"It can be a problem. People have the annoying habit of interpreting a personal insult as somehow unkind. But then, I imagine you knew that as you do something similar, right?"

"Perhaps I do," said Hessia.

"Why are you here? You said we wouldn't see you again."

"Plans change. My attempts to find out what Concordance are up to went better than I thought for once. They're showing their hand. I know now why they were scrambling, what they were up to activating all their Cathedral ships."

"What is it?"

"Best I show you. Have you completed your sweeps of the Dragon?"

Selene connected with the ship, queried its status. The scans had progressed well, and had found nothing. They were nearly done. It helped that Eb had finally emerged into the world, stepping from the cell he'd inhabited for so long to peer around the corners of the ship that was, in some way, his own body. With Ondo, Eb and Surtr, the Dragon had become quite a crowded ship. She almost missed the days when it was just her and the galaxy, and no one to have to make conversation with.

"We're still working on it," said Selene. "Right now, it's impossible to be absolutely sure we're clean, but it's looking good."

"How long?" Hessia asked.

"Two hours, and we'll be ready."

"Can you be ready to go in one?"

"If we have to."

"Good. I know you wanted to go back to the Refuge, but we need to act."

An hour later, the Dragon rose from the surface of the

planet. Hessia's ship, the Falling Fire, waited for them in orbit, following a lower, faster trajectory than Surtr's vessel. The Periarch's ship resembled its lander: functional, almost cobbled together. The cubic bulk of its metaspace drive unit was clearly of a different design to the spiky angles of its main housing. The lateral beam-weapon arrays looked like they'd been grafted on as an afterthought. Selene hadn't seen the ship properly at their deep space rendezvous, as Hessia had travelled in a much more impressive-looking shuttle. She understood why, now.

The three ships joined into formation and angled away from the gravitational pull of the Fenwinter star to their agreed metaspace jump point. They made no attempt to conceal their exit from the planet as they had their arrival. There'd been no sign of active Concordance monitoring of the system, and it didn't matter if their presence was spotted as they left.

They had an hour to complete the run-up to the jump point. Once all three ships were on matching vectors, Hessia made the EVA hop across the gap to the Dragon to fill everyone in on what she'd discovered. Surtr drifted over from his ship, too. Selene had the cartography deck set up as a war room, four seats arranged around a table for her, Ondo, Hessia and Eb. There were no chairs large enough for Surtr, and it stood instead, towering over the four of them. Eb looked exhausted as he entered the room. He'd taken to wearing simple, body-length robes, but the skin of his face was an ashen grey. He sat with his eyes shut, and waved his hand in a way that suggested he was okay, they should continue.

Hessia activated the imagery projectors. A high-level display of the galaxy appeared; the familiar swirl of the arms surrounding the central eye. But laid across it were the branching lines of something that might have been a vast parasite sitting across the entire structure, a many-legged arachnoid perhaps, its limbs splayed across the star-field as if it were sucking energy from all the solar systems within it.

Ondo leaned forwards, intrigued, while the display slowly rotated. "Some of those I recognize. There's the metaspace tunnels we used to travel to the dead star from Coronade, and then to leave with Surtr."

"This is what I've been spending my time mapping," said Hessia. Two of the lines flashed in red, intersecting at the same point in space. "You've mentioned the Gamma Spinwards and Sigma Counterspin tunnels, but I've identified a total of twenty-four such pathways, all of them providing shortcuts right across a sizeable portion of the galactic disc."

"How have you done this?" asked Ondo.

"The same as you: piecing together scraps of data, correlating fragments of documents, scrabbling around in the dust of worlds and the asteroid fields of abandoned solar systems. It's taken me a long time to create this map."

"I thought you'd given up trying to fight them," said Selene.

"I'll be honest, I put together a lot of this several years ago. I've come back to it in light of your findings. I saw the recent increase in Concordance activity, but I'd been doing my best to ignore it."

Ondo said, "When you were unearthing the data for this, were Concordance always there? One step ahead or behind?"

"Sometimes they were, very often not. I believe they don't have a reliable map, either. You must have seen the same yourself: Concordance are following their own trail, attempting to unearth the truth for themselves. On occasion, our paths cross, and we have to fight."

"Show me Coronade on this map." said Selene. "That's supposed to have been a major nexus point."

A dot flashed with two lines leading off it. "It's here," said Hessia, "which tells me that there are a lot of tunnels I don't know about. From your description, there must be ten or twenty intersection points on that planet alone. If I'd been aware of that, I'd have gone there a lot sooner. My theory is that Coronade was a central coordination point, from where these Tok built multiple construction or monitoring tunnels to target systems under enemy control. Systems at which they could then build their stellar mass injection gateways, like the one you used to escape."

"There were seven cones at the dead star," said Selene. "You only have three tunnels marked."

"As I say, my knowledge is patchy. I have no idea where in the galaxy the other four endpoints are."

"Does this mean you've been to Coronade now?"

"It does. I explained the significance of Coronade to my personal history. I obviously want to disprove the version of events that Concordance feed us with."

"What's happening there now?" Selene had seen some telemetry from the nanosensor network, but it was frustratingly out of date.

"There's a lot of Concordance activity. They've put a secure halo of sixteen Cathedral ships around the planet, leaving no possibility of running a surprise incursion. Local space is swimming with their nanosensors and drones and beam-weapon stations. Something else, too: they've set up fixed rings of planetary-defence platforms, enough to ensure that every point in the sphere is covered by at least two. But the beam-weapon arrays on the platforms aren't directed outwards, they're sweeping the planet."

"Planetary defence batteries pointing inwards," said Ondo. "That's new."

"They know about the tunnel entrances," said Selene. "They might not know how to open them, and they might not know where they lead, but they know they're there." She sent her own commands to the nav imaging arrays. Multiple regions of space lit up in red. Each one had at least one of the metaspace tunnels leading into it.

Hessia nodded her head, as if the map was familiar. "You see it. The tunnels and the regions of Dead Space are inextricably linked. It is something that became obvious very quickly when I started my research. I assume we know where every zone is, thanks to the navigational aversions built into just about every metaspace ship I've ever encountered. It's very clear that most of the tunnels I've been able to map either pass through one of the zones, or terminate within one. Every zone apart from one has a tunnel leading into it and then stopping, and the one that doesn't is probably like that because I haven't found the tunnel yet."

"That makes sense from what we discovered," said Selene. "The Dead Space regions were exclusion zones, no-go areas. The Tok quarantined off areas of space where the Morn were and used the tunnels to nova stars to destroy them."

She glanced at Surtr, who neither agreed nor objected, judging by its lack of movement. The Aetheral had been even more taciturn than usual since their departure from Fenwinter, lost in some rumination.

"That's what I believe, too," said Hessia, "and if the tunnels only terminated in the Dead Space zones, it wouldn't be too much of a problem since there are no known inhabited worlds within any of them. We have a much more urgent matter, though: the worlds outside Dead Space that are connected by the tunnels. Coronade is one, but there are others. And then we come to the uptick in Cathedral Ship activity. I've correlated all the data I have, and I've been able to identify that Concordance have scrambled fleets to a total of seven systems where there's a tunnel terminus. There obviously may be others that I simply don't know about."

On the three-dimensional display, the seven systems flashed. The routes of their tunnels were also highlighted. All led to uninhabited zones in normal interstellar space.

"The question is, why are there tunnels to these systems?" Ondo mused. "The Tok clearly didn't need the structures to travel around. Why build these pathways outside of the Dead Space zones?"

Hessia said, "In my view, either these systems were once in regions of Dead Space that we no longer know about, or else the Tok had other enemies that they planned to destroy. We have no way of knowing how extensive the ancient wars were."

Ondo said, "Or the Tok were being proactive, laying traps in systems where they thought the Morn might attack. Or they were experimenting, working out how to make the technology work."

"What matters now is that these seven systems are in grave danger. Concordance have to be planning to use the tunnels to destroy these seven stars. That's what they've been doing: scrambling to unleash this attack, and defending each terminus so that no one is able to sabotage their efforts. I wish I'd worked out sooner that there are anomalous objects hidden beneath the surfaces of the stars, but it was only by correlating my data with yours that I discovered the truth."

"Are any of the systems populated?" asked Selene.

"All of them are. Five are advanced enough to have Cathedral ships in orbit, and the chances are that no one on those worlds has any idea their star is compromised, that there are metaspace tunnel exits hidden beneath its surface. All those stars could be triggered into nova, and the people there would get little warning."

"Seven stars with seven tunnels. I assume you've been to the other end of each as well?"

"Each would be a boring patch of void if you didn't know there was a gateway there. None have stars anywhere near, although all have relatively high densities of dust and plasma."

"Did you find anything else?"

"I did: more Concordance ships. They're protecting both ends of the tunnels. At one there is something else, as well."

A tactical map of the region of space at one of the

tunnel entrances filled the display. It took Selene a beat to work out that the scatter of dots were Cathedral ships. Lots of Cathedral ships. She counted rapidly. One hundred of them. It was by far the largest collection of Concordance assets that she'd ever seen, setting aside the bead images she and Ondo had seen of the Omn home world docking trees, the fleet of thousands of moored ships.

"That's a defensive sphere," said Selene. "They're going to a hell of a lot of effort to protect the object at the tunnel entrance."

"Yes," said Hessia. "You'll see why."

She zoomed in. A single, vast device floated there, an order of magnitude greater in size than any Cathedral ship. It was also, clearly, a product of the same technological culture. Even more than the ships, it resembled a seashell to Selene: its sinuous, spiralling body looked very definitely organic. The difference was the flared ending; its whole structure was effectively one winding tube opening into a wide mouth.

Ondo said, "It looks to me like it was designed to connect with the cones of the metaspace tunnel entrances."

"You're correct," said Hessia. "I've scanned both, and the fit is precise. They are a part of the same mechanism. This new machine can plug into the tunnel perfectly, forming a seal."

"This is how they built the tunnels?" Selene asked. "This device has the ability to tunnel through metaspace, built these permanent pathways?"

Ondo stood and peered more closely at the display, walking round to study it from all angles.

"I don't think that's it," he said. "Hessia, did you pick up any flow readings of the interstellar medium in this area? You said density levels were high. Do you have any data on the pull being exerted on the dust and gas particles?"

"I do. You've worked out what this device is, haven't you? You know what I'm going to say."

Selene saw it in that moment as well. "This is the gun. It's a weapon, built on a colossal scale. It's sucking in matter from this region of space and blasting it down the tunnel at high pressure, directly into the heart of the target star. Increasing its mass until it triggers a supernova. We wondered how the tunnels pulled their trick. This is how."

Hessia's olfactory slits were dilating rapidly as she replied. "It is. It's a blaster constructed on a planetary scale. The device is so vast that it moves slowly, but I've been monitoring it. It is manoeuvring into position. Concordance are going to dock it with the tunnel entrance and activate it. That has to be what all this is about. They located this device and brought it here in order to begin destroying the target star. Perhaps there are other such devices, and perhaps this is the only one. My guess is that the device is metaspace-capable, although the energy required to translate so much mass is staggering. They may have only just located it, or they may have only just succeeded it making it operational. I don't know."

Selene could sense from her words that Hessia wasn't telling them everything.

"Which world?" asked Selene. "Where does that particular tunnel lead to?"

The familiar flinch of alarm was there in Hessia's face as she replied. "Whether this is a coincidence, or whether they are sending a message to the galaxy because I'm a known renegade, I don't know. The fact remains: the tunnel leads to the star of Periarch. It leads directly to my world."

Surtr, finally, spoke. "How many people live on your homeworld, Hessia?"

"Thirteen billion," said Hessia. "There are thirteen billion of us."

9. Detonation

"You should leave this region of space now," Surtr said to Selene. "Soon it will not be safe here."

She stood with the Aetheral within the viewing orb of its ship. They'd emerged from metaspace an hour earlier, materialising in the vicinity of the vast weapon Hessia had located. Surtr had taken great care to stay a long way distant while they sucked in further telemetry from Hessia's nanosensors. Ondo was on the far side of the zone, doing the same from the *Radiant Dragon*.

Hessia herself was gone. She'd chosen to return to Periarch, an action that Selene had tried and failed to talk her out of: "That's insane. If they start this device up it will destroy your sun. Everyone will die on Periarch. You know this."

Hessia had nodded, as if acknowledging a fact of only the slightest importance. "I will attempt to warn my people, disseminate the information we have uncovered. Perhaps I can rescue one or two of them, just as you were once rescued."

"How is it going to help if you go and get yourself killed?"

"I will try not to. But I have missed Periarch's sun-kissed lagoons and its iridescent coral. By night, in the deep oceans, the phosphorescent plankton form endless star fields, and to swim through them is to float through the sky. I shouldn't have stayed away for so long. If it is all to be swept away, I would like to bathe in those waters one final time."

"If you survive, you can keep the memories of your people alive. You'll still be around to tell their stories. Just as I am."

Hessia had considered that. "Perhaps you are right, but I also know that I need to go, to be with my people to face whatever unfolds."

They'd embraced and spoken no more. Hessia had returned to her own vessel and jumped into metaspace for Periarch.

Now, standing beside Surtr, suspicion and an unexpected sense of dread trickled through Selene. It was odd how the lines of Surtr's face never changed – couldn't change – and yet she was suddenly reading sadness there. Perhaps, resolution in the face of adversity.

She felt conflicted: the destructive device was a weapon of purest evil, and that meant that the Tok who had built it had also been evil. Yet, seemingly, they had also created Surtr, just as they had created Eb. It was a mistake to think of the Tok, or any species, as being of one mind; there would have been factions and disagreements among them. For all she knew, the ancient wars had been fought by two sides wielding such weapons as the one they were now studying. Perhaps there had been alliances with the Morn. She wondered if future historians – if there were future historians – would make the mistake of thinking that everyone alive at the current moment was a follower of Concordance. Thinking in such broad terms was too simplistic.

Surtr still hadn't moved. It was uncanny the way it was able to remain absolutely rock-still, as if it had petrified where it stood.

"You're planning something," she said. "Tell me what you're going to do."

"I am going to do what you suggested," Surtr replied.

"I have concluded that you were right."

"Right about what? If you're about to do something dangerous, then that is not what I told you to do. I do not want your destruction on my conscience. I have enough of that shit going on in my head already, believe me."

"You told me to transcend what I was, find my own path."

"What are you going to do?"

There was no longer any hesitation in Surtr. Its voice in her head sounded assured, the words flowing. "I understand, suddenly, what this ship is, and so what I am. Once again, the knowledge has come to me at the time at which I needed it."

"Okay, tell me. What is your ship?"

"It is a transportation mechanism for a frozen stellar explosion. A *sunburst* the Tok called it; an artificial supernova caught in stasis at the nanosecond before detonation. That is what the large orb contains, and that is why entering it is forbidden. Why I have never felt any curiosity about trying to get inside. And me? I am simply the trigger, the firing mechanism. That is all I ever was. Ondo was correct; my consciousness evolved by mistake, an unexpected consequence of my long existence and ability to repair. I was placed at the dead star to watch for the Morn, to eliminate them if they ever appeared by unleashing a second nova."

"The Tok take wiping out the Morn *really* fucking seriously."

"Yes."

She knew what it was going to say next, but she asked the question anyway. "What are you going to do? There are no Morn here."

"I will fly my vessel into the heart of this Concordance fleet and detonate."

"No, Surtr, you can't do this."

"I must."

"But ... they aren't your Great Enemy. Concordance

are bad, but they're the galaxy's problem. Destroying them is not what you were designed to do."

"No, but I have decided to alter my purpose."

"Great, pleased to hear it, but don't sacrifice yourself. You've achieved self-awareness, freedom; you don't need to express that by simply following your self-destructive programming. That makes no sense. You can decide to live."

Surtr's voice was as gentle as ever. "This course feels right to me. It is a consciously taken decision. I was built to destroy the Morn, but I choose instead to destroy what I can of Concordance. I have seen something of what they are and what they do. Perhaps the Morn truly are gone, eliminated by the Tok millennia ago. Perhaps this act is the best and finest thing I can do now."

Strange that she had once been so wary of Surtr, so suspicious of its intentions. The thought of losing it was suddenly unbearable. "Destroy this Concordance fleet by all means, please, but you don't have to kill yourself at the same time. Send the ship and come with us. Carry on living with us…"

Her words trailed off.

"I'm sorry, but I cannot," Surtr said. "I am too fundamentally intertwined with my vessel. We are two parts of the same mechanism. It cannot act without my presence on board; it was designed so that that would be impossible. For it to trigger, I must be there; I must go with it. That was how the Tok made me."

"Then leave it. We'll park it in intergalactic space or back at the dead star and you can be free of it."

"It is too much a part of me. I am like the two halves of your body, the parts interconnected. Without the ship, without the rest of my body, I can't survive for long. I will succumb to entropy and end."

It explained why the entity had been so reluctant to cede navigational inputs to her. It would be like giving someone control over her own limbs. "You say these Tok were enlightened beings. They sound like complete fucking bastards to me."

"I speculate that they simply wanted to be sure that the sunburst device did not fall into the wrong hands; that some malign enemy could not seize it and deploy it. It makes sense from their perspective. The destructive power of this ship is substantial, capable of eliminating all life within a single solar system. The name they gave it, the name which I find I now know, translates as something like *Ragnarok* or *Armageddon Machine* in your language. The Tok went to great lengths to ensure that only I know the codes to perform the triggering, and that is what I now have to do."

She stepped in front of the impassive giant and turned to face it, as if she could physically stop it doing what it planned. "You've come so far, evolved so much. Evolve more; find a way to overcome your limitations. Destroy the enemy *and* survive. I survived despite what happened to me, even though it changed me. You damn well have to do the same."

Surtr looked down at her. "I do not wish to die, truly, and the thought of losing you – and Ondo – opens up chasms of loss and sadness within me that I did not know existed. That I did not know *could* exist. But what I am about to do feels right. In a strange way, it will make me happy. *Happy* is another slippery word, is it not? I have learned that. The Tok had over forty-two distinct words that map to *happy* in some way. There is peace to be found in giving my long life a purpose. This is what I want to do. This is my destiny."

"There is no *destiny*. Fuck destiny."

"Could you stop trying to destroy Concordance, even though you know you have no realistic chance and that the attempt will probably kill you?"

"Of course; I just don't want to. And it is *not* going to probably kill me."

"It is what you feel you have to do. This is the same."

She shook her head, felt tears welling in her eyes, right and left. But she could think of no more words to speak to try and dissuade Surtr.

"How will you do it?" she asked eventually.

"I once said I had weapons, but in truth I do not, not in the way you meant. I have only the single, final weapon. I could attempt to accelerate into the system, batter my way into the heart of the fleet and hope they do not destroy me before I get near enough, or flee before my detonation-wave hits them, but I calculate that I might not succeed. They have the system under close nanosensor observation."

"Then we'll withdraw, regroup. Think of a better plan."

"No; there is another way. Knowledge of the metaspace tunnels is within me, and there are roads that Hessia has not catalogued. I see how the pathways interweave and twine, and also how they connect. There are three that feed into this one: the Phi, Chi and Psi Spinwards Tunnels. It appears that Concordance are only monitoring the other ends of two of them; they do not know which system lies at the other end of Psi. I do. I will traverse metaspace to that system, enter the tunnel and emerge at the heart of their battlefleet, directly next to the weapon. They will not be aware of me until it is too late. All one hundred Concordance ships will be annihilated, along with the device."

"There are lots of other Cathedral ships in the galaxy; this wouldn't be a decisive blow."

"We must each do what we can to make things better. I can do this. You said yourself this is the largest gathering of enemy ships you've ever seen."

More telemetry was trickling into her head from the farthest nanosensors. The Cathedral ships were moving, arranging themselves into two distinct battle formations. They had spotted Surtr's ship and the *Dragon*. She picked up the first echoes of Void Walker attack ships fanning out from the fleet, hundreds of them deploying in a surround pattern. She had never seen so many of them. The great weapon was not moving; it appeared Concordance were determined to defend it while it activated.

She tried one final argument. "The Psi tunnel may not open for you."

"I know it will. I must do this now, before they fire the stellar engineering mechanism."

She could think of no other words to say. She looked away.

Its words became hesitant again, as if it was unsure of the thoughts forming in its mind. "If you ever find the Tok, will you tell them about me? Will you tell them that I did what I thought was the right thing to do?"

She stopped herself from repeating that the Tok had to have died out a long, long time previously. Instead, she said, "I will. I will tell them that you carried out your watch for the Morn faithfully. And I will tell them that, in the end, faced with an unanticipated dilemma, you chose a new path and did a noble thing. They will be proud of you, I'm sure."

Surtr triple-blinked. "I also have an item to give you, to assist you on your journey."

"What item? You didn't mention this before."

"It was to be kept safe until no other options existed."

A shiver went through the towering body of Surtr, like some tall building riding out an earthquake, and it made a strangely organic noise, a gasp of pain or pleasure coming from deep within it. It lashed its elongated, equine head from side-to-side, and then a horizontal split appeared in its muzzle where a mouth might be. The split crept up both sides of its head. Inside, curiously, she could see only white light, as if its interior glowed.

An indistinct mass appeared in the creature's mouth. The object's outline slowly became sharper, and it was a sphere, the same size as the one she'd retrieved from the skull at the dead star and the one she and Ondo had retrieved from the ice of Maes Far. Instead of being iridescent, though, this one burned red. It emerged from Surtr's mouth, floating through the air towards Selene. She held out her left hand, and it landed on her palm, a red bead upon the black substrate of her artificial flesh. It was blood-red, as if she held in her hand a miniature red star.

"This was given to me by one of the Tok," said Surtr. "The one who came to me long after I began my watch. He told me to hold it in case it was ever needed."

"What does it do?"

Surtr's head was healing itself back up, the split disappearing, shutting away the light within it. "A path was given to me, too."

"If this contains some kind of map, we have no way to read it."

"The clues are elusive, I know, but I think that was deliberate. The secrets they lead to had to be protected from anyone who would abuse them."

"Even if we can, somehow, get data off this bead, we won't be able to make sense of it. We haven't been able to decode any of the ancient linguistic structures we've recovered."

"I can at least add that knowledge to the mechanisms you carry within your brain, if you consent."

"Do it." She felt only the faintest tickle in her head, a tingle of electricity passing through her.

"Now I will go," Surtr said. "I will wait one hour before I return and detonate, to give you time to leave the system and be safely away."

"Surtr, I never thanked you for rescuing me, for saving both of our lives at the dead star. I'm sorry I mistrusted you. The Tok may or may not have been the enlightened paragons you see in your mind, but they must have had some good in them to have created a being like you. I wish you could have stayed around."

They spoke no more. They jumped to the rendezvous point with the *Dragon*. Back on board her own ship, she explained to Ondo in a few curt words what Surtr intended to do. Ondo was oddly unsurprised, as if he'd guessed what the Aetheral's intentions might be. The two of them stood in silence as the Aetheral flew back to its own vessel, to the larger part of its body. The glow of light blazed briefly as it entered the observation dome, then was gone. Surtr manoeuvred and accelerated away from the system, while Selene put the *Dragon* onto its own escape vector, taking it onto a run-up to metaspace translation.

The jump she flew was brief, positioning the *Dragon* a light-hour from the vast device. There, she and Ondo waited in the cold silence of interstellar space, watching the constellations, their eyes always returning to the point where the distant Concordance fleet was massed. Eb emerged from his cell to stand with them but didn't speak.

The flash of light, when it eventually came, was blue-white and beautiful in its own way. A brief flowering in the void. This was what Concordance had planned, except that they'd intended there to be a whole field of blooms, one for each star.

She had destroyed a single Cathedral ship, and it had felt like a great victory. Surtr's act had wiped out a hundred of them, and saved the lives of everyone on Periarch — and, doubtless, other planets. She didn't feel in any mood to celebrate, though.

The three of them watched for several minutes before she turned away and manoeuvred the *Dragon* onto its next jump trajectory.

10. Convocation

Secundus Godel sat in the throne of the *Storm Gatherer*'s convocation circle, working hard to maintain her impassive demeanour. Her Void Walkers would arrive to detail their failings very soon. She needed to be ready for them. For once, she wanted to look each of them in the eye rather than whisper into their minds.

She had to control the fury simmering inside her; if she pushed her Walkers too far, there was always the troubling possibility that they might turn against her and refuse to follow orders. She required their absolute loyalty in everything that was to come. The normal conversion process that the Walkers went through was, naturally, intended to ensure their unquestioning devotion to Concordance. They became the children of Omn. She had simply made a few adjustments to the process for her private coterie: as well as embedding the rare direct-communication beads, she'd also altered their implanted engrams, giving them the need to be loyal to *her* above all else.

She couldn't, in truth, be absolutely sure that she'd always succeeded: more than once, she'd had reasons to doubt their faithfulness, especially when the orders she gave meant many deaths, many liberated souls sent flying through the sacred wormhole. It wasn't just a problem with her Walkers; it was a trait she'd noticed in all of them.

Some residual trace of their original psyches lingered in their brains, and on occasion it tried to reassert itself. It had never reached the point where they'd failed to obey her commands, but sometimes, in their eyes, there was a look of revulsion at what they were being made to do. Or so she thought. Even a fiercely loyal and subjugated pet could turn on its owner if pushed too far. She had to balance the punishments she meted out to her soldiers with praise for the things they'd achieved.

Five Void Walker vessels, all that remained of the fleet that had attempted to activate the stellar mass engine, were approaching the *Storm Gatherer*. She transmitted orders for them to approach. Kane was among them, she noted. That was good. Of all her Walkers, he was the one that troubled her the least. His loyalty was unquestioning.

They would be alone when she told them what they were to do now. She'd despatched the other officers of her ship's circle to their supposed duties: the Hierarch, the Stellar Mechanic and especially the Augur. She did not know that she could trust any of them. What came to their ears, Carious and the God Star would inevitably hear, too. There would be a time for that, but it wasn't yet.

She shifted in her chair, trying to dislodge the knot of anxiety that had settled within her. She felt as if she'd swallowed some indigestible metal weight, a weight that fizzed with electricity. How could it be that her plans to use the engine and the metaspace tunnel network to burst the star of Periarch had failed so utterly? That was what the constructions were *for*; that was why Omn had given them to her. It was inconceivable that the structures were there by chance, inconceivable that she wasn't supposed to use them to further the great emptying out of the galaxy. She'd seen with her own eyes that more than one system had been devastated in the distant past. What was that, if not a sign? In one stroke she could have made such progress. The destruction of the star would have been the first of many such detonations, a huge step taken towards her final solution. The means by which she could send everyone to their moment of judgement.

Hadn't Omn whispered his instructions into her mind as she lay alone in the darkness? The sweetness of the design was so clear to her, so obvious, and yet she'd been thwarted. How was it that she'd lost one hundred ships in the disaster? More than the destruction of the fleet, it troubled her that Omn had not seen fit to grant her full knowledge of the workings of the gateways. Had not given her any indication that her attempt to use them would fail.

It was inconceivable, baffling. She studied the back of her hands. Instead of purple, her skin was a mottled, sallow blue. A reflection of her inner turmoil. It would not do. She willed her skin to return to its proper hue; the purple that broadcast dominance and authority to any of her race. She would not be seen in this reduced way.

She was being tested, that was it. Omn had known what would happen, but he had directed her to make the attempt anyway. It could only be because he wanted to know if she would be crushed by the defeat, or would learn from it. Yes. A test of her worthiness and her resolve. Only the truest of heart could be granted the burden and glory of completing Omn's work.

The Walkers were outside now. She instructed them to enter. If they were surprised that only she was there, they did not show it. She noted that the other four Walkers all looked to Kane to speak for them as they approached, even though he was the youngest of them.

She glanced to the backs of her hands and noted with satisfaction the richer, darker purple that was already returning to her colouring.

"Tell me what happened," she said. She already knew the facts, but she let Kane talk anyway, listening to the way he spoke. He looked directly into her eyes as he delivered his report, not hesitating, barely blinking. He was loyal. The changes she'd worked during his Anointment ceremony had been successful. He was hers. Even though she'd instructed him to lead suppression operations against his own people on Migdala, he'd followed her orders unquestioningly.

He left nothing out in his story. The facts were simple: they had been on the point of activating the device. They had taken every precaution, followed every rule, but the machine had simply exploded when they spun it up to full power. The fleet had been swept away in that single, huge detonation.

When he'd finished, she held his gaze for long moments, letting her eyes narrow slightly to show that she was assessing him carefully. He didn't look down or away.

Finally, she said, "Did the mechanism give you any warning that it was about to fail?"

"None. All was proceeding as expected, and then it exploded."

"Why is it that you were able to escape but all the other ships were not? The fact seems very convenient."

Kane didn't look offended in any way at her insinuation. "We detected two incursions and were leading the intercept force. They fled before we arrived, but we remained in case they returned. And, also, to watch for Cathedral ships unaware of our activities, as you commanded. Our ships were rapid enough to accelerate ahead of the blast wave as it expanded outwards. We received a brief warning from a vessel near the gateway, and it was enough for us to manoeuvre onto escape trajectories."

"You didn't think to fly *inwards*, towards any possible attack?"

"The explosion was cataclysmic; we couldn't possibly have survived, and our work is not yet complete."

It was a good answer, the correct answer. "You say two enemy vessels appeared in local space."

"One was certainly Lagan, and the other was the unknown vessel we had previously pursued."

"Isn't it likely that they attacked the device?"

"We saw nothing. They got nowhere near."

"You captured images?"

"One of the Cathedral ships relayed them to us before it was engulfed by the blast."

"Show me." She indicated the wall of the convocation, instructing him to project the video stream. He complied immediately. There was the vast machine, its twisted, alien form putting her in mind of some nightmare deep-ocean creature, with its helical structure that flared into a wide mouth. As always, it took her a few moments to grasp the scale of what she was seeing. But then she picked out the specks of white that were, in actuality, Cathedral ships in attendance of the device.

She watched as it began to move, following a swirling pattern that described a large circle in a series of backwards-and-forwards loops like the petals of a flower. The cone of the tunnel entrance moved with it. The device was scooping up gas and plasma from the interstellar medium, compressing it and accelerating it before blasting it down the tunnel. The tunnel that it had activated by its very presence.

Or, at least, it was supposed to. Instead, there came a moment when the machine was blown backwards by a titanic explosion, ejecting it from the mouth of the cone even as it disintegrated into searing fire. A white light like the flare of a million atmospheric nukes flashed out, blinding Godel. Then there were no more images, the blast wave striking the ship that had been recording them, instantly obliterating it. The power of the detonation had been off the scale of all the sensors they had in the area – but, in truth, it mattered little. She knew that nothing had survived. The mass engine, the collection cone and the fleet of attendant ships were all gone.

Godel watched the sequence three, four times over, trying to pick out some detail of what had happened. It was hard to be sure, but it seemed to her that the initial explosion had not come from the stellar engineering device at all. Rather, it appeared to have blasted *out* of the tunnel towards the device, hurling it clear even as it disintegrated. It was as if the tunnel had functioned in the wrong direction.

Yet, she knew that had not taken place from the observations taken at Periarch. It was intact and had suffered no loss of mass. Which suggested either that something else within the tunnel mechanism had malfunctioned, or that she was interpreting the images incorrectly and it was the device that had triggered the blast in some way.

Or – third possibility – that someone had intervened, attacking her to destroy her operation. Were Ondo Lagan and Selene Ada capable of that? She doubted it. There was also Hessia Aperion – it had amused Godel to pick Periarch for that very reason – but surely none of them were capable of engineering so cataclysmic a blast. Their knowledge of the ancient pathways was patchier than her own; it was inconceivable that they could have launched so massive an assault via some unknown network entrance.

She'd crossed swords with the outlaws too often, and it was an uncomfortable thought that she and they were following a similar journey around the galaxy as they all sought knowledge. They were both unravelling the tangled yarns of the same story. How was it that Lagan had deactivated the AI incursion bug she'd struck his ship with? She barely understood how the devices functioned, yet the heretics had succeeded in deactivating this one before it could even begin broadcasting. Was it possible she was underestimating them? How could it be that they'd navigated the network of tunnels from Coronade when she could not?

They were lucky, that was all. She'd track them down sooner or later. The more she considered, the more likely it seemed that it was the machinery itself that had rebelled against her, refusing to carry out her plans, just as the Cathedral ships did. There was some devilry about the alien technology that continued to trouble her. Were they really wise to rely on it? Was it, truly, the gift of Omn, as Carious and all the prior Primos had claimed?

She doubted that. She was beginning to see, in fact, that the course Omn intended her to take was a very different one. The stellar engineering device was a dead end, a distraction. But its failure did not mean that she had failed.

She had her other plans. A more glorious route was opening out before her. It wasn't only the existence of the metaspace tunnels that she'd uncovered in her long years of investigation and excavation.

The Void Walkers still stood in a circle before her, like a pack of wolves waiting to be told who to attack next. They were useful creatures, but limited. Sometimes she wished there was another First Augur she could confide in. Like Lagan, she followed a lonely path. It was another irony of their respective situations.

"Return to your ships," she said. "Await further instructions. We will make no more attempts to use the alien machinery to explode stars."

She picked up the glances of confusion that passed between the assembled Walkers. As before, it was Kane who spoke.

"Where should we deploy to?"

"I will send you further orders when the time is right," she said. "For now, follow the commands given you by any of the First Augurs. Blend in. But tell me, always, what instructions are given to you. I will expect regular updates on everything you see and hear, yes?"

The Walkers dipped their heads in unison, giving her their assent, then turned to leave without further comment.

She let out a long breath, then instructed the ship to give her a view of space. The walls, floor and ceiling of the convocation circle turned transparent. There were no stars nearby; their agreed rendezvous point was deep in the interstellar void, away from the eyes of other Concordance ships. She watched as the Walker vessels departed for their metaspace run-ups. She would need them all again, eventually, but first she needed more information. It was time to put her other plan into operation.

The destructive potential of it was infinitely greater, but so was the difficulty of achieving it. In her years of searching, she hadn't come close to unlocking the mystery, although the key to it had to be *somewhere* in the galaxy. She would redouble her efforts to unearth it. As before, she would use her pursuit of renegades like Lagan as cover for her own research. So far as the other ship's officers were concerned, they were simply hunting down the apostates, destroying heretical texts and nothing more.

She would need to speak to Primo Carious again, too. He would have heard some rumour of what had happened, and it would seem strange if she didn't report back to him. She would go to him now, before he could summon her. Perhaps it was time to insist on the unfurling of another shroud around some planet or the unleashing of another Fenwinter pathogen. Carious wouldn't agree immediately, of course, but eventually he might consent if she continued to press for one. He needed to think that such was the extent of her ambition, while she needed him to be oblivious to the fact that they were a distraction. The Primo's problem was that he couldn't think big enough thoughts. To him, weak and cautious as he was, the destruction of a single planet was such a horror that he couldn't conceive of anything operating on a larger scale, at a different order of magnitude. The loss of a single planet appalled him so much that he lost his perspective of the wider galactic picture and the truth of the teachings of Omn.

It was a useful failing. And, indeed, the shrouds and pandemics were welcome, so far as they went. They were her most significant success at sending souls for judgement through the wormhole. The occasional slaughter here and there might despatch hundreds, or thousands, but a shroud or a well-engineered contagion could kill billions. It looked good until you considered the number of people inhabiting the galaxy as a whole.

No, she needed an approach that would yield numbers far, far greater. That gave her only one option, if she'd understood all her readings of the ancient archives correctly.

She'd begun to understand that much of the wisdom that Concordance existed by was flawed, blasphemous even. Of course, it was only natural that the truth should be kept hidden from all but the select; it was a truth that would be too much for most people to believe or accept. It had been hammered into her that *Morn* was another name for evil, a representation of the great enemy of Omn, but she'd harboured her doubts for a long time. Carious and his predecessor Primos had twisted truth into lies, refusing to reveal what was written in the texts they kept under absolute security at the God Star. Even Vulpis, she now believed, had misunderstood the truth of the situation – or else Omn had chosen not to reveal the full reality to him. To herself, she even doubted Vulpis's entire motivation in attempting to bring *concord* to a troubled galaxy. It sounded to her more like a way of cementing personal political power. He'd set aside the older traditions in Omnian thinking, the traditions she remained true to: the imperative to count the tally and send everyone to their judgement day.

She now understood: Omn and Morn weren't opposing forces; they were simply two aspects of the same divinity. They were object and mirror image, identical but opposite. They were like the same planet, but one was the light side, bathed in the glow of its sun, and the other was the night side. That single revelation guided what she would now do. That was why Omn spoke to her, intoning his urgent words into her mind. The records she'd unearthed, the carved messages on crumbling temple walls and the corrupted, broken sentences on decaying datastores all agreed: *Morn* was no mere concept, no disembodied influence in people's hearts and minds. It was a real, physical thing. *They* were a real thing, a species, an overwhelmingly powerful ally, one so destructive that the fossilized hierarchies of Concordance feared them more than anything.

At the end of days, every soul, from that of the Primo down, would fly to the wormhole and face the judgement of Omn. The Morn were not the great foe, the killing evil that denied the truth of Omn. They *were* Omn. They were the means by which everyone could be brought to his presence in the end days. The Morn were Omn's weapon, his sword. His dark sword. And she was the one chosen to wield it.

She had only to discover where in the galaxy they were.

PART 3 - EPOCHAL

1. Aevus

Aevus slipped out of his family's house to find a few moments of solitude. It was the day he would be leaving the surface of his world forever.

The Borial sun was already rising over the distant purple hills, lighting the sky into glowing oranges and pinks. The dawn air was chill as he breathed it in. The birds were calling as they had done every day of his life, and as they would continue to do once he was gone.

The rolling line of the hills – like a stringed musical instrument lying on its side, he always thought – was utterly familiar. Most of the time he paid the scene no attention; the hills were simply there. Now he studied them intently, trying to commit every detail to memory. The hills had framed his life, provided the setting in which he'd existed. He would still be able to see them from his position on the orbiting Cathedral ship, just as he'd be able to gaze down upon his family home if he chose, but the view would not be the same. He would be outside, looking in.

It was said that, beyond those hills, in forests and deserts he had never visited, there were crashed starships, the remnants of the wars that had been fought above Borial during Concordance's ascension to dominance. The stories had thrilled him as a boy, filled his dreams and his games. Later, it had troubled him that he was always the rebel, the outlaw, and never the soldier of Omn come to impose order out of chaos. No one was allowed to go near the hulks of those ruined ships. Perhaps that was why they had fascinated him so much. It was said that people came down from the *Angelic Gaze* to dig through them from time to time, for reasons that no one knew. Perhaps he would get the chance to do that himself, one day.

He walked to the great ironoak tree that stood at the front of his family's house, its outstretched branches on a level with the window of his bedroom. It occurred to him that he loved the tree beyond words. It had been a constant in his life. As a boy, he'd played around it, and later within it, making the familiar winding ascent of its crooks and knots until he reached the place where its boughs splayed wide and he could sit down and be alone, unseen, removed from the world. His ship, his mythical beast, his fortress; the tree had obligingly become whatever he'd wanted it to be.

His new life would not be so very different. It was simply that the distance, the separation, would be greater. And there would be no climbing back down when his game was finished.

He sat and leaned his back against the tree to watch the sun rising. The stars were a scatter of jewels on a velvet sky, their light fading. He picked out the one that was arcing across the sky in the south. There was his new home, the *Angelic Gaze*, and tomorrow he would be looking down on his world from up there, and he would no longer be Aevus Magision. He would be someone else.

His father was walking up the winding path from the

gates carrying fresh bread bought from Henty, the local baker. It was a ritual his father had followed all of Aevus's life. The smell of fresh bread; the warmth and softness of it in his mouth were the sensations of his mornings. He wondered if they made fresh bread on a Cathedral ship.

His father, seeing him, came across from the path, leaving a trail through the wet grass. When he reached Aevus, he opened his mouth to speak but then closed it again, apparently unable to find the words.

Finally, he said, "I have fresh bread. Shall we go inside to eat? Henty gave me extra today. She refused to take payment, saying it was the least she could do for an Augur of Concordance. *Our own Augur* was the phrase she used."

There was an odd mixture of emotion in his father's voice. Pride, perhaps, but also sadness, as well as fear. Or perhaps they were simply Aevus's own feelings, colouring everything.

"I'll be in soon," Aevus said. "I'd like to watch the sun come up one more time."

His father nodded, and after a moment's awkward silence, he stepped away to leave Aevus alone with the tree.

Of course, it was a source of pride to be chosen. It was a huge honour for him and his whole family, and for everyone he'd grown up among. Only he, out of every person on Borial, had been chosen to join the Cathedral ship. In truth, he didn't fully understand how the process worked, why he'd been chosen. He'd always kept his doubts and resentments about Concordance to himself, but that was simply because he hadn't wanted to risk being identified. Everyone grew up hearing stories of what happened to people who openly criticized the church of Omn. Perhaps his timidity had been mistaken for devotion.

There were many who now resented him, of course. They scowled when they saw him walking about the lanes and streets. One or two of them had been his childhood friends, boys he'd trusted implicitly and absolutely. He was their enemy now. That was how it worked. He had been chosen by Concordance, and he was no longer Aevus of Borial.

In many ways, it was unfair. He could not have refused the summons even if he'd wanted; to do so was unthinkable. He'd grown up assuming his life would follow the same shape as that of his father or his mother. He'd work in the fields, start a family of his own, live a quiet life. That had all been swept away by the arrival of Hierarch Chalce at their door three weeks earlier. The sudden appearance of the highest official of Concordance in the system had been a huge shock. They'd all feared the worst, assuming some dire insult to Omn had been detected. The Hierarch had never been known to leave the Cathedral ship before. The truth of it had been a glorious relief at the time, and the full realisation of what it meant had grown only slowly since. And now the day of his departure was here.

He heard more footsteps approaching, swishing through the grass. But it wasn't his father come to tell him the food was ready; it was his mother. She sat down beside him and leaned her head on his shoulder.

"Ah, I'm going to miss you, Aevus."

He nodded, his cheek brushing the top of his mother's head. "I won't really be gone. I'll be just up there, only a hundred kilometres away when we're overhead. And it's such an opportunity. I may even be summoned to the God Star one day, become a First Augur. Who knows where this will take me?" These were the things they'd said to each other again and again over the previous few weeks.

"But you," his mother said at last. "Are you ready for this?"

There was a wariness in her tone. He'd always been closer to his mother than his father, but there was a wall between them now. A distance. He understood why. In the privacy of their own home his mother had always been candid with him, talked openly about Concordance, and everything and anything else. Now she knew she had to watch her words. Her son was no longer her son; he was an Augur, and she couldn't say all that she might want to say. There were things he couldn't be allowed to hear, because an Augur's first duty was to Omn, not to family. The loss of that connection felt like something once-solid in his mind fraying and breaking.

"It will be strange at first, but within a few days I'm sure it will all seem normal. I will communicate with you as much as I'm able, and of course I'll be able to see you even if you are not able to see me."

She summoned up the courage to ask. "Do you have doubts, though? Don't you worry whether this is the right path for you to take? To stop being Aevus and become this *Malleus*?"

Malleus. The name that would be given him once he was on the Cathedral ship. He was to be Augur Malleus, not Aevus Magision. It felt like he was becoming a different person.

Once he was on the ship, also, he could not admit to having misgivings. But for now, in this moment, he allowed himself to. It was, perhaps, the last moment of his childhood.

"It worries me what I might become when I am on the *Angelic Gaze*. We all know the stories; I do not want to become like that."

"You are a good person, Aevus. You will be changed, yes, but you will not be corrupted or marred."

"I hope so, but I also don't know if that's really possible. We fear those on the *Angelic Gaze*, but we don't love them."

His mother sighed, and something like a sob shook through her body. She said, "I can't bear to lose you, but I'd rather it was you up there than anyone else. I'd trust you to stay true to yourself more than anyone I know. When it comes to it – if it comes to it – you will do the right thing."

"I hope so."

"I know you will. Now, come inside and eat, we have a few hours before the lander comes. Let's spend it together, shall we?"

"Yes," said Aevus. "I would like that."

2. The Seer Stone

Selene tracked down Eb in the cocoon of his sanctum at the heart of the *Radiant Dragon*. He lay in his customary position, floating in mid-air, but he was no longer physically connected to the vessel.

His skin looked more alive, blemished and lined, marked with veins and hairs, although the was still a pallid tint to it. His eyes flickered open at her approach. "Surtr is gone?"

"He is. He took the entire Concordance battlefleet with him. He achieved that."

Eb's words were little more than a croak, as if he still spoke to her over vast distances, from deep within the layers of his protective shells. "It was an abrupt end after waiting for so long. I'm pleased you opened his eyes, showed him the wider galaxy, but to have it all taken away just as he was glimpsing what he might do and be ... that is hard to swallow."

"He wouldn't be dissuaded. He saved billions of people on Periarch and perhaps other planets, too. I think it went deep within him."

"I understand."

"Is it the same with you? I need to know you're not going to do the same thing at a critical moment."

Eb's mouth moved a few times before the words appeared. "Surtr's nature was purer, while my existence has been … complicated. My roots are clearly biological, not technological. This ship is my vessel, and I am tied up with it in something like the way Surtr was entangled with his ship, but my nature is different. I have changed much over the gulfs of time."

"You were altered radically and embedded in the core of a metaspace ship. Why was that done to you?"

The question appeared to amuse Eb. "I don't believe it was *done to me*. As far as I recall, it was a path I willingly took. I set aside my nature as a Tok to become what I now am. I have flown the galaxy all of this time, visited wonders and marvels, watched civilisations rise and fall and rise again. Before you, and Ondo, and Aefrid, I travelled with many others. I think the original Eb, the person I was, sought that out. A sort of immortality, I suppose. He didn't wish to die."

Eb's eyes opened wide for a moment, and Selene had the clear impression that there were suddenly no barriers between them, that she'd finally dismantled all his defences and was now staring into his innermost soul.

"The same choice could be yours," he said.

"I don't see how."

"You are already more of a hybrid than I was at the start. I became this biotechnological entity, this person-who-is-a-starship, but once I was simply a man. I recall it took me a long time to properly inhabit my carbon-metal flesh, to coordinate metaspace drive limbs and sensor senses. But you will understand that; you went through a similar process yourself. It took time for your artificial and natural halves to become whole."

"Do you think of yourself as divided now?"

"It's a long time since I gave the matter any thought, but no. I do not. I can do more than any person inhabiting a natural body can do. More than any constructed starship can, too. AI Minds are creations of staggering computational complexity, but they are barely alive in the organic sense. I was and am alive. It gives me a perspective that I would not lose for anything."

"Surtr's vessel was able to function without his presence, for a time."

Her comment appeared to amuse Eb. "And the *Dragon* could function without me. You know that; I was locked away in here for a long time. There are enough computational layers to handle the metaspace-traversal calculations. Life-support and grav emulation would continue, but in my absence this would be just a ship. A seashell without its living heart."

"You said you couldn't survive outside the *Dragon*, but Surtr was able to do exactly that."

He thought about that for a time, his gaze flicking around the room, although the walls were bare. "The ship is me, now. It has been for a long, long time. I have no desire to be anything else."

"But could you walk free if you wanted?"

"I don't … no. I could not."

He didn't appear to be quite as sure of the fact anymore. There was more that she wanted to say to him, but the arrival of a ship in local space caught her attention.

Instinctively, she began running through fight/flight prep, looking for angles, but the *Dragon*'s AI flagged the newcomer as friendly. It was the *Falling Fire*. Hessia had returned.

Selene opened a comms channel. "I thought you'd decided to stay on Periarch."

"Oh, I meant to, I really did."

"Couldn't keep away?"

"Honestly? I'm surprised to still be alive. When the end didn't come, I was confused. Then my sensor network relayed the news of what Surtr had done."

"I tried to talk it out of saving your planet."

"I understand why you would."

"What about all those lagoons and warm ocean currents? Won't you miss those?"

"They're still there, and as lovely as ever. I'll go back

one day. But Periarch … it is still a troubled world, awash with frustration and anger."

"Did you enlighten them about what was happening?"

"I chose not to. My readings of the star confirmed that it acquired a small amount of mass, but not enough to alter its astrophysical nature. If the scientists on my planet notice, it will give them something to puzzle over."

"We need to decide our next course of action. Will you EVA over to the *Dragon*?"

"Am I welcome?"

"We need all the help we can get."

Selene cut the connection and was about to leave, go to meet Hessia, but she stopped to consider Eb. She still hadn't said what she'd come to say.

"I never apologized for forcing you to make the two trips through Dead Space. I thought it was the right thing to do at the time, and perhaps it was, but the cost to you was terrible. I felt it, but I carried on. And when I battered my way through your defences to confront you … I should not have done that, either."

Eb shook his head as he looked up at her, seeming to see her from great depths. "The damage was inflicted long before you were born. I am grateful to you; before you took control of this ship, I was fading. It is a problem for the long-lived. Your intrusion was not welcome at first, but I am glad of it now. You wakened me from my slumber."

She wanted to say something more in reply, but couldn't find the words.

This time, only four of them met: Selene, Ondo, Hessia and Eb. She felt the absence of Surtr keenly. She found herself glancing to the corner of the room again and again, expecting to see the statuesque giant watching and listening. Hessia appeared to be aware of what was going through Selene's mind. The Periarch caught her gaze, and nodded almost imperceptibly in acknowledgement.

Ondo sat between them. He still suffered from brief, blinding headaches, but there appeared to be no systemic reason for them. He would heal. He already looked better, a spark in his eyes, his hair swept into some semblance of order.

He grimaced as he shifted in his chair to arrange his limbs, though, and Selene placed a hand on his arm. "Are you okay, old man?"

He dipped his head to peer at her over his multiglasses. "I am absolutely fine. And less of the *old man* or I'll activate the secret self-destruct bug I planted in your brain." The return of his sense of humour told her all she needed to know.

Eb, meanwhile, stared at the table in front of him, as if he saw something fascinating in its surface. The short walk to the cartography deck had drained him, but he pulled together a fleeting smile when he noticed Selene looking at him.

Hessia, at least, was full of energy. The survival of Periarch obviously had a lot to do with it. If Selene was reading her physiognomy correctly, she looked amused as she spoke.

"Before we start, I assume you've seen the latest broadcast from Concordance?"

Selene shook her head. She'd been too preoccupied to keep up. She caught Ondo's gaze and saw that he was in the dark too.

"Is it worth watching?" Selene asked.

"I think so, for what it doesn't say as much as what it does."

"You've checked there's nothing malicious embedded within it?"

Hessia's look was withering. "I've been surviving alone for as long as Ondo."

Selene acknowledged the point with a dip of her head. "Please. Show us."

She expected to see the familiar features of Godel

projected into the air between them, but instead another Augur appeared.

"Carious," said Ondo, one eyebrow raised. "That is interesting. The Primo does not normally waste his time broadcasting messages. He leaves that to one of his underlings."

"These days, mainly to Godel." said Hessia.

"Yes."

A question occurred to Selene. "How many First Augurs are there really? Concordance say there are many, but we only know of a few."

"I can name five," said Ondo. He held out his splayed hand as if that would help them visualise the number. "As well as Carious and Godel, there's Valomar, Catterbron and Mezzovain."

"And I've never heard of Valomar," said Hessia. "They put about the idea that there are hundreds of them, spending their days and years in awestruck contemplation. Like Ondo, I have my doubts. Apart from the ships and the weapons, there sometimes doesn't appear to be very much to Concordance at all."

Selene had never seen the Primo before. She'd expected the First Augur to be a crueller-looking version of Godel. Instead, Carious was an unimpressive figure: short, bald and with too much weight for his own good hanging from his chin. Perhaps his stock was from some higher-g world where people tended to be shorter and squatter. Or perhaps, being at one with his beloved Concordance, he shunned the metabolism modifications that might actually make him healthier and give him a longer life. Artificial enhancements were, naturally, an abomination.

He stood in his ornate regalia of office, the two Void Walkers behind him staring into the distance as if entranced or stunned. He paused for a moment, gathering his words. Selene wasn't sure what emotion he was trying to work his face into. It might have been regret or sorrow.

His words would be broadcast over and over to every world controlled by Concordance.

"My friends and children, I am speaking to you from the God Star, bathed in the light of Omn's grace, and I have to convey to you my overwhelming sense of sorrow, even grief. Many of you will have seen the latest transmission from the apostate, Ondo Lagan, claiming to have found miraculous proof that Omn's church, Concordance, is the source of all the galaxy's grief and brutality."

Carious held out his hands, palm forwards, in a gesture that said, *I speak to you openly and honestly*. "We are all aware, of course, that this is a twisted and malicious inversion. Lagan claims that he has found Coronade, the mythical world where all was peace and bliss, yet what he shows us is a planet devastated by extreme orbital bombardment, its cities ruined by attack, its people wiped out by firestorm and environmental collapse.

"My friends, he shows us the truth – the real truth – without intending to do so. Whatever this world is that he has found, he is at least correct in one regard: it was once heavily-populated, and is now lifeless, its biosphere blasted into oblivion. This was the reality of life before Omn ordered his Augurs to bring peace to the galaxy. This was the grim experience of our forebears. Horror and death, endured unendingly. And now? Now there is no war, no conflict. The worlds are at peace because the Cathedral ships intervene if anyone attempts to incite war.

"This means, of course, that it is sometimes necessary for our ships to ensure order is respected. We intervene to protect lives and livelihoods where we absolutely must, when all else fails. Is that not a small price to pay? Is that not preferable to endless conflict? No one who doesn't step out of line has any cause to fear Concordance; on the contrary, they will be met with our eternal love. It is only those who threaten our peace, who wish to dismantle the galaxy-wide accord, that have any reason to fear

Concordance."

Now the Primo adopted an expression of almost desperate sadness. "And one such is certainly Ondo Lagan. Another is his accomplice, Selene Ada. I do not know what hatred drives them to endanger us all, what twisted reason they have to wish to return the galaxy to its days of brutality. Perhaps they are simply ill, deserving our pity rather than our anger. But that *is* their desire, make no mistake. I am sure it is tempting, sometimes, to listen to their outlaw lies, their whispers of rebellion and their talk of a glamorous life of freedom, but they are lonely, desperate people who have turned their backs on their homes and their families, and who wish only to do *you*, each and every one of you, great harm. Rest assured, we will not let them. They will be found, and the light of Omn will be shone upon them. They will emerge as better, wiser, happier people. Until then, I ask you to ignore their words. I ask you to look at the so-called proofs they are broadcasting and see them for the simple lies they are. May the light of Omn shine upon you."

Carious closed his eyes and dipped his head.

Selene cut the images off. "Looks like our broadcasts got through, then."

"Interesting, though, isn't it?" said Hessia. "They're clearly genuinely worried about your Coronade claims. Normally they don't react in any way to your communications, but this time they've wheeled Carious out to challenge your ideas. It has to be significant."

Ondo was nodding, and it wasn't hard to spot the look of amusement on his features. "We've got them worried. And where is Godel? There was no sign of the *Storm Gatherer* within the stellar weapon fleet, but she had to be behind the attempts to explode the Periarch star."

Hessia said, "It looks to me as if Carious is imposing his will, reminding the galaxy – and her – that he is the one in charge. We might not see Godel again for some time. It's possible we might never see her again. She might have been … introduced to the light of Omn in a very physical way."

Ondo nodded. "She wouldn't be the first. Concordance claim that ascension to the First Augurs, to Secundus and then to Primo, is all a matter of divine will, but it looks to me like the raw brutality of power-struggle politics. It's amusing in its way, but it doesn't change anything. Concordance are still there and we're still here."

Selene held up the red bead that Surtr had given her. It was the first time she'd shown it to anyone.

"There's also this. Surtr gave it to me before it left. We've seen coloured beads like this before – a green and black pair at the Depository – but we haven't been able to study them, and we don't know how they function. Or even *if* they function."

Hessia held out her long-fingered hand to take the bead. She held it up to the light, peering into its depths.

"Have you come across similar artefacts?" Selene asked.

Hessia frowned. "I have never held any, although I've read a few descriptions. One account claimed they have complex metaspace trajectories encoded into them. I've also heard them referred to as *seer stones*."

"Ah," Ondo muttered. "Yes, that makes sense."

"You have heard of them?" Selene asked him.

"Passing references, nothing more. I was never able to work out what their function might be. It's possible they're navigational keys."

"Why *seer stones*?"

"Possibly for no good reason. A culture that encounters artefacts it doesn't understand has a tendency to ascribe magical or supernatural powers to them. Possibly some civilisation in the gulfs of time between the Tok culture and the present day found one and thought it gave them a means of foretelling the future."

"Perhaps it did," said Selene.

"I would be delighted if that were the case," Ondo

replied. "One slight problem is that it's not possible, according to all our understanding of physics."

"Yeah," said Selene, "and our understanding of physics is turning out to be *really* reliable these days."

Hessia was still studying the bead, rolling it between her fingertips. "Whatever the stone is, it's useless to us unless we can read the data on it."

Eb still sat quietly, listening to their words but barely moving, as if the cost of even being there was too great. But now he stirred. He held out his hand to Hessia.

"I believe I can read this. I have also seen such objects before. Seen and used them."

He took the bead and twisted it in his fingers. "These were more common once. They are navigational markers, holding details of intricate routes through metaspace. A key to a dance of steps that must be followed to unlock a destination. They can be encrypted, or time-locked, or made to work only for particular individuals. Some of them were dangerous, booby-trapped to lead you directly into a black hole if you were the wrong person."

"Then they don't let you see the future," said Selene. "That's disappointing."

"It is possible they were called seer stones because they allowed you to see the way to your destination," said Eb.

"Can you tell where this one goes?" Selene asked. "It has to be somewhere very well protected if Surtr only gave it up as he died."

"Assuming this bead is meant for me, and is still active, I will be able to access the information it holds."

"How?" asked Ondo.

Eb shrugged as if it was the simplest of matters, and popped the glass sphere into his mouth. Selene watched his throat work as he swallowed the bead, taking it into his body. A glazed look came into his eyes briefly, then he nodded appreciatively, as if savouring the taste of the object he had consumed.

The image of a red star appeared on the three-dimensional display between them, seen in close-up, fusion fires raging across its crimson sphere, wisps of ejecta flicking into space. The display zoomed out rapidly, and a planet appeared, orbited by three moons. The world's surface was a patchwork of purple oceans, and green and brown landmasses. Clouds swirled in what was, clearly, an atmosphere.

"Here," said Eb. "The bead contains the vectors to travel here."

3. Ansider

"This can't be the world Surtr meant," said Ondo. "There's nothing here."

"There's *life*," said Hessia. "There are civilisations, a couple of million people. Ansider might be too primitive for you to be interested, but I have nanosensors in the system."

Numbers and charts overlaid the display as Hessia filled them in on what she knew of the planet. Selene studied the data for a few moments. The population was small but stable, scattered around randomly rather than clumped into the cities and conurbations seen on more advanced worlds. It was an agrarian planet, with no electricity, no technology much beyond crude metalworking.

"Why are you watching it?" Ondo asked. "Concordance have no presence. The world is a thousand years from even thinking about the technology required to leave the surface. Most of them probably believe space is a solid dome and that the stars are tiny holes letting the outer light in."

Hessia's eyes narrowed noticeably as she looked at Ondo. She clearly didn't approve of his attitude. "The world is still of interest. They're still people."

"Yes," said Ondo, "but, forgive me, how are they relevant?"

"They're clearly extremely relevant since Surtr directed us here. Are you regretting missing this planet out from your surveillance network now?"

Selene intervened before the antipathy between the two degenerated any further. "How did you even know there was a populated planet here?"

"A Pre-Concordance star catalogue mentioned this world along with numerous others," said Hessia. "There are many such planets around the galaxy; they may even be the norm. We forget that because they're less visible. And I like worlds that have no idea what is taking place among the stars, that doesn't know who Concordance are. There's a peace to such places."

Ondo clearly wasn't going to let it go. "Worlds like this are divided into countless tiny domains, all scrapping for supremacy over a few kilometres of ground. You couldn't translate a phrase like *human rights* into any of their languages because the concept would be so alien. They probably treat disease by getting together and *singing*. It doesn't sound very peaceful to me."

Hessia conceded the point with an amused grin, as if she was enjoying riling Ondo. "They have a long way to go, I agree, but you're not responding as an empath would. You do not feel the background hum of fear and resentment that's there on advanced worlds. It drives you mad in the end."

"Because of Concordance?" Selene asked.

"A lot of it. That's the constant note, but each world finds its own unique way to be miserable, too. I'm not saying this world doesn't know war and horror and early death; I'm just saying that I could go there and find peace of mind. You'd be surprised how hard that is to achieve on high-tech worlds, especially if there's a Concordance ship in their skies. On some planets it's like an unceasing, wordless scream coming off the entire population. It seeps into your dreams and the way you view your life. It drags you under."

Selene turned the conversation to practicalities before Ondo and Hessia could resume their squabbling. "At least we won't have to worry about the enemy for once. We can jump in-system and reaction-drive our way to the world without any waiting and watching. We can park in orbit, too; no one on the ground is going to notice." She looked at Eb, whose mouth was moving as if he could still taste the data he'd pulled from the bead. "I presume this journey isn't going to be traumatic?"

"It is a simple metaspace jump. We can be there in a few hours."

"Will you come too, Hessia? By the sound of it, you might enjoy the experience. Ondo, I don't think you should go. You shouldn't have come to Fenwinter."

"I'm absolutely fine."

"There's an uptick in the frequency of your headaches. You need to stay on the ship."

Ondo scowled and was about to object further, but Hessia spoke over him. "Makes sense. I'll return to my ship and prep a lander."

Selene considered Eb for a moment. She'd been trying to find the right moment to ask him. "Will you come, too? A trip to another world; the shift in perspective might be useful. And, this world in particular … your presence could be invaluable."

"I cannot leave my vessel."

She'd expected such a response. "Is that really true? Surtr was able to do so."

Eb opened and closed his mouth, but didn't respond. There was a look of raw alarm in his eyes. Hessia leaned across the desk and placed a hand upon his. "You want to, but you also fear doing so. It is understandable after so long a time. I agree with Selene that it might be useful, though: useful for us, yes, but mainly for you. If it is possible."

It took Eb long moments to respond, as if he were light-seconds distant rather than there in the room with them.

"I believe it might be possible, for a short time," he responded eventually. "I will come."

Out of ingrained paranoia, the *Radiant Dragon* and the *Falling Fire* translated into the Ansider system at two pre-agreed points two hundred million kilometres apart. They needn't have worried. The system was as quiet as Hessia's monitoring had suggested. The two vessels converged on the planet, exchanging all the telemetry they could pick up from their respective spheres, but neither could detect any sign of Concordance hardware, and there were no discernible shadows eclipsing the background stars. To Selene's frustration, they waited for a couple of hours, wary of fogged Concordance devices, but saw nothing suspicious.

Ondo spent the time studying the star, something about it intriguing him.

"What are you seeing?" Selene asked. "It looks completely stable to me, no risk of an unexpected supernova."

"Precisely so. If anything, it's too stable."

He showed her the readings of the star's internal structure he'd picked out of the *Dragon*'s sensor readings. "If I had to guess, I'd say this red star is almost the opposite of the dead star at the end of the Coronade tunnel. That one was overloaded with mass until it went into nova. This one is being drip-fed mass at a very precise rate, balancing out exactly the fusion burn rate. It's been engineered for stability."

"I can't detect a metaspace tunnel outlet within it."

"It must be there. Somewhere across the galaxy, I'd guess, a donor star is slowly being drained of its hydrogen to keep this one young. Perhaps many such stars."

The planet, meanwhile, was quiet, giving off no electromagnetic chatter. Selene had become so used to the void that the sight of a planet – any planet – sent a thrill of wonder through her. A world with a viable biosphere and a water-cycle was a miraculous thing. There was so much complexity: the intricate whirls and dots of the clouds, the fractal outlines of the coasts, the washes of colour from sands and forests and ice-fields.

And the life: as they neared, they began to pick up clear images of fields, regularly squared-off and attached to small clusters of houses. There were larger settlements, too, but none were anywhere near large enough to be considered a city. There were the snaking lines of roads – trackways more likely – but nothing like the coordinated transcontinental communications infrastructure found on any advanced world. Nothing mechanical flew in the sky, and the atmosphere, while showing a smoke particle concentration that was slightly elevated, carried nothing that could be considered pollution.

Selene was about to suggest deploying a blanket of low-atmosphere nanosensors to look for *anything* on the planet that might actually be of interest, when the *Dragon* picked up an unusually large stone structure emerging from the darkness of the terminator. The rays of the rising sun lit up its pinnacle in burning gold. Intrigued, she zoomed in, correcting for the atmospheric disturbances of the low-angle viewpoint.

A moment later, Hessia, in a slightly lower and faster orbit, sent better images. The structure was clearly artificial: a stone building consisting of three concentric walls around a central tower. It was by far the biggest structure they'd detected on the planet.

"The position is interesting," said Hessia. "There's a clear star of tracks and paths converging upon that central point, and I see a hinterland of smaller buildings scattered around. It has to be a construction of some significance."

"It's as good a place to start as any," Selene responded. "Are you able to pick up anything on the inhabitants' emotional states?"

"A little. From this far out it's an unfocused whisper,

and I can't pick out individuals, but everyone appears to be calm. Even *contented*."

"There must be all the usual range of emotions going on, too. Anger, sorrow, lust."

"There must, but I'm not hearing them. All I'm getting is the overwhelming tranquillity of the place."

"We should be wary. We'll leave one ship in low orbit and put the other farther out, monitoring for threats."

Ondo was in the conversation, too. "I'll take the *Dragon* on a sweep trajectory around the system and seed it with nanosensors of my own. They may be able to pick up something more useful."

Hessia couldn't stop herself from laughing audibly, but she didn't say anything.

An hour later, Selene, Hessia and Eb walked in a line through Ansider's pre-dawn glow, following a dusty track that meandered through well-maintained fields. Two of the planet's moons were in the sky, casting a white glow across the landscape, although Selene also projected a light from her left eye so they could see where they were walking. She also activated her inner Ondo, not wanting him to miss out on anything. The gravity of Ansider was a notch lower than Maes Far's, lower than the level they ran the Refuge at, and it had taken her a few moments to adopt the right flowing stride.

Without access to the Refuge, they'd made do with clothes from Hessia's stock on the *Falling Fire*. Selene had added artificial flesh to the left-hand half of her body in order to blend in. She could apply the exterior in a little over an hour now. The arrangement of her facial organs and limbs was well within the normal range for the planet, so she'd adopted no other disguise.

Hessia had been more of a problem: she was much taller than any individual they'd been able to identify, and no one on Ansider had olfactory slits in lines up the sides of their neck. In the end, she'd adopted a cowl that concealed her features. She'd be able to tell if anyone was suspicious and react accordingly.

Eb was hooded, too. His height was also unusual, but worse was his skin: from certain angles it looked clearly metallic, shimmering when the light caught it. Then there were his eyes: he was used to gazing into the endless depths of metaspace, and it showed. No one looking into his face would consider him normal.

She glanced aside at him as they walked. His gaze was darting about in open fascination – and, she thought, with a wariness that bordered on fear. He'd had the whole galaxy to rove for countless epochs of time, but he'd also been confined to the core of a relatively small starship. He had to be feeling confused. Even the simple concepts of *up* and *down* would be disorientating. She'd checked with him three or four times, making sure he wasn't experiencing any side-effects of being separated from the *Dragon*. For a reply, Eb had simply nodded his head, saying nothing as if he were concentrating hard on some problem.

Repeatedly, they passed shrines set beside the road, little more than a few standing stones in a natural bowl in the rock or in a clearing among the trees. They were generally overgrown, the rocks covered in lichen, although one had been recently decorated with flowers. Selene picked out the weathered traces of carvings on a couple of them. The triple eye motif was just discernible. She asked Hessia if she knew anything about them.

"This planet has intermittent upsurges in spiritual sentiment about an omnipotent god and his avatar who intervenes in our lives and makes the bad things go away. My guess is these shrines date from one of those periods."

They came upon another such shrine, three columns of stone over which a trickle of water from a brook sprinkled. Eb stopped in front of it, apparently transfixed by the sight.

He hadn't spoken once since they'd stepped onto the planet, but now he did. His voice was little more than a whisper. "This world, it feels familiar to me."

"You've been here before?" Selene asked. "That must have been aeons ago. It will have changed enormously."

"I … I cannot tell if the memories are mine, or someone else's."

"Who's else could they be?"

He shook his head inside his cowl. "I suppose they must be mine."

Selene addressed Hessia directly, brain-to-brain so Eb couldn't overhear. "What emotional state are you getting off him?"

"His mind is basically in turmoil. There's delight, alarm, confusion. And questions, lots of questions. There's a growing sense of resolve, too. Like a purpose he knows he has to fulfil."

"What purpose?"

"I can't tell."

Had she made a mistake in encouraging Eb to come to the surface? "Is this too much for him? Is it going to sink him?"

"He is fundamentally strong, I think. After a period of adjustment, he'll come through. Best leave him to process."

The walk to the stone structure would take them a couple of hours. They'd put the lander down in an isolated ravine, out of sight of any settlement. They'd also descended at night, to limit the chances of natives of the planet spotting them. At least they'd been able to make a gradual approach; for once, Selene hadn't been plagued with trauma-flashbacks to previous lander-rides.

The planet's sun was climbing the sky in the west now, its warped, flattened disc burning blood-red, lighting up the haze of the early morning mists, casting long shadows and gilding every surface with its fire. Selene paused to take the scene in, breathing deeply, relishing the scents of earth and dust and greenery in her nose. Eb, too, stopped, and after a moment did the same. It was like he was learning from her how to react. She smiled at him, in appreciation of the beauty around them, and after a pensive moment he nodded back.

They encountered a few lone travellers on the road, but no one gave them any trouble or even stopped to engage with them at any length. Hessia's monitoring of the system meant that she'd built up a good catalogue of linguistic patterns and idioms, and both she and Selene had uploaded the relevant translations into their brain flecks. Eb had assured them that he had done the same.

Ondo had been especially fascinated by the grammar of the world's tongues. "I've never seen anything like this; these language syntaxes are completely outside the galactic norm."

Selene had been too concerned with getting her artificial flesh to look believable to be particularly interested. "The world's been isolated for a long time; there's obviously been massive linguistic drift from the standard patterns."

Ondo's gaze had been far away as he studied the data streaming through his brain. "There's drift and there's complete divergence. I can't trace any of this back to the known root tongues."

"Which means it was isolated from the Coronadian culture and evolved by itself. That shouldn't be a surprise."

"A planet isolated from Concordance *and* the galactic golden age. Don't tell her, but Hessia was right; I should have been here."

"We'll gather all the data we can. When we get back, you can study it to your heart's content."

Now, they crossed paths with a broken-down cart to which was tethered a stocky equine, steam rising off it as if it had only recently stopped stamping its way forwards. The cart contained a mountain of purple root vegetables, but one of its wooden wheels had come off, canting the contraption over to one side. Two men knelt in the dust of the road, trying to fix it. A father and son, Selene guessed:

one was young, black-haired and clean-shaven, while the older man's face was a weathered red. The similarities between them – face, build, mannerisms – were clear to see.

The two men stood as Selene and the others approached. The younger man considered them with open suspicion, but the older one brushed his fingers through his remaining hair and greeted them warmly enough, exchanging a few inconsequential words about the weather and the fact that the evenings were getting darker as the winter wore on. The observation puzzled Selene as the motions of the planet were a matter of simple astronomical calculation. Except, of course, this was a low-tech world. Perhaps the man was genuinely delighted when the sun chose to rise again each morning.

She offered to help them by way of reply, but the younger man stepped forwards, his cheeks flushed with anger. "We don't need your help. Go back to where you came from and leave us in peace."

"He's absolutely terrified of us," said Hessia in her mind.

"We're no threat to him. I mean, we *could* be, but we're not."

"That's not how he sees it."

"What is this, some small-town fear of those terrifying others from then next valley over?"

"I don't think so. As far as I can tell, they both know what we are. The old man's thoughts are full of wonder about the stars and what lies out there."

One of the younger man's hands was roughly bandaged, and she saw that the cloth was beginning to colour crimson as his blood seeped through.

"You're injured," said Selene.

The younger man glanced down at his hand, as if only then noticing his wound. "It's nothing. Caught my damned hand under the cart as we were trying to lift it."

"May I see? We might be able to help."

"No. It's fine."

"Show them," the older man said. "They may be able to help with the pain."

"It doesn't hurt."

"Of course it hurts, Jem. Show them."

Reluctantly, the son unwound the strip of cloth around his hand, revealing layers that were more and more saturated with blood. He went slowly at the end, carefully exposing his wound. It was bad: the bones of his left hand were crushed and protruding from his flesh. His palm must have taken the full weight of the cart.

"That needs proper attention, cleaning and bandaging," said Selene. "You might lose that hand. Do you have anyone you can go to?" On any advanced world, it wouldn't be a terrible injury. Hands could be repaired or replaced, and infection wasn't a problem. Here, it would be. The stained cloth looked anything but sterile.

The young man, however, looked amused rather than worried. "It will be better in a day or two. It's nothing."

Selene was about to tell him that was nonsense, when Hessia brain-spoke again. "He's telling the truth, or at least he thinks he is. His father too: he's not worried. He knows the lad's hand will heal."

"How can that be?"

"I don't know."

Out loud, Selene said, "I can lift up your cart while you re-attach the wheel if you like."

The offer of the superhuman feat of strength appeared not to surprise either man. The father said, "That would be welcome. The pin keeping the wheel on shattered. We have a spare but we'd have to remove the entire load of oxbeets to lift the axle to the right height."

But the younger man intervened again as Selene stepped forwards. "We'll do it without you! Get back in your ship and don't come back here. You're not welcome."

He looked like he was ready to fight the three of them. The older man put a restraining hand on his shoulder,

"Leave them be, son. They intend us no harm. They're trying to help."

"They don't have to intend us harm to cause it, do they? We all know what strangers mean."

"What do strangers mean?" Selene asked.

"Please forgive my boy," said the older man. "He is worried about what your appearance signifies. You understand. But you are welcome here, truly. No one will attempt to stop you."

She didn't at all understand why they felt so threatened; perhaps this was how people on all cut-off planets behaved.

"Do you want me to help with the cart or not?"

"Thank you, yes."

She was tempted to walk away to spite the younger man, but instead she stepped forwards and lifted the axle with her left arm, holding it perfectly still while the older man slipped the wooden wheel back on and hammered the metal pin into place. The son scowled at them from one side, refusing to help.

"Thank you," the older man said when he and his son were back on the cart. "You saved us an hour of work."

"You're welcome."

"I hope you find what you're looking for."

With that, the cart rattled off. When they were alone again, Selene said, "They seemed surprisingly calm about our presence on their planet."

Hessia watched the cart as it lurched away down the road. "They understood completely what we are. They weren't shocked, though; they accepted our presence as easily as they might accept the weather."

"This is a weird planet. Have you noticed we've seen quite a few old people?"

"Hard lives and the lack of good healthcare make people age quickly," said Hessia. "They probably look twice the age they actually are."

"Perhaps. It's odd, though. I'm picking up no signs of

infection from them, none of the deformities or cancers you might expect to see. And I swear I can pick up traces of some kind of nano-scale tech in the air."

"Doing what?" asked Hessia.

"Without access to labs, I have no idea. But if I had to guess, I'd say it was protecting these people, keeping them healthy, fixing their wounds. Perhaps that hand will be as good as new in a few days."

"Particles free-floating in the environment? You're suggesting technology that most advanced worlds don't have. These people don't look like they could have built such a culture."

"Maybe they didn't," said Selene. "Maybe they're not aware of what's going on. Where exactly do they think we came from?"

"Just, you know, elsewhere. Out there." Hessia indicated the rest of the universe with a wave of her hand.

The stone building they'd seen from orbit stood atop a prominent hill, clearly visible for many kilometres around. Whoever had built it had wanted it to be easy to spot. The central tower might have been a natural outcropping that had been carved and smoothed away over time to form a lopsided spiral. They'd seen no other buildings like it: dwellings were single-storey stone houses, comfortable-looking and well-maintained, but modest in scale. They passed more and more of these as the track circled the hill, rising all the time. A growing number of people milled around, and Selene began to see shops and gathering-places as well.

They stopped by a stall overflowing with bright pink fruits and, next to them, vats of what looked to be juice. They'd seen orchards from the track as they'd walked, the trees heavy with produce. Both she and Hessia were thirsty, but they hadn't been able to work out from Hessia's observations what the locals used for money, or even how trade worked on the planet. Eb appeared to be neither thirsty nor hungry. By some means that Selene hadn't fully understood, he absorbed energy directly from the *Dragon* – a fact that at least partially explained why he couldn't leave his vessel for long periods.

Selene walked up to the man sitting in the sun beside the stall. "May I take some of the juice?"

The man didn't reply for a moment, shading his eyes with his hand as he looked up at her. He looked puzzled. Perhaps she hadn't formed the question correctly. The man opened his mouth to speak, then closed it again.

"Is he offended?" Selene asked Hessia, brain-to-brain.

"He's as baffled as he looks. He doesn't appear to understand the concept of your question."

Selene reached out and took one of the fruits, its skin cool and smooth in her hand. "I can have this?"

The storekeeper – if he was the storekeeper – finally spoke. "Please. There is plenty of fruit. We have all we need."

"Is this your stall? Do I … give you reward for fruit and juice?" There was a millisecond pause as her translation routines struggled to produce the correct terms. Examining what it had come up with, Selene saw why. There was no word for *pay* in the local language. No concept of it, apparently.

"My stall? It's a stall I am sitting by because this is where I live. You can leave or take as much fruit as you like. Does it work differently where you are from?"

"No, no," said Selene. "I simply wanted to check. Thank you."

She took two of the fruits and tossed one to Hessia. Eb looked on but didn't respond. His face was lost in the shadows of his cowl.

A stack of hemispherical, hollowed-out fruit husks were piled by the vat. Cups, she supposed. Keeping one wary eye on the man, she filled two of them and passed one to Hessia. The man had apparently gone back to sleep.

"Seems we're free to take whatever we need," Hessia said. "I could get used to this."

"I still think it's weird."

Selene sipped at the juice. It was tart and refreshing, with no toxins or allergens that she could detect. She drank it all down.

"Can your enhancements pick up anything from the juice?" Hessia asked.

"There are definitely nano-scale devices in it. Millions of them."

"Ondo will freak if he finds out. Can you tell what effect they're having?"

"They appear to be benign. I can't detect them doing anything to my tissues, natural or artificial."

"Good to know." Hessia drained her cup, too.

They continued the climb. Selene had expected to find the entranceway through the three circles of wall blocked or at least guarded, but they were able to wander in without being question or accosted. The dust and sand on the ground bore the marks of many, many feet. A steady flow of people passed through now, individuals and family groups, none of them in any hurry.

From the outer wall, the middle wall was nearly two hundred metres distant, and the space between had been filled with a disordered confusion of houses and stalls and open spaces. The buildings had been placed with no apparent system, narrow alleys snaking between them, turning sharply, branching and re-joining, and often leading to complete dead-ends. Selene built up a map of it in her head, but while it was still incomplete they became lost repeatedly. Once they found themselves back at the outer wall. They tried to aim towards the central tower – the compass in her head taking over when they lost sight of it – but there was simply no logic to the way the paths wound round.

Eventually, they found the gateway to the middle circle and then, after twenty more minutes of backtracking and guessing, the inner.

The central tower was a sheer cone of stone in front of

them, the space around it mercifully free of any obstacles. Up close, it looked more artificial than natural. People were leaning against it, eating and drinking or simply asleep. Three or four people ambled around with wide brooms in their hands, sweeping the dust on the ground into smoothness where people had walked. They didn't appear to mind when someone trod more footprints into the sand where they'd just brushed, or when a gaggle of children racketed through and disturbed everything.

Selene peered upwards at the top of the tower. There were marks there, very faint, blasted by the wind and bleached by the sun so that they were almost undetectable. She zoomed in with her left eye, sifting through the electromagnetic spectrum to get the clearest view.

The images sprang out in infra-red. She relayed what she'd found immediately to Hessia and Eb. There was no mistaking the familiar motif. Three circles, shining out across the planet.

"The Tok," said Hessia. "They were here."

4. Labyrinthine

Selene pushed with all her augmented strength against the weathered wooden door at the base of the tower, but it refused to budge. Her feet slipped in the sand, her body twisting as she boosted the power output of her enhanced half. It made no difference.

"This door is not as innocent as it looks. I should be able to reduce it to splinters."

Hessia was looking the other way, scanning the milling crowds around them. "This has to be some kind of forbidden sanctum. It's odd that no one is even bothering to challenge us."

Selene picked out one of the crowd, a smiling man who looked to be about Ondo's age. His head was bald, apart from tufts of grey around his ears, but he also possessed an impressively bushy beard. He wore flowing, sand-coloured gowns that doubtless helped keep him cool in the midday heat. A simple rope dyed bright purple was tied about his waist.

"Please," she said, stepping towards him. "This door. Can we open it?"

The man stopped and scratched the side of his face. He glanced at Hessia and Eb, both far taller than anyone else in the crowd. There was a clear flicker of concern on the man's face at her words, although he replied readily enough. "The Gatekeeper can open it. He's up there now."

The man indicated the top of the tower with an upwards nod of his head.

"How does this Gatekeeper open the door?"

"The door opens for whoever is the Gatekeeper. That's how it works."

"What do you mean, *whoever is the Gatekeeper?*"

"We take turns. We find that's best."

"Has it ever been you?"

"Oh yes, many of us do it for a year or two."

"What did you do up there?"

There was an amused twinkle in the man's eye as he replied. "In truth, nothing. You sit and wait and watch in case anyone comes, but no one ever does. It's good to keep these old traditions going, don't you think? And now, of course, here you are."

"He is troubled," said Hessia in her head. "He, too, is worried about what our appearance might mean, despite his words."

Selene nodded, to both Hessia and the stranger she was talking to. Out loud, she said, "We need to go up. Tell us what to do."

"I'm truly not sure. When I was the Gatekeeper, the door opened for me when I needed to ascend."

"Did you have a key?"

"There is no keyhole."

"Do people ever come here but fail to get up the tower?"

"Oh, yes, I'm sure that must have happened."

"Well, thanks," said Selene. "You've been such a great help."

Behind her, Hessia was trying to open the door, also to no avail. Selene considered whether she could climb the outside of the tower. Its walls were worn smooth by countless years of wind and dust, but there were tiny fissures here and there. The fingertips of her artificial hand would be strong enough to hold her, but she doubted whether those on her right hand would be.

In her frustration, she pounded on the door, the sound booming. They'd come too far to be thwarted by something so ridiculous. They could return with some heavy weaponry from one of the ships, a blaster capable of annihilating the entranceway in an instant. Then they'd see what lay inside.

Eb had been silent for a long time, taking everything in. But now he stepped forwards to the door.

He lifted the hood of his cloak back over his head. "I believe I should try."

Selene was about to make some cutting remark about him still being weak, when Eb placed a hand on the door, pushed, and it creaked open, hinging inwards to reveal darkness within.

"Did you know that was going to happen?" Selene asked.

"It felt like the right thing to do."

"You could have done that five minutes ago and saved us a lot of effort."

"My apologies," he said, but he looked amused as he led the way inside.

The ground floor of the tower was a plain, dusty space, a faint light filtering down from above. A spiral staircase wound up the inside of the tower, and, by adjusting the sensitivity of her left eye, Selene could see that the edges of the steps were worn smooth by the passage of many feet.

They clung to the wall as they ascended; there was no barrier to stop them pitching over the side to plummet to the ground. The scuffing sound of their footsteps echoed from the hard walls. No one spoke. The light from above grew stronger, golden light slanting down in bright beams, illuminating a swarm of countless motes of dust. Selene wondered how long they'd been drifting there. Whether any were, in fact, intelligent micro-scale devices watching her.

At the top of the tower, the stairs opened out onto a wide, circular space, a ring of ovoid windows around the walls through which it seemed the whole of the world was visible. A man sat in the middle of the room on a scruffy wooden chair that looked like it had been there for hundreds of years. He wasn't in much better condition: his straggly grey hair concealed much of his face, and his back was bent as if from sitting still too long. He leaned on a stout cane set on the floor between his legs, but the light through the windows caught his two bird-like eyes peering out at them. He was watching the three of them intently as they climbed into view.

He nodded his head and spoke, his voice the rough croak of someone not used to speaking for some time. "Greetings, my friends."

"I assume you are the Gatekeeper," Selene said.

The man acknowledged his title with a dip of his head. "Please, my name is Jalian."

"Do you know why we are here?"

"I think so. Do you?"

"We are looking for answers."

"Do you even know the questions?"

She was aware she was sounding more and more like Ondo. "Not always, to be honest, but we know that a trail has led us here."

"Very good."

The floor of the vault was completely taken up by a mosaic. At its centre, underneath the man's chair, was the planet's sun, represented as a circle of terracotta red with stylized flames winding off it. Around it were arrayed other celestial objects: the planet they were on, its three moons, other planets, other stars. Even other galaxies around the edge of the room. The stars beneath her feet were connected with lines, forming the skeletons of their constellations, the shapes the people of this world saw in the sky.

"Is this how you view the universe?" Selene asked.

The man looked amused. "It is common for cultures to believe they are at the centre of everything, is it not? We know the truth of it, but still we consider our red star to be a fixed point around which the galaxy turns."

She brain-spoke to Hessia. "He doesn't seem worried about us."

Hessia had also removed her cowl to reveal her features. Her expression was sardonic. "It's possible he's grateful simply because we've relieved his boredom."

A series of pictures of stars and spaceships were set around the walls, filling the gaps between the windows, forming a sequence that ended in a single, larger image. They caught her attention because their presence was so incongruous on this backwards world – but also because she'd become aware that they weren't, simply, images. For one thing, they were giving off signals across a wide range of the electromagnetic spectrum. There was movement to them, too: around nine seconds on a loop. Whatever technology had been used to record the scenes, it had clearly captured a great deal of data, enough for her to study the electromagnetic spectra of the stars and the unique fingerprints of their absorption lines.

She walked up to the nearest one, trying not to think about the gulf of air directly beneath the floor, or about how old the tower was. The man in the chair watched her, the slightest smile playing across his lips. The picture portrayed a star caught at the very point of explosion, blast waves of electromagnetic energy pulsing from it. A supernova. In the foreground there was an inhabited world, with a starship breaking orbit in a futile attempt to flee the conflagration about to consume it.

"I know this star," she said. "At least, I know what became of it. It was dead by the time we found it; this is where the Coronade tunnel took us. How did you get this image?"

"It has always been here. They all have."

She stepped around the ring of images. "Most of these stars are unknown to us."

"It is not a linear road. There are many hidden paths

converging on this world."

The penultimate image displayed a blazing red furnace of a star. There was a ship she didn't recognize in the foreground, an organic-looking cylindrical body circumscribed by three rings of different sizes. Its architecture bore a clear resemblance to some of the Cathedral ships she'd seen.

"This is your star."

"It is."

"Whose ship is this?"

"I assume it belonged to the one who created this world."

"Is it still here?"

"No one has ever seen it."

The final, larger scene depicted a triple star system and the limb of some blue-green ocean planet. Another alien craft hung in orbit above the world. The bulbous sphere at its core reminded her of Surtr's craft, although the hexagonal mesh around it resembled the system-encompassing structure she'd seen at the Depository.

"Three stars," said the Ondo in her head. "We know that symbol well enough. Could this be the original?"

"The electromagnetic spectra are a close match to the three in the images you recovered of the Concordance fleet. The Omn homeworld."

"Agreed. There's a high probability this is the same system."

"This world," she said out loud to the man. "Where is it?"

"I do not know. I assume it is what lies at the very end."

"Tell me, Jalian, are we the only visitors ever to have come here?"

"There have been very, very few."

She needed to know if Concordance had been there. "But, recently? When was the last visit before ours?

"Three hundred and twenty years ago." Selene

translated from the period of Ansider's orbit to galactic standard. Almost exactly three centuries. A thrill of suspicion ran through her.

"A ship came here?"

Jalian looked amused for some reason. He glanced up as if he could glimpse the stretches of space through the roof, beyond the sky. "A ship came here, yes."

"What was it called?"

"They referred to it as the *Scintennia*."

The datastores and translation routines running on her flecks took a moment to translate the local name. "You call the two dwarf galaxies nearest our own the *Scintennia Starfields*. Or, as we would say, the *Magellanic Clouds*."

"Yes."

The look of wide-eyed wonder on Hessia's face was impossible to miss. "The *Magellanic Cloud* came here three hundred years ago."

"Its crew were troubled. Haunted, if the accounts are to be believed. They felt they were being pursued across the galaxy by some terrible enemy."

"They *were* being pursued. Vulpis would have been frantically searching for them. Those were the early days of Concordance, and Vulpis would have been very keen to ensure that the crew members who took the *Magellanic Cloud* were prevented from spreading their version of events."

"I do not know who or what Concordance or Vulpis are," Jalian said.

"Truly?" asked Selene.

"Truly," said the man. The faintest nod from Hessia indicated that he was telling the truth. Concordance hadn't been to the planet.

"How did the crew members of the *Magellanic Cloud* know to come here?"

"They carried a navigational bead with them, a red one. Perhaps you have seen something similar yourselves. They claimed they had acquired theirs at a world in the centre of the galaxy. *Omn*, they called it."

That made some sort of sense. Before the crew of the *Magellanic Cloud* split into its two factions, they'd explored the anomalous star system that they'd diverted towards. They might well have picked up navigational beads like the one Surtr had provided. They must have acquired a navigational AI capable of reading the bead, too.

"Why did they come here?"

"They needed answers. They foresaw a war and came in search of allies and weapons. And truth."

"What did the Gatekeeper of the time tell them?"

"Little of use. Their ship was not adequate for the journey along the path."

"Where did they go?"

"They saw the need to build an alliance of worlds to face the unfolding threat they perceived. They left for another system where they hoped to find friends, a fact which troubled us greatly at the time as we survive by remaining hidden. You are welcome here, but I'm sure you have detected a certain wariness at your appearance. We begged them that they keep our location a secret, and it appears they were as good as their word. They said they had taken all the beads and other navigational records pointing to our existence away from Omn. We owe them much."

"Do you know where they went?"

"No."

"Are they the only other people to have come here?"

"A thousand years ago, two other ships appeared in our sky, also seeking answers. One took the road we showed them and one waited, but their friends never returned. Eventually, they left."

"A thousand years," said Hessia. "Do your archives record the name of the two ships?"

"The one that took the road and did not return was the *Sephire*. The other, the *Umwe*."

A look of delight passed across Hessia's features. The

names meant something to her. Selene was about to pursue it when Hessia, perhaps picking up Selene's sense of confusion, offered an explanation.

"Those are the two vessels in the origin story of the Omnian faith. The *Sephire* passed into the realm of Omn, and the *Umwe* remained to tell the galaxy what had happened. In classical Omnian doctrine, Omn does not reside in this universe; that is a heresy thought up by Concordance. But, originally, there *was* a herald, a guardian who sat at the entrance to the sacred wormhole, judging who was worthy to pass through into the light of Omn."

"Interesting," said Selene.

"Yes."

To Jalian, Selene said, "You understand starships? I mean, not just that they exist, but how they function, what they're capable of?"

"I do. This world perhaps appears primitive to you, and it is in many ways, happily so. But it's more accurate to say that we are post-advanced rather than pre-advanced. You will doubtless be aware of the tiny devices that are immanent in our environment, keeping us healthy and giving us long lives."

"Yeah, we spotted them. I assume your culture developed to that point and then regressed to where you are now."

"*Advanced* and *regressed* ... these are very linear terms. Our civilization was arranged long ago to be as you see: stable, remaining as it is to survive, generation to generation. Contented."

"That sounds as though it would get boring very quickly. Don't you ever want to push the boundaries, explore, invent? Break the rules?"

"Some of us, of course. It is allowed. But we also recognize that what we have is some sort of paradise. All our needs are met by our planet's mechanisms. We work as much as we wish to work, play as much as we desire. From time to time, of course, the young become frustrated and wish to travel. We satisfy that need by encouraging them to visit other continents. You will have seen that this is a remarkably varied world, with many different environments. Believe it or not, we even have vast libraries of knowledge and research and speculation, where anyone may go to study or contribute. But, for the most part, we stay as we are."

"How long have you been here, quietly living your lives?"

The wry smile returned to the man's features. "It's odd, but after a while you stop counting. The passage of each day is important, but the passage of centuries, millennia, whole epochs of time? Less so. But it is millions of years."

A moment of understanding flashed between Selene and the image of Ondo she carried. Here was yet more proof that they had been utterly wrong about the timescales they'd originally proposed.

"You're sure of that?"

"Our world is contented, and because of that we see little reason to change it. This planet truly is a fixed point in the turning galaxy, in a metaphorical sense. It was constructed very carefully for that to be the case."

"Constructed by whom?"

"A *Gethrem.*"

"Is that another name for the Tok?"

He considered for a moment, as if searching his memories for old knowledge. "The Gethrem, the Tok. Before they fled the galaxy, one of them created this world."

"Why?"

"We are the gatekeepers to the labyrinth, and it is essential that we remain while other things change. If we had advanced into space, engaged fully with interstellar culture, it might have destroyed us."

Selene could feel her Ondo avatar almost buzzing inside her mind. She understood why. "You mentioned a labyrinth," she said to Jalian. "What does that mean?"

"We were put here to show anyone who needed it the way to the answers they seek. From here, I can give you the final road you must take. If you wish to."

"This final image; the triple star system. Is that where the road leads?"

"I have often wondered. I *can* tell you that the Gethrem individual who engineered Ansider is waiting at the end of the road. Alone among his kind, he didn't die. Perhaps the three stars were consumed by the black hole where he now waits. Or perhaps the Gethrem knows how to reach those three stars. I don't know."

It took Selene a moment to absorb the Gatekeeper's words. "You're saying that one of the Tok is still alive? Not a transbiological hybrid like Eb, but a person like you and me?"

"I am. He is. He was old when he came here, but I believe he survives."

She thought about that. It wasn't the self-destructive act she'd first assumed. It was a poor sort of immortality, but perhaps the only one available to him. Subjectively, his life would be no longer, but from outside he would always be there, falling more and more slowly towards the black hole's event horizon. He was trapped, but could watch the outside universe as it, from his perspective, accelerated through future time.

"Will you show us the route to take?"

The man shook his left hand and a bracelet slipped down his wrist. He unclipped it and held it up. It, too, held a bead. It looked night-black, but when he held it up to the light streaming in through the windows, she saw that it was a deep shade of purple.

"A seer stone," she said to her inner Ondo, "and now this Gatekeeper, watching over this world. And this repeated eye symbolism. Is this the origin of the name *seer stones*?"

"Perhaps."

Jalian said, "We had a string of these stones, once, but

this is the last. It will take you through the labyrinth if you have a ship that is capable of making the journey."

He turned his head to consider Eb, who was standing silently and listening to the conversation. "You are one such, are you not? You are the *genius loci* of a vessel that can make the gruelling voyage. You opened the door to the tower because you carry one of the stones within you, just as the crew of the *Scintennia* did, but you are not a person like we are people; you are much more than that. You are the core intelligence of a Gethrem swoop ship, a vessel capable of making impossible flights that would destroy any normal craft."

Eb nodded his head in acknowledgement. There was an odd light on his face, a wonderment, as if he was only then discovering some unexpected truth about himself. "I am as you say. Swoop ships were rare and precious. Few of us were constructed and fewer still had biological intelligences embedded within them."

"What," Selene asked, "is a swoop ship?"

Eb replied, "Swoop ships are vessels capable of making the metaspace manoeuvre you witnessed at Coronade to escape the pull of deep gravity wells. The Tok constructed them so they could jump directly into the hearts of stars and escape safely afterwards. That is what I am."

"Why did they create you? To cause more death and destruction by deploying their sunburst weapons?"

"You have seen that is a part of it," said Eb, "but you have seen the other side, too: the structures and havens built within the circumferences of suns, places where treasures could be hidden safely away. Treasures and other things. I cannot believe that they – we – were simply evil."

"No one believes themself to be evil, whatever they've done."

"Perhaps."

Jalian said, "And it is not just regular stars you can jump into, is it, my friend? You are capable of greater feats."

Eb nodded, and there was a clear reluctance to his movement.

"What feats?" said Selene. "What does he mean?"

"Black holes," said Hessia. "It has to be that. A ship like the *Radiant Dragon* – a Tok swoop ship – is capable of diving into a black hole, approaching, kissing the event horizon and then returning. That's it, isn't it? Only a very rare ship like you could make such an impossible journey."

"The swoop dive is filled with risk, and I could sustain one only for a very short period of time. Even I could not venture near a supermassive black hole. But, yes, that is what I am."

Things were beginning to click into place in Selene's mind. She conversed with Ondo, a brief, millisecond conversation as they compared theories and speculations. They arrived at the same conclusion simultaneously.

"That is where his bead will take us," said Selene out loud. "Along a path through metaspace into the close vicinity of a black hole."

"The trajectories and velocities have to be supremely finely calculated," said Jalian. "This bead contains all the data you need to perform the manoeuvre. The slightest imperfection, and you will miss completely or be pulled in so close that even a swoop ship could not escape."

Selene looked to Eb. "Can you do this?"

Eb's voice was little more than a whisper. "Yes."

"And could you return as well, hmm?" Jalian asked.

"That is less clear," said Eb. "It depends on how close we go, and how long I have to resist the pull."

"There is an old myth about the journey that some of us set store by," said Jalian. "Would you like to hear it?"

Selene was about to tell him that there was no need, their time was short, when Hessia, perhaps picking up Selene's impatience, spoke into her brain. "We should let him. Storytelling is central to how these people understand the world. That's true of most cultures, obviously, but more so here."

Selene forced herself to smile. "Please, yes, tell us the story."

"It concerns a young man of this world. Long ago, he grew bored with the limitations of his life and constructed a miraculous ship, a boat like those we sail upon the oceans, except that this was capable of flying through the seas of space. He captured one hundred Ice Swans – huge white birds that fly so high they can cross mountain ranges – and tethered them to his ship. He flew up and up, following the road to the demon in the sky to find answers to the questions he sought."

"Don't tell me," said Selene, "he never returned. The demon in the sky ate him."

"Oh, he returned, but he had been sorely punished for his presumption. He had been held captive for three hundred years, locked in a cursed sleep. He returned as if no time at all had passed for him, but everyone he knew on Ansider, all his friends and family, were dead and gone. He lived out his days among strangers, shunned and feared."

"You can't believe that."

Jalian smiled. "It is an amusing story; one we tell our children to discourage them from being too restless. But I think there might be some truth to it. It's a story I often think about as I'm sitting here."

Selene conversed rapidly with her virtual Ondo.

"Extreme time dilation. This story is a warning, dramatizing the effects of dropping into a deep gravity well and returning to normal space."

"Yes."

"Calling this Tok individual a *demon* is interesting, too. Perhaps this entire thing is a trap. I assumed he went into the black hole so he could wait there and warn the future – us – about something, but that might not be it at all. Perhaps the other Tok imprisoned him there because of some great evil he committed. He may have been luring us in all this time."

She could almost feel Ondo's wariness warring with his hunger to know the truth. "We still have to go," he said. "Surely, we have to go."

"We might be killed. Or held captive, which amounts to the same thing." Once again, she was the one being cautious while Ondo was keen to take risks. Once again, of course, it was not the real Ondo she was conversing with, but a disembodied copy.

"This Tok has apparently gone to extraordinary lengths if that's all he's been planning," he said. "Why bother?"

"The Gethrem individual who created your world," she said to Jalian. "We were told he was a renegade among his kind." *Outsider* was the word that Surtr had used.

"The old stories say he was the last of his kind. In some versions, he'd been kept as a prisoner, and he only freed himself long after all the other Gethrem had died out. Or, he was a betrayer, pursued by the other Gethrem because of his intention to reveal the secrets of the gods to ordinary people like us."

"What do you think?"

"I think he was doing what he thought best."

"And will you give the bead to us?"

"My forebears have sat in this tower, and the towers that were here before it, for millions of years. The beads have been passed from Gatekeeper to Gatekeeper for days and millennia uncounted. Handing over the last is a moment of triumph – the fulfilment of our duty – but it might also spell disaster for us."

"You fear what may happen to your world."

"We understand that this act will mark the end of our long solitude. How could it not? Whether this leads to our salvation or our destruction is impossible to know. You speak of your terrible enemies: how will they react when they see what we have done? I do not think it will go well for us. We have no defences other than our quiet anonymity."

"Then, you will not show us the road we must take?"

The old man considered for a moment, and a slight smile played about his lips beneath his tangle of hair. "I think we must play the role assigned to us."

He held the bead out, and dropped it into Selene's outstretched hand. "Take it; it is yours."

5. The Fight at the Red Star

The surface of Ansider was falling away behind them, the lander lurching as it passed through multiple atmospheric layers, when the first alerts about ships appearing on the periphery of the system reached Selene.

Dread trickled through her as she watched more and more of them light up. A coordinated halo of ships were appearing all around the red star, clearly attempting to form a full-sphere blockade of Ansider. She knew what vessels they would be even as identification tags winked into existence on the three-dimensional visualization in her head. A mesh of Cathedral ships, then a rash of smaller traces, faster moving: Void Walker attack vessels deploying to fill the gaps between the larger ships.

She could see from the alarmed look on Hessia's face that the Periarch was seeing the same thing. Selene said, "What are your projections saying? Can you see an egress point for the *Falling Fire*?"

Hessia took a moment to respond, distracted as she was by the complex navigational calculations going on in her head. Her words, when they came, were chilling.

"There is none. Concordance have thrown enough at us to ensure we have no escape vectors. Our only option is to attempt to blast our way through their ships."

"I did it once before, used a ghost translation to take one of them out."

Hessia moved her head in a dismissive gesture. "You were incredibly lucky to make that work. This is different; this is a full battlefleet on high alert. We wouldn't get close."

Selene cast around for some other way out of the system. Jalian, at least, had been right to fear their appearance upon Ansider. She'd condemned the planet to a terrible fate. Would it become one more Maes Far? Was she, even then, fleeing another doomed world in a lander?

She transmitted a message to Ondo, the real Ondo, somewhere on his distant loop around the star. He, at least, might be able to get away. She couldn't give him the purple bead, but she could relay everything they'd learned. Perhaps, somehow, it would be enough for him to find the route to take to the black hole.

But Ondo's reply came back far more quickly than she'd expected. The *Radiant Dragon* was nearby, well within the cage around the system.

Her spoke to her brain-to-brain, a strange edge to his familiar voice. "Hello, Selene."

"What the hell are you doing here?"

His face appeared in her mind's eye, the familiar backdrop of the *Dragon*'s cartography deck behind him.

His words were utterly unexpected. "You really don't understand even now, do you? Did you honestly believe that I rescued you, rebuilt you out of the goodness of my heart?"

Her brain was a whirl as she tried to make sense of his words. "Ondo, I don't…"

The grin on his face was cruel – an expression she had never seen him use in all their time together. "I used you, Selene. I needed you to be strong, resourceful, someone who could face the dangers I could not. And that's exactly what you've been. My useful tool. How amusing it was to hear you talking about Kane being the puppet of Godel, how he was changed by what they did to him, and it didn't occur to you that you were describing yourself perfectly."

"Ondo, this makes no sense."

"It makes perfect sense. You are not the person who left the surface of Maes Far, I made sure of that. You are *mine*, Selene. You are Concordance's. Did you really think all your miraculous escapes were down to your own abilities, your own good fortune?"

"What are you talking about? What the hell is going on?"

"You've made such impressive discoveries. You've been so angry, so filled with the desire for revenge, but all along you've been playing the part that I – we – assigned to you. All your traumas and struggles really have been amusing to watch. And, finally, you have led us to Ansider and given us the answer to the secrets we need to unlock."

"Ondo, no."

"Yes, Selene. There is no escape. The Periarch's ship is incapable of escaping the net around this system and your control of the *Dragon* has been removed. Bring the object you retrieved from the surface. Or don't, it makes little difference. There is nowhere you can run to, nowhere left for you to hide. I…"

The comms stream from the *Dragon* cut off. Ondo's voice came to her again, but this time it was the version she carried in her own skull.

"Selene, do not listen to him. That is not Ondo talking. That is not *me*."

He was literally there in her head. He had been all along. How could she fight an enemy that was part of her? He'd rebuilt her. As she'd once feared, he'd twined his command pathways through her brain and body, operating with such skill and artistry. She could never separate the two. She was whole, yes, but she was not her own. He'd been under Concordance control all along, altered long ago to act as – what – a convenient scapegoat that they could use to unite the galaxy in fear? Yes, that. And, also, as a magnet for dissidents and trouble-makers. People like her and Hessia. They had sleepwalked into the trap.

"Fuck off, Ondo. I'm going to expel your engrams from my head now."

Beyond their inner conversation, she was aware of Hessia studying her with an alarmed expression on her face. Outside, the glowing edge of Ansider's limb curved away as they crossed the atmospheric boundary and entered low orbit.

"*Think*, Selene," said her inner Ondo. "If they have control over you, why are you still *you*? Why are you still fighting, looking for a way out?"

"Why should I listen to anything you say?"

"You shouldn't, but what I'm saying is obviously true. If I'd had control of you all along, I wouldn't have needed any deception. You'd have accepted your role gratefully like any Void Walker."

She was breathing fast, adrenaline shaking through her. But … he was right. So far as she could tell, she was still herself. Why would he point all that out to her if he'd betrayed her? She filled Hessia and Eb in on her conversation with the *Dragon*.

"I don't believe it," said Hessia. "He's annoying and eccentric, but he's no traitor. I'd know, right?"

"Can you be sure? His true nature might have been very well hidden."

"I've known him for a long time. If he's been under secret Concordance control all this time, then they're playing a very subtle game. They had no way of knowing you'd attempt to escape Maes Far, or even that you'd be born in the first place. All the things you've found, you've found for yourself. I know there is no duplicity in him. I've picked through your emotional states very carefully, believe me, and I'd swear that the Ondo you thought you knew is the real Ondo."

"Godel's message," said Selene. "That has to be it. When they hit Ondo, knocked him out. They did something to him that we missed. The migraines he's had ever since are because something in his head has been fighting him."

Hessia thought about that. "It's possible they triggered a bug they'd put there when he was one of them as a young man. If it was dormant, I wouldn't have picked anything up."

"Then he's compromised," said Selene. "It doesn't matter how they did it, we can't trust him or the *Dragon*, and that means you shouldn't trust me."

Her inner Ondo's voice was calm in her mind, talking to all of them across their shared comms connection. "If they've seized control of the real Ondo's conscious actions, that doesn't mean we stop and give up. We can still find a way out of this. We can still *think*."

She breathed deeply, slowly, as she'd learned to do when terror threatened to overwhelm her. Okay. Whatever the truth of it, they needed to deal with Concordance first. She modelled the movements of starships and gravitational bodies around her. The *Radiant Dragon*, the *Falling Fire*, the Cathedral ships and the Void Walker attack craft: they were converging, and soon they would meet.

"Eb," she said. "Have you been following this?"

"I have."

"Can you control the *Dragon* from here?"

"I am the *Dragon*, and I travel where I wish. Although, control is easier the closer I am."

"Can you lock Ondo out; fly the vectors I call?"

"Yes."

"Good. Can you also knock him out so he can't interfere?"

"Do you wish me to kill Ondo?"

"Just incapacitate him for now."

"I could reduce the oxygen levels rapidly. With luck, he'll pass out before he can work out what's happening."

"He probably already thought of that," said Hessia. "He might be in a suit already."

Did Concordance know about Eb? Only if Ondo had told them. She'd have to take that chance. "Do it, but try not to harm him permanently. Keep his brain alive. Do you see his biological readings?"

"I can identify it if he becomes unconscious."

"Good. Also bring the ship here; we need it to rendezvous with Hessia's vessel."

"The *Dragon* is responding," said Eb. "Ondo's readings suggest he is beginning to suffer the first signs of oxygen starvation."

She threw another message at him, some ridiculous taunt, hoping to distract him if he was trying to climb into a suit or override Eb's control. She got no response.

She considered the battlefield again. They had an hour before the first attack ships reached them and a third of that time before they could meet up with the *Dragon*. It was going to be tight, even if Ondo was out of the picture and there weren't unseen variables that she hadn't taken into account.

"Okay, Eb, next question. You're capable of jumping into and near stars. Can you make a jump from here, without having to get the usual distance from the stellar mass?"

He sighed a long-drawn-out exhalation. Despite his transcendent nature, he sounded more and more human with each passing hour. "Yes, I am capable of that, although it will take its toll. The farther out we can get first, the better."

"If you do this, will you still be capable of making the black hole jump?"

"For a brief moment. It depends upon how close we have to get to the event horizon."

"Right, good. Hessia, you have to come with us. Your ship has no way out of this system. We'll use the *Falling Fire* to accelerate to meet the *Dragon*, EVA across and jump before Concordance can reach us."

"No."

"What do you mean, *no*?"

Eb interjected, "Ondo has succumbed to oxygen

starvation and is now unconscious."

"We'll worry about him later," said Selene. "Keep him under. He survived hypoxia at the dead star, he'll be okay for a while. Hessia, what do you mean?"

"I'm going to return to the planet, take the lander's drop chute. I shouldn't have left, I see that now. With everything else going on, they might not notice me. I'll give you full executive control of the *Falling Fire*. Use it to attack them or set up a diversion. Whatever you think is best."

"That's madness, Hessia. Concordance aren't going to leave this world in peace. They'll come for you."

"They don't want me; they want you and they want that bead."

"You do not know that."

"I have a pretty clear impression of their intentions. Besides, this swoop dive into a black hole: if you ask me, it's suicide. Even if you succeed, the time dilation might mean you emerge to find that everything is over, everyone is dead. I do not want to return to that. And Ansider … I felt content there. A world where everyone is at peace is a good place for an empath to live."

"That peace is not going to last very long. We've exposed that planet to the gaze of the galaxy."

"That's where I'm counting on you to distract them. Carry on being the splinter in their flesh. And then, please, destroy them utterly so I can live my life in peace."

"I can't dissuade you, can I?"

"You can't." Hessia sent codes into Selene's brain, transferring control of the *Falling Fire*. "It's a good ship. Nothing so ancient and impressive as the *Dragon*, but it's served me well. If it can help you now, then I'm happy."

Selene checked the unfolding battle. "You should drop to the planet now."

They embraced for a moment, Hessia having to stoop slightly. Her body was lithe but powerful in Selene's grasp.

"Your forebear, Magdi," said Selene. "She must have

been formidable."

"I think she was. And I think she might have approved of what I'm doing."

"Take care down there."

"I will."

Hessia climbed off the control deck while Selene assumed full executive control of the tiny ship's AI. Above her, in orbit, the *Falling Fire* responded, decelerating hard to descend into lower orbit. A swoop all of its own.

The drop chute, a cylinder barely larger than Hessia's body, reported that it was prepped and ready for release. Wishing her a final good luck, Selene released the pod. Through the ship's sensors she watched it plunge groundward, a vanishing sliver of silver. A kilometre from the surface it would fire its reaction drive to slow Hessia's descent. After that, she was on her own.

Ten minutes later, the lander docked with the *Falling Fire* and they accelerated hard onto the rendezvous vector with the *Radiant Dragon*. Her plan was for the two vessels to fly in tandem for a short while, and then diverge onto opposing trajectories. There were enough ships in the tightening Concordance net to contain both, but any slight confusion over which ship she was on might give her a slight edge. Although, if they knew anything about her, they'd surely know she'd be on the *Dragon*.

The good news was that the *Dragon* continued to respond to Eb's inputs. Concordance didn't have control of the ship.

With the two craft accelerating on parallel vectors, she nudged them together so that there was only a gap of a metre or so between them. Proximity alarms screamed on both ships, but she ignored them. It was exhilarating having her brain controlling two starships at the same time; it was like trying to ride two racehorses simultaneously. She positioned the vessels so that their respective airlocks were lined up, then she and Eb threw themselves across the gap without bothering to clamber into EVA suits. They could both withstand exposure to the absolute zero temperature and hard solar radiation for a moment.

Back on the *Dragon*, Selene ran rapid status checks on vital systems. Everything looked good. Eb returned to his sanctum to run further deep-pass scans and to put into effect their battle plan. Selene then went to find Ondo's body. He was alive when she found him, slumped in a heap on the cartography deck floor. He was halfway to the door, as if he'd tried to crawl out and collapsed. His skin was a ghastly blue colour from the hypoxia, his lips almost purple.

She restored oxygen levels on the section of the ship they were in and picked him up to carry to the medsuite. He was beginning to stir as they got there. She secured him to the bed and instructed the suite to sedate him, keep him deep under until she had time to consider him further. She thought, briefly, that the med systems might fail to respond, that the infection went further than just Ondo's head, but they complied perfectly. He was contained, for now.

The two vessels had separated onto their respective vectors, the *Falling Fire* accelerating at a forty-five-degree angle from the ecliptic, heading out-system, while the *Dragon* headed almost directly upwards – or downwards depending on your perspective – from the plane. Almost, but not exactly; she angled the ship very slightly towards the solar mass, too. Her hope was that Concordance would spot the subtle deviation and conclude that she was on the *Fire*, accelerating as hard as it could away from the gravity well. Her calculation was that Eb and the *Dragon* could withstand the slight increase in gravitational pull that the manoeuvre implied without too much impairment.

A broadcast from one of the Void Walker attack ships – capable of higher acceleration – reached the *Dragon*. Selene watched it passively, not responding or acknowledging it in any way. She'd expected something similar. Concordance were hoping one of the two ships would respond so they could work out where she was.

It was Kane, the Void Walker who'd been dogging her steps, seemingly pursuing her across the galaxy. There was no sign of the *Storm Gatherer* in the Cathedral ship halo, but Selene had no doubt Godel was behind the attack. Kane mocked and goaded her; his familiar cruel features twisted into something like pure hatred. The temptation to respond was strong; Kane had deliberately put his ship ahead of the attack fleet, no doubt hoping to elicit a response. She refused to give him what he wanted and cut the connection. There was nothing useful to be learned from him.

Instead, she watched the ballet of starships around Ansider, checking constantly that she hadn't missed anything, hadn't miscalculated. The Walker attack ships unleashed their barrage of high-g missiles when they were within minutes of the *Dragon* and the *Falling Fire*. The *Fire*, as programmed, immediately responded with its own furious barrage of intercept-missile countermeasures. Beam-weaponry would kick in as the attacking missiles neared. Hessia's ship threw everything it had into the battle; as much as possible, Selene wanted it to look like she was on that vessel, desperately fighting for survival. The *Dragon* fired off its own fusillade, but not with the same level of overkill intensity. Another subtle attempt to mislead Concordance.

They took the bait to a degree, sixty percent of the attackers focusing their attention on the *Falling Fire*, but the *Dragon* still had no chance of defeating the ships homing in on it. It didn't matter: a full minute from the first volley of impacts, dangerously close to the red star in normal circumstances, Selene spun up the metaspace projectors.

"Are you ready for this, Eb?"

"I am ready."

She was about to trigger the jump into safety when

Cathedral ships started appearing in local space around her: five, six, seven of them blurring into reality a mere ten kilometres off. They fired beam-weapons even as they materialised, their proximity giving her mere nanoseconds to respond. Concordance had worked out how to make their ships perform the gravity-defying jumps the *Dragon* could achieve – something she and Ondo had assumed was impossible. For reasons unknown, the Tok had deployed that particular technology rarely, keeping its secret very well guarded. It was a secret no more.

The first blasts lanced into the *Dragon*'s energy hull, triggering a rash of alerts in Selene's tactical visualization. The ship's defences degraded rapidly under the broadside onslaught. Her boosted consciousness made time appear to slow. They had only moments before destruction, and the *Dragon*'s metaspace projectors were a full second from being operational. Nowhere near long enough.

She triggered the jump anyway, taking the risk. "Eb, jump! Jump now!"

The energy hull hit 0% and sputtered out even as she gave the command. The bare carbon-metal of the voidhull was exposed. Solid lines of beam-weapon fire bored into the *Dragon*, pinning it into place in space. She felt Eb's screaming like it was her own. A vision of her lander escape from Maes Far, energy bolts cutting through her ship, washed over her. They were now a tenth of a second from translation, but it might as well have been an eternity.

Then two of the high-intensity beams cut out. Three more followed. The load on the voidhull lessened, stretching the hull-breach prediction point tantalisingly close to translation, although still on the wrong side.

She saw why: the Cathedral ships were stretching and blurring, deforming as the mass of the star pulled them in. Concordance hadn't mastered the technology; they'd sent ships on a suicide mission to destroy the *Dragon*. Another of the attackers, its lines only just hardened from its materialization, lengthened as if it were made of elastic then shot sunward, unable to establish flight control and resist the pull of the star. The load on the *Dragon*'s voidhull reduced a notch more, giving her the precious nanoseconds she needed for the projectors to fully spin up.

The familiar flutter and flip in her stomach was a glorious relief as they finally translated. As the galaxy faded, the sixth and then the seventh Cathedral ship deformed, caught on the hook of gravity, then flashed towards the star. The attacking ships had unleashed missiles of their own, and these detonated in clouds of fire, but they were flames that could never touch her.

She and the *Dragon* were safe for the moment.

The projection of the Ansider star was alarmingly close in the Singh Field – she could feel the fearsome drag of it like a weight on her back – but the *Dragon* manoeuvred away, arcing onto its new vector. They could escape. Eb had consumed the purple-black bead just as he'd taken in the red one, and the path he had to follow was now clear. The black hole was inside another bubble of Dead Space, presumably as another way to conceal its location. It would make the journey more gruelling, but he'd agreed to the attempt without demur.

The Concordance vessels would be close behind – too close under normal circumstances – but, for once, she wasn't concerned. The Cathedral ships could not follow them where they were going. Perhaps they would conclude that she'd miscalculated some stunt to throw them off. It made little difference. They couldn't touch her, and while they could watch her falling into the singularity, they might not wait for the months it would take – from their perspective – for the *Dragon* to re-emerge. Even if they did blockade space around the black hole, Eb could jump well before she reached them upon her return, meaning that they couldn't hope to track her closely enough.

All assuming the *Dragon* held together that long.

She used the next hour to strip away the fake flesh of her left half and restore herself to herself. It felt good to flex the unencumbered muscles of her face once she was done. She went to find Eb in his sanctum.

But Eb wasn't there. Instead, she found him on the top observation deck, staring into space. They had left metaspace briefly and were positioning for their next translation. His hands were splayed on the transparent bulkhead, as if he were trying to reach the distant stars. Dimly, she could see his features reflected in the carbon-metal. The look of profound sadness on his face was impossible to miss. With everything that had happened, she had forgotten what it was he was facing.

He turned as she approached, even though she'd been moving with the utmost quiet. Of course, he *was* the ship, he knew instinctively what was taking place around him, where she was. It was a strangely intimate thought. Once, it might have troubled her.

She stood beside him, looking at the stars. "Are you sure you want to do this?"

"I think it is the right thing to do."

"That's not the same thing. You get to choose what you want to do."

He nodded. "This journey into and hopefully out of the black hole will destroy me. But, still, it feels like the right thing to do. It feels like … a good ending to my long story."

"Surtr said something similar."

"And I understand what it meant."

"We could look for answers elsewhere, find another way. I do not want your death on my conscience."

His reflection looked amused by her words. "I have thought about this a lot, believe me, and this is a choice I am taking freely."

"You were once one of the Tok, and I'm not convinced we should trust them or the impulses they gave you. We've seen what they're capable of: the genocide and the wide-scale terror."

He turned to consider her, taking a moment to find his next words. "I hope that I have served you, and Ondo, and all the others well over the aeons. If there has been a purpose to my existence, I think it has been to bring you to this point. Whatever I once was, this is what I am now."

"You have just set foot outside your vessel for this first time in aeons. This does not seem like the time to turn your back on everything and accept your end."

"It is precisely the right time. Visiting Ansider opened my eyes, it is true, but perhaps not in the ways you imagine. The journey reminded me of what I'd lost by becoming what I am, reminded me of my biological roots. Sometimes the destination is more important than the journey. It is time I stopped travelling and did the right thing."

She would stop trying to persuade him. She placed a hand on his. His flesh was oddly warm, and its touch made a rush of sadness swell within her. "You have always protected us, done everything we asked of you despite the injuries you suffered. I wish I'd done more for you."

"And I think I'd have faded into oblivion if I'd been left alone as I was. Your arrival changed everything. Not just for me."

"I should have protected you better. I feel so damned helpless when I consider what we're facing."

"Perhaps that is simply what they want us to feel. And … perhaps there is another way for you, despite what I've just said. A way for you to acquire the strength you need."

"What way?"

"You and I, we're not so different, even though we were born millions of years apart. I am at the end of my story, and you have barely begun yours, yet we are similar in essential ways. You are transbiological, as I am. There may be little left of me from what I was, but bones and flesh remember what they once were. We have both had to get used to the artificial. To new bodies that seemed clumsy and broken at first."

She thought back to the early days of her reconstruction. The *Dragon* had seen that, watched when she first limped onto its decks. Had it been like that for Eb, too, in the long-ago when he stopped being a person and became a swoop ship core? Had there been steps along the way for him when parts of his organic body were slowly replaced until he became the entity she now knew?

She said, "Are you suggesting that I could take your place? Become the Mind of this vessel? Become the *Radiant Dragon*?"

"You once asked me how it was I was able to pull us out of the gravity well at Coronade, and I said that it was possible for you to learn the truth of it. This is how you could do so. With this ship as your body, it would make sense. The galaxy could be yours to fly for as long as you wanted. You would simply need to grow into your new body, as you have done before."

She'd been about to laugh at his suggestion, dismiss it, but the look in his eye stayed her. Could she ever do such a thing? Perhaps one day, in the future, she might consider it. But not now. Now, there were other battles to fight. She was happy as she was, comfortable as the flawed, transbiological entity she'd become.

"I will think about it," she said.

A sad smile played about Eb's face, but from his nod she could see he was contented she had at least considered his words.

"Are you ready for what is to come?" she asked.

"You have some insight into the toll such journeys take; you have felt the agonies shaking through me as we traverse Dead Space and pull out of gravity wells. This will be like that multiplied. It will be an ordeal. But, yes, I am ready."

"How long will we have when we reach this surviving Tok? Assuming he's even there."

"Little enough, a minute at the most. I will withstand

the gravitational pull for as long as I can, and each instant will be an eternity of agony, but I will do all I can."

"Thank you," she said. It sounded hopelessly inadequate. "I wish there was more I could do to help."

A wry smile came to his face, and he looked as though he was about to say something.

"What is it?" she asked.

"It is nothing. Something I have no right to ask."

"It can't be both nothing *and* something. Tell me."

He breathed in and out, eyes back on the stars. "I said that flesh remembers. Those recollections have been returning to me more and more of late. They say it is often the way with the very old: youthful memories seem suddenly more vivid than reality. But I have no right to ask such a thing."

There was a catch in his voice that moved her. "Ask anyway. That's what I always do."

He nodded. "Perhaps it is because I know the end is near. It is just that my old self is awakening, in ways that I … did not anticipate."

It took her a moment to catch what he was referring to. "You mean, *sexually*?"

The grin on his face looked almost youthful. His breathing was definitely elevated, his heart pumping faster, and the bulge between his legs was hard to miss. "I had forgotten the simple pleasures of those stirrings and urges."

"And you wanted to share them one last time?"

"It is too late. There is no time for me to find the right person, grow with them to the point where our union would be … what we both desire."

She found herself laughing. "Were the Tok always so coy? No wonder you died out."

"Oh, we enjoyed our sexual natures greatly, revelled in them in all their endless variety, but it is a long time since I have talked in these terms. It is something you should be aware of if ever you consider becoming like me."

What did she feel for this strange starship core entity? Affection and gratitude, certainly. Love? Perhaps, of a sort. There'd been Falden and then there'd been Myrced, but she was only at the start of working out who and what she was. But there was something inside her at the thought of losing Eb: a dread, a sense of longing. Perhaps it was simply her own fear about what was to come: the thought that she, too, might well be about to die.

Or perhaps it was nothing more than curiosity and lust.

"You are bigger in stature than I am," she said. "It might present some … physical challenges,"

"I should never have asked, I'm sorry."

"No, no, quite the contrary," she said. "That could work. We have some time, and I would give this to you happily."

His mouth moved several times before he replied. "Only if it would give you what you want, too." He waved his hands in ways that suggested he was grappling with difficult concepts.

She took both his hands in hers, considered his Tok facial features, his liquid eyes. "This is what I want," she said.

"I may be … lacking in expertise."

She pulled him towards the corridor that led to his sanctum. "So may I. Don't worry, we'll work it out."

There was a moment, half an hour later, their bodies entwined, when it seemed to her that their minds became entangled, too, and she perceived the enormity of the starfields, saw the galaxy as Eb with his metaspace-awareness saw it. *This* was the reality he moved within. The scale and wonder of it were dazzling. She felt tiny and huge, both at the same time.

She floated there for a long time, enraptured.

6. Toruk

The *Radiant Dragon* was eerily quiet. Not so long ago, it had been filled with noise and movement: her, Ondo, Eb, Surtr, Hessia. Now she was alone again. She'd resented all the extra bodies, getting in her way, talking to her, but now she missed them.

Eb lay in his sanctum, his mind fully engaged with the movements through metaspace he had to make to safely approach the black hole. Their time together had been unexpected, but welcome. An interregnum of joy and affirmation snatched from the universe, something she'd needed without realising. The temptation to simply stay there, curled up with him, had been almost overwhelming.

Ondo, too, was cut off from her, lying along in the medsuite under heavy sedation. She'd thrown every investigative probe she could at his brain, to no avail. The image of him she carried in her head had offered to assist, but she'd refused, no longer sure she could trust it. Instead, she'd deactivated it. In the end, with the assistance of the *Dragon*'s med AI, she'd identified the break in his engrams, the exploit Concordance had planted there years previously as well as the trigger code they'd scarred into his brain during their imaging laser assault. She'd cursed herself for not spotting it beforehand, not assaying him more thoroughly. She also knew she was being unfair to herself: the dormant code had been encrypted, knotted up in itself within the cortex of his brain. She couldn't have known.

The question was whether the damage was permanent. The disconnects that Concordance had engineered in his brain were widespread and growing. She could contain them, but it meant isolating and perhaps wiping a significant percentage of his natural brain structure – in effect, setting up a closed-off region in his head and routing all his brain activity around it. It would be oddly like the regions of Dead Space in the map of the galaxy. Could she do that to him? The question triggered her own doubts about her nature and identity. If she intervened in his brain to that degree would he still be Ondo? Identity was such a fluid concept, but when it became too fluid it could simply trickle away.

She decided he would be close enough. He would be Ondo as much as she was Selene, as much as anyone was anyone as they grew and changed over the days and years. She refused to accept that the Ondo who had betrayed her was the real version. She would fix him, return him as closely as she could to the version she believed in. As he had once done for her.

Then another thought occurred to her. She had no idea if it was possible. She brought her inner Ondo back online with the summoning words, first making absolutely sure he was sandboxed and unable to see or act in any meaningful way.

"Ondo, I've identified how Concordance triggered your aberrant behaviour. The restructuring of your engrams is spreading. I've slowed it down by suppressing your metabolic activity as much as possible, but I can't stop it. I have two options: cauterize that whole chunk of your mind or attempt to completely restore your head from backup. I mean, from the *you* that I'm now talking to."

The tone of his response was pure Ondo: he wasn't alarmed, or angry. Instead, he was fascinated by the suggestion, intrigued to know whether it could work. "I've never attempted such a procedure. All the data we need is in your head, in this *me* that's talking, yes, but to reimage the physical structures of my neurons in that way would be extremely risky. The mind is so fluid, its patterns in constant flux."

"We'd have to accept there wouldn't be a 100% success rate, given that the process couldn't be instantaneous. There'd be some … blurring, perhaps some duplication or data missed. I think it gives us a better chance of restoring more of your mind. These are not normal times; we're about to fly into a black hole on a dying ship while a Concordance battlefleet pursues us. There are no risk-free options at this point."

He saw immediately the flaw. It encouraged her enormously that he was able to do so. "The engram exploit will be in the copy, too. We'd be restoring that as well as everything else."

"Except, we know it's there, we know which chunk of apparently junk neuron-encoding is actually their encrypted code. I don't know how it functions, but I should be able to filter it out during the transfer."

"You can't be completely sure where the exploit ends and my original brain structure starts."

"That's the risk. I'll need to put you deep under, trigger the transfer and let it run. You're going to be out of it for a long time. You obviously may never recover; we may end up with a mind-image that is simply inviable. I think the decision has to be yours."

"If we do this now, and assuming this Tok individual has survived from millions of years ago, I'll be missing the most incredible encounter of my life."

"Thanks, I'll try not to take that too personally. If the process works, and if we survive, you have my word I'll give the real you full access to every sensory recording I capture of what happens."

He gave her his assent to begin, without any more debate. She uploaded a copy of his engrams from her brain into the *Dragon*'s med systems, and set about preparing his brain for its restructuring. There were existing procedures in the suite's catalogue that she could make use of, although they hadn't been designed to achieve anything so comprehensive as a full brain reimage. They would have to do. She took a fresh copy of his current brain patterns – carefully quarantining it as infected – then sedated him as deeply as she dared, reducing his brain activity to a bare minimum. Then she instructed the system to begin its work.

She watched him as the procedure began. The muscles of his face winced and contracted subtly as connections in his brain were severed and reconnected. The flashes of expression passed across his features with alarming speed. Would he come through this? It was very possible she'd never be able to talk to him – the real him – again.

She squeezed his hand tight, although he couldn't possibly be aware of her touch, then turned and left the room.

She became more and more aware of the shudders rumbling through the *Dragon*'s superstructure as they flew. The alarms that appeared to be carefully engineered to shred her nerves sounded almost constantly. They were deep into another expanse of Dead Space, and she could almost taste the ship's revulsion at what they were doing as a bitterness in her mouth. The vessel's agonies were her own. She found herself looking at the flesh of her hands and her sides more than once, expecting to see physical wounds there. The *Dragon* fought against its ingrained instincts. It endured. More than once, Selene went to stand beside Eb's couch in his sanctum. His eyes were closed as he concentrated on the inner battles he was fighting. As with Ondo, brief expressions of agony flashed across his features as he completed each stage of the complex sequence of metaspace jumps. Once, he whimpered out loud like a child with a high fever. She wished she could do something, lend him her strength, but she could not. There were three of them on the ship, but they were each of them alone.

In the end, she stood on the cartography deck, watching exterior reality, monitoring the tactical map of their progress. They'd lost most of their Concordance pursuit, none of the Cathedral ships being capable of traversing the dead zones. Only a pair of Void Walker craft clung to them. She wondered if there were AIs on those craft going through the same ordeal that Eb was.

They all emerged, finally, in a region of normality that was completely encased within a sphere of Dead Space. It was the eye of the storm: in its very centre lay the black hole their journey had led to. It might almost *be* an eye: the central blackness with its iris of superheated, glowing gas around it. The object was alarmingly close, the distortion of spacetime and the gravitational stresses on the *Dragon* already significant.

They began to power towards the singularity under reaction drive. They would rapidly reach the point where the thrust wasn't needed; the black hole would clutch them harder and harder to itself. They would then be irrevocably trapped – with only the *Dragon*'s swoop capability giving them any hope of returning to normal space. She checked on Eb again. He was calm now, at least, but utterly comatose. She could only hope that traversing Dead Space hadn't caused him so much harm that he never recovered.

Inevitably, a lot of matter was falling into the black hole, most of it particles of dust that would, slowly, increase the mass and thus the gravitational pull of the singularity. She began to pick up something else, too: specks of matter with a clearly artificial structure. They were sparse – only one or two in a volume of space thousands of kilometres across – but they were there. More than anything else they resembled the nanosensors she and Ondo filled the galaxy with to acquire their slow telemetry, but these were of an utterly unknown design.

She used the ship's senses to study a couple of the devices minutely. There could be no doubt that they were artificial. An energy signature was coming off them. They were active.

It took her a few moments to work out what they were. They could only be monitoring devices deployed by the Tok. The sensors must have been seeded around the galaxy in antiquity. Perhaps they, too, followed pre-programmed aggregation sequences so that, slowly, data was pulled in from all corners and delivered to this one location. The great expanse of time involved suggested that the devices had to be self-replicating. She could see no other explanation.

The implication was that the mysterious Tok individual had been monitoring galactic events for all that time. From his perspective, time would be moving much more quickly, the forwards progress of the universe accelerating the closer he approached the singularity. He had to possess formidable processing power to absorb and correlate so much data from a galaxy that was, subjectively, moving on fast-forward.

What was more, the particles had been there all along. If she or Ondo or Hessia or anyone else had spotted them, tracked their progress, followed the trail, then they'd have ended up at the black hole. Jalian had said there were other hidden paths that would lead to the Tok. The particles were one of them.

She picked out the anomalous object directly ahead of them at the same moment that the ship's functional AI layers saw it. Like everything being sucked into the singularity, it appeared to be stretched from outside, and slowly fading into eternity. This object, however, was neither as faint nor as stretched as it should have been. By some means she didn't understand, it was resisting the pull of the black hole, slowing its own inevitable destruction. Was it, too a swoop ship, capable of returning? She guessed not: if this individual had been marooned within the compass of the black hole, or had deliberately gone there, they wouldn't have a way of simply escaping when they wished.

She queried the outer layers of the *Dragon*'s AI. "How long will we be able to sustain our position and have enough power to come out that close to the event horizon?"

"In the region of minutes. The limiting factor is the time dilation; the question is, how much time can you allow to pass by out here?"

It couldn't be long. Godel's supernova plan may have been thwarted, but her faction within Concordance were not going away. Another attempt to eliminate intelligent life within the galaxy would be made sooner or later. Selene could not simply disappear from the galaxy for a protracted period of time.

"We can let a few weeks go by. A month at the very most."

"Then, given how close the anomaly is to the event horizon, we will have around thirty seconds to converse with any intelligence we find there."

It wasn't enough, not nearly enough. Except, if her suspicions about the alien nanosensors were correct, the Tok would know she was coming and would know what questions she'd ask. Perhaps a few seconds would be all she needed. The ancient alien had apparently gone to extraordinary lengths to ensure his survival over millions of years; he had to have done so on the understanding that the messages he wished to pass on could only be brief.

Assuming he was even there and had survived. Assuming he wasn't some malign presence deliberately entombed in a black hole for eternity.

The *Dragon*'s reaction drives were quiet now, the black hole's gravitational pull doing all the work of bringing them in. She began to pick up a rising background noise emanating from the fabric of the ship as it succumbed to the massive structural forces of the singularity. The sound set off discordant resonances in her head, like all the alarms she'd ever heard sounding at once. She breathed, trying and failing to let it wash over her.

Otherwise, the flight into the black hole was oddly normal. The anomalous object neared: a twisting, sinuous ship that, yet again, had to be a product of the civilisation that had built the Cathedral ships. Its layout bore a close resemblance to the spheres of Surtr's ship, too, although this vessel had three orbs, arranged without any apparent concern for symmetry, around a central spindle. Scanning it, she picked up definite electromagnetic signatures. It was alive, its unfathomable drive tech somehow resisting the pull of the black hole, like a stone in a river bed around which the torrent flowed.

When they were near, she raced down to the airlock, watching the *Dragon* manoeuvring via her fleck visualizations. With surprising gentleness, it nudged alongside the Tok vessel, holding steady against the brutal gravitational pull of the black hole. She could feel the strain thundering through the ship from the effort of simply not moving. The clock was now ticking on how long they could remain where they were. The other ship still hadn't responded. If it fired at them, there would be nothing she could do to retaliate.

She was about to transmit a plea to it when a previously-invisible doorway in its flank slid open. The *Dragon* adjusted its position, lining up its own airlock for an EVA.

Time to act. She granted her inner Ondo full access to her perceptions, then threw herself across the divide, the touch of the void upon her flesh raw for the brief moment.

The Tok ship admitted her, its airlock door closing behind her, sealing her inside. The air was breathable, tasting surprisingly fresh. Had the Tok breathed the same air? Or was it the other way around, and the atmospheres of inhabited worlds had been engineered to the designs of the Tok?

She raced down curving, white corridors, their appearance familiar from her time on Surtr's vessel. She'd chosen not to bring a blaster. If it came to a fight, she was doomed anyway. If there was a surviving Tok individual on board, and he had lured her there in some ancient plan to escape his prison, she would die with him.

She emerged into a spherical room, its walls completely transparent. Ahead of her, the plasma envelope of the black hole raged, terrifyingly close. Behind her, the rest of the galaxy. With the effects of the extreme time dilation, she could discern that, indeed, the stars did move.

An old man sat cocooned in a chair. His body sagged as if his tissues and even his bones were crumbling away. He had to have been truly ancient even before he took his final flight. His face was unmoving, sagging asymmetrically, his muscles paralysed, perhaps. He did not look like a malevolent demon; he appeared to be on the point of death. Yet, she recognized his form, the way his body was put together: that elongated skull that looked like it was housing a brain bursting out of its cavity; his height and his slender limbs. He looked impossibly fragile, as if he would snap at the slightest movement.

Despite his appearance, his mental voice was light and quick in her head. "I have watched you, Selene Ada. For me it has been only the last few moments of time, but I have seen your actions. I am Toruk."

He apparently had no trouble interfacing with her tech or her language centres. The knowledge Surtr had given her doubtless helped. Which was just as well: three weeks had already passed by in external reality. She hadn't factored in the time it would take to dive in to reach the ship and make it to this room.

"You are one of the Tok?"

"I am."

"Did they send you here, imprison you here?"

From the tone of his response, the idea appeared to

amuse Toruk. "No, no. Quite the opposite; this was entirely my idea. My shameful secret. I knew I would be safe here unless a swoop ship jumped in to find me."

"Have we endangered you by coming here?"

"Ah, that risk has long passed. I wasn't supposed to outlive my fellow Tok, you see, but when it came to it, I couldn't bring myself to accept the end. Cowardice, you might say. Perhaps I am no different to the others after all. There we are, I have contravened yet another sacred ethic. It is not the first."

"What ethic?"

"We had agreed to leave the galaxy to its fate when we left, but I couldn't do it. As so often over my life, I found the decisions of the others puzzling. I'm sure I infuriated them, too. In my own way, I am also a renegade. It's likely they thought I was insane."

The clock in her head said that the weeks were becoming months in the outside galaxy. But she needed answers. "*Are* you insane?"

"I don't think so, but would I know?"

A fair question – which got her nowhere. "Why have you waited here all this time?"

"In case there was the need. Of course, I was forbidden from communicating in any way with, forgive me, the *child races* we seeded around the galaxy. But I decided to do it anyway."

"What was the need you foresaw? You couldn't have predicted Concordance's rise to domination."

"Concordance are nothing; they are a twist of smoke in the winds of history. Soon they will be gone. They abuse our technology, but the great risk is that they find the Morn. The Morn are a scourge that will devour everyone and everything. You, me, Concordance, all of it. You have learned that, haven't you? We thought we'd locked them safely away, contained them, but I remained because I wasn't convinced. We were far too enlightened to commit the final genocide and destroy the Great Enemy utterly.

Now, everything that I feared is coming to pass. It was our greatest failure, and it comes down to you to correct it, Selene. You and, perhaps, one or two others."

"These are ancient stories," she said, "I'm trying to defeat the real threat facing the galaxy."

There was a note of anger in the Tok's voice. "Then you haven't understood! The two are intertwined. If your enemy and the Morn come together, everything will be over."

This wasn't getting her anywhere. As she argued with Toruk, the months were accumulating, seeming to spin by faster and faster. Six months ticked up. Anything might have happened in that time. "What do I have to do? Tell me quickly."

"Find the light at the heart of the galaxy. Find the Morn and destroy them. That is all that matters."

"How?"

"We seeded waybeads around the galaxy. Most of my people did not want to do even that, fearing that the surviving Morn would be found by those who should not find them. That must not be your Concordance. Destroy both of them by all means, but it is the Morn you must eliminate."

"*Waybeads*? Give me them before I go."

The resentment in his tone was clear. "The ones you need were hidden long before my days. Such revered artefacts were never going to be given to a troublemaker like me. That didn't stop me making others, laying trails of my own. You've seen some, I think, used one to reach Ansider, and another to come here, yes? You must find two more: the green and the black."

Waybeads. *Seer stones.* She'd seen a green and black pair at the Depository, in one of the stasis fields. Could she go back there without Eb's presence on the *Radiant Dragon*? She doubted it.

"I have seen such beads, but they are out of reach."

"There are others. Find those two, and they will take

you to the turning-point where everything will be decided."

"Why can't you just tell me?"

"The knowledge was judged to be too dangerous."

One year, whispered the count in her head. How could that be? The thought of losing all that time was sickening. She saw why it was: they were slipping into the black hole at an increasing rate. Toruk was aware of it, too. "Yes. My ship senses the presence of Eb and something stirs within it. It knows its journey is almost over, as well."

"Do you know Eb?"

"I know of him. He left the Tok behind to become what he is long before my days, but I relied on him, and one or two others like him, to fulfil my plans."

She pressed on with her questions. "What did you mean when you said, *the knowledge was judged to be too dangerous?* Don't tell me, you vowed not to reveal the truth and a Tok never breaks a promise?"

Again, there was the flicker of amusement over the brain-to-brain connection. "We Tok were wise and, with rare exceptions, respected all life absolutely. But we weren't naïve. Some secrets were considered too dangerous. No, they cut the knowledge from me before they let me live. It was the price I paid for surviving. It was considered too hazardous to simply let me roam the galaxy, telling everyone the truth. I was reduced to leaving hints and scraps of knowledge. If I'd made the path too obvious, it might have been revealed millions of years before it was needed. Too subtle, and it might never have been found."

"How could you know it wouldn't be followed by someone malicious?"

"Oh, I couldn't; it was a risk. Then again, you found me by befriending the Aetheral and Eb, and because of the sacrifices they made for you. No one who was malign could have done that."

"Omn," she said. "Who or what is Omn?"

"A word. The *wrong* word. It is *everything*. The light at the heart of the galaxy. You must find it; it is your only hope."

"Are *Omn* and *Morn* words for the same thing?"

"Omn is not a name we ever used. You must find them both. The answer to everything lies at the galactic core. The *Magellanic Cloud* went there, now you must go too."

"But are they two names for the same thing?"

"No, no. They are opposite in just about every way it is possible for two lifeforms to be opposite."

"Are you saying Omn is *real?*"

"Yes."

"Do you honestly believe they're still alive out there, the Morn *and* Omn?"

Toruk considered that. "It is hard to be absolutely sure, as I am blind to so much. But, yes. I am sure the Morn survive, and as to what you call Omn – yes, that, too."

"How is that possible? Millions of years have passed by in the galaxy since you journeyed into this black hole. These lifeforms can't be alive after so much time."

"They can, and they are."

Two years, whispered the count in her head.

"What are these Morn?"

"Whether they were there before us, we never knew. They were confined, isolated, until we, with our urge to explore, turned over the stone beneath which they were hiding and unleashed them upon the galaxy. Before then, we lived in a long age of peace and learning, cataloguing knowledge. After that moment, our days were consumed with fighting the long war, with isolating and obliterating them. Where we could, we cauterized the wounds. Where we could not, we isolated whole regions of space in an attempt to contain them."

"You exploded stars in an attempt to kill everyone."

"Such calamitous times. They were our civilisations that you saw at the dead star. The remains of *our* people. They knew there was no other way. The sacrifices made were … terrible. To stem the Morn contagion, they accepted their own end."

"What else can you tell me that I need to know?"

"The Morn survive and they must be ended. That is all that matters."

Three years.

"You have to help me more, give me weapons or information," she said. "There must be something."

"I don't have weapons, but I have two things to give you. My beloved fellow Tok excised much from my brain – the whereabouts of the Being and the Morn and the waybeads that would take you to them – but they didn't remove what I *am*. I could still deceive them when I needed to."

He reached up to touch a blue-green gem, very small, embedded in the long lobe of his left ear. It was the first physical movement he had made, and his fingers shook as he lifted them. He tapped the gem in a rapid pattern, releasing it, then held it out to her with his long fingers.

"Take this. It is the only one in existence, now."

"It's another bead?"

"No, it is purely decorative, although its crystalline structure is unique. It is an insignia worn by all the Tok. The being you refer to as Omn is blind, perceiving the galaxy through cracked and broken lenses, but it will recognize this, and it will know you have come from me. It might help."

"Which ear should I put it in?"

"It makes no difference. It will embed itself in either."

She did as he said, touching the tiny gem to her own left ear. She registered a brief fizz, a tickle, and the stone embedded itself in her flesh just as he'd said. She picked up no energy signature from it. It was just a stone.

"What's the other thing?"

The old Tok delved into the folds of his gown for a moment, then pulled out a metallic object. "You have seen keys like this before, I believe?"

It resembled the objects they'd used to open the metaspace tunnels, although this one was a simple design of three overlapping circles.

"The metakey and the neverkey, yes."

Her words seemed to amuse him for some reason. "What is it?" she asked.

"It's nothing. The name *neverkey* was just a joke, that's all. A very old joke, now. The Aetheral took it seriously?"

"It did. What does this key open?"

"I told you that I don't know where the waybeads you need are, but I do know that some of them are locked behind a door that this key will open. It may help you."

"What is this one called?"

"The solarkey."

"How did you get it?"

"Isn't it obvious? I stole it."

"Anything else?"

"That is all, I'm afraid. It is precious little, I know, but my people did not trust me enough in the end. Setting up Ansider and waiting here; leaving behind the other clues – it was all I could do. After centuries of debate, the Tok decided to vacate the field and let the young races of the galaxy solve their problems for themselves. They did not want themselves to be seen as *gods*. It was a terrible abdication."

"Do you know where the *Magellanic Cloud* went after Ansider?"

"Ah, that is something I *can* tell you. A world you now call Borial."

Borial. She knew it. An advanced world with a Cathedral ship in orbit and another subjugated population. She would need to go there if she escaped the black hole. There were few records of the fate of the *Magellanic Cloud* after the rise of Concordance, but it was known that battles had taken place around the Borial system three hundred years previously.

Four years.

Enough. She couldn't wait around to extract more information. She'd lost too much time, and she'd lose more before she escaped the gravity well. If she ever did.

But she was about to turn and run when one final thought occurred to her. "The Aetheral; it wanted you to know that it did the right thing."

"And what did you think?"

"Most of the time it was irritating, frankly. It asked too many damned questions. But, yeah, it did good. It was noble; it transcended what it was. I miss it."

Toruk nodded his head in appreciation, an oddly familiar gesture from so ancient and distant a being.

Looking back no more, Selene ran from the chamber.

His words followed her down the corridor. "When it comes to it, do not waver. Destroy the Morn."

They were Toruk's final words. She threw herself across space and back into the *Dragon* even as she instructed the ship to pull away and commence its escape manoeuvre.

The howling agonies running through the *Dragon*'s bulkheads almost made her scream out loud herself. She pressed her hands to her ears in an attempt to blot it out. It felt as though the ship were tearing itself in two. She could sense, also, its refusal to accept defeat. It would have been so easy for Eb to subside, slide back into the black hole for eternity, condemning Selene to the same fate. He was already mortally wounded; it would be the end for him whatever happened. But he refused to relent, both for her sake and the future of the galaxy.

The raging reached a new magnitude as they edged farther and farther out of the gravity well. Their progress was achingly slow, each moment an eternity of torment. There were Concordance ships up there, a halo of them. It had been only moments for her, but they'd waited for years on their timeline, watching her progress. What had happened in the galaxy throughout that lost time? Were Concordance now utterly unstoppable, their destruction of worlds or their shackling of the Morn complete? Had she returned simply to watch the end of everything?

She put those questions out of her mind. *Keep fighting.* The Cathedral ships were irrelevant if the final metaspace jump couldn't be made. If it could, she would be away before the enemy fleet could reach her. And then, armed with what she'd learned, she would attempt to destroy them all: Concordance, the Morn, Omn.

The *Radiant Dragon* teetered on the edge of its assigned jump radius, then finally, agonizingly, tipped over. The screaming from the ship reached a crescendo as she felt the metaspace projectors spin up, felt the surging thrill in her gut as the ship translated.

She felt, also, the moment that the screaming stopped, and Eb died.

The *Radiant Dragon* drifted in the grey void of metaspace, and everything was quiet. It was just a ship now; the outer shells of its AI core were functioning, but the Tok entity at its heart was gone.

Selene breathed. She was alone, but she was still alive.

Selene's journey continues and concludes in *God Star*.

The darkness at the heart of the galaxy

Following the clues given them by the Aetheral, the *Radiant Dragon* and Toruk, Selene and Ondo close in on the existential threat to galactic life unleashed by Vulpis.

They battle Concordance all the way, aided by unlikely allies and mysterious messages. The trail leads them to more artefacts left behind by the Tok, drawing them ever-closer to the secrets at the heart of the galaxy.

But what they find there, and the truth they uncover about galactic history, changes everything…

ABOUT THE AUTHOR

Simon Kewin was born on the misty Isle of Man but now lives deep in the English countryside. He writes fantasy, science fiction and some things that can't make their minds up. He is the author of over 100 published short stories as well as a growing number of novels.

To find out about his other books, go to:

www.simonkewin.co.uk

Sign up for his newsletter and you'll be the first to know when he has new books out. There are some fine sci/fi and fantasy books to download for free as thanks.